Mr D Dancy
3 Neame Road
BIRCHINGTON
CT7 9DU

CW00865600

WAR
BROTHERS

By Patrick Slaney

From the author of The Diamond Chain

Copyright © 2013 Patrick Slaney

The right of Patrick Slaney to be identified as author of this book has been asserted in accordance with section 77 and 78 of the Copyrights Designs and patents Act 1988.

All rights reserved. No part of this publication may be reproduced, stored in a retrieval system, or transmitted in any form or by any means, without the prior permission in writing of the publisher, nor be otherwise circulated in any form of binding or cover other than that in which it is published and without a similar condition including this condition being imposed on the subsequent publisher.

All characters appearing in this work are fictitious. Any resemblance to real persons, living or dead, is purely coincidental.

Chapter 1

I lay awake enduring the silence of the prison they had incarcerated me in. The cold was unbearable, my bedding, what there was of it, was soaked through, and it was all made worse by the moss growing on the moisture laden walls of my cell in the outbuildings of the old Bavarian castle in the city of Munich. There was the stench of urine in the air. What little clothing I had been left with was totally ineffective against the cold chill of winter in this dungeon of a place. Would I have to suffer much more of this and the answer to that question was, probably not. Branded as a traitor, I had been told that they had only one way of dealing with traitors and that was to shoot them. My excellent service record with the Luftwaffe, and my job as a test pilot for the new Me262 jet engined fighter would not save me from the death penalty.

For my sanity, I had tried to keep track of time, but I had given up the task of trying to work out whether it was morning or evening. I no longer had any interest in knowing what day it was as if I didn't have a future there was no point. My will to live was a desire of the past. My battered and tortured body just wanted to rest, and, at this stage, I would welcome the release of death. My body and mind had suffered enough and couldn't take much more of their treatment. I couldn't even hang myself as they had anticipated my thought processes and left me with nothing that I could use to make a noose. Part of their torture was to let me suffer the agony, leaving me with no way of escaping. The nights were a refuge as they never came to get me until the early morning and, although I couldn't sleep, I had time to think, and, what little comfort I got came from my memories.

I was now twenty four years of age having been born in 1917 in the North German port of Lubeck. I don't remember much about my early years, when Germany was struggling to recover from being heavily defeated in the First World War. I lived with my mother and her parents in a small terraced house in a suburb within walking distance of the centre of the city. They managed, by various means, to get food to survive when food was practically non-existent, but survive we did. We were luckier than most as my granddad, my grandfather on my father's side, owned a bakery, and we had a daily supply of bread.

When I was old enough to understand, my mother told me that my father had been killed fighting for Germany at the battle of the Somme in 1916 before I was born. I was told by some of the neighbours, who had lived in the area for a long time that they thought I had a twin brother, but nobody ever explained to me what had happened to him. My mother never brought up the subject, so I assumed he had died quite young in a similar fashion to many other babies at that time. I learnt later that in the period 1917 to 1920, when there was such a shortage of the basic food stuffs and also outbreaks of disease, such as the flu of 1918 that the infant mortality rates were unusually high.

Germany was not a suitable place to grow up in during the 1920's. There was not only the deprivation, but it also was extremely dangerous to go out on the streets as there were a lot of political marches and unrest surrounded these marches. The suburb of the picturesque old town of Lubeck that I lived in was called St Lorenz Sud. I was able to walk to school and also to play in an enclosed public park close to my home. This park, totally enclosed by a high stone wall, was a fantastic haven for young boys. There was an old quarry that we could catch fish in, grass we could play football on and bushes and trees, we could hide in or climb. It was my escape from reality.

Even the most basic of food was rationed, and often we had to go hungry, so I loved to escape the confines of my home and go to the park as often as possible. For some reason, the hunger pains weren't so hard to bear when I was playing outside. I know that my mother and my grandparents often went without, and added their share to mine, to prevent me

4

from suffering from malnutrition. I also noticed that valuable items were disappearing from our home. I suspected that this was a way of getting money to buy items on the black market. Despite the shortages, I grew up into a healthy child able to withstand the diseases that were claiming so many of the young people in the town in those years.

As I was growing up, I remember frequently looking at a picture of my father in his uniform that sat on a table in my granddad's bakery. I had never met him, so it was the only connection that I had to my natural father. He seemed remarkably tall to my young eyes, and he wasn't just tall but was well built to match his height. Even though he was just a photograph to me, I was extremely proud of my father, and I missed him. My granddad was always telling me to eat up and behave so that I would grow up to be a man like my father.

In the winter of 1926, my grandpa, the grandfather on my mother's side, who I lived with, died. He had not been well since he had been injured in the war and every winter he had struggled to survive. He had been invalided out of the army in 1915 when the gas, being used by the German army against the French, had been blown back into their own trenches at the second battle of Ypres. He had never fully recovered from the disastrous effects of the gas. In the warmer summer months, he seemed to be able to breathe normally; however, once the cold damp days of winter came he wheezed and coughed for hours on end. The funeral service was held in the local Lutheran church, and then the internment took place in the local graveyard. My mother went to the service in the church, but didn't go to the grave side ceremony as it was frowned on for women to attend. I had to go with my Uncle in her place.

Living in the house with my grandpa had not been a pleasant experience. As a result of the damage to his lungs, he was always coughing uncontrollably. He was extremely irritable and, as I was the smallest in the house, he was always shouting at me. They had moved his bed into the kitchen which was the only room that was heated, so to escape from his tirade, I had to go and play in the park. In winter, when it was bitterly cold outside, and there was deep snow, I couldn't escape to the park so had to stay indoors. I hid away in my bedroom keeping warm under the bed covers. I felt guilty at being very relieved when he died, but pretended to my mother that I was as sad as she was.

My grandmother seemed to give up her desire for living after that, and she only outlived my grandpa by about four months. So within a very short period of time, we had gone from a family of four to just my mother and me. My mother worked in the bakery run by my granddad. Up to the time my grandparents died they had taken care of me when she was out at work as she commenced work each day at 6:00 am. The bread and cakes had to be ready and freshly baked for the Customers when the doors opened at 6:30 am. The bakery was closed every Friday, but open every weekend. With their deaths, there was no one to look after me, and I had to get myself up and off to school every morning during term time. On a Saturday and a Sunday, I went to my granddad's bakery and made some pocket money by delivering bread around the area.

I was a quiet child well able to look after myself. Being brought up surrounded by grandparents made me respectful and aware of other people. I had friends in school, but when I wasn't in school I tended to keep to myself. There wasn't a lot of happiness around with people being so badly affected by what was going on around them and the struggle they had simply to survive. Smiles were few and far between.

Looking back now to those days I realise that we just existed. The only day that my mother had off from her work was Friday, when the bakery was closed, and she used that time to catch up on the washing and keeping the house clean. I supposed she loved me, but there wasn't much expression of love in our house. We survived from day to day, and I was just glad that I didn't have to go and live somewhere else.

Just after my eleventh birthday in March 1928 my mother, when she arrived home from work, told me to sit down as she had something to tell me.

'Markus, Frau Peters talked to me in the shop today, and asked me if her son Walter could come and stay with us for a little while.'

'Is that the fat Walter in my class at school?' I asked.

'Yes; Walter that goes to school with you. Her husband has just got a job in Munich, and she wants to go with him. Their only option at the moment is to stay with relations there. Unfortunately, the relations don't like children, so she can't take Walter and Olga with them. She offered to pay me if I cared for Walter.'

'So he would come and live here; like a brother?' I exclaimed, very excited by the idea.

'Exactly! You could either share a room or he could sleep in the bedroom over the hallway.'

'I wouldn't want to sleep in the same room as him Mum. If I fell out with him for some reason, I would have nowhere to go to get away from him.' I liked Walter, but at times he could be extremely annoying, and I liked to escape to be by myself on occasions.

'Well, I told Frau Peters that I would talk to you and give her an answer tomorrow. I take it then that I can tell her yes?'

'Yes Mum, it will be great to have him here as we can do everything together.' Having Walter around would lessen the loneliness that I felt when my mother wasn't around.

The following Monday Walter moved into our house, and I now had a brother in residence. He wasn't as good at waking up in the morning as I was, so the first problem that I had with him, was getting him out on time for school each day. At least he didn't get grumpy when I pulled him out of bed. After school, we usually went to the park, and the quarry to keep ourselves amused. I felt a lot safer with the two of us always together. I was starting to grow quite tall for my age and Walter was also well built and strong. The bullies tended to find someone else to pick on. My mother had told me that my father had been quite tall at just under two meters, and she was expecting me to grow to a similar height.

They started up a junior football team in the local stadium which Walter and I joined. It was only a ten minute walk from my house, so it was easy to get there. They used to play matches most weekends and then practice one night during the week. I was much bigger than the other children in my age group so was always the first one picked for the team. Walter had two left feet and was a little fat, so he always was one of the last picked.

After practice one evening, the leader of the group, a twenty six year old man called Stefan Mulder, called me over and said that he wanted to talk to me.

'Markus, I have noticed you and how much effort that you put into your play. You also are always on time for practice.' I always made a big effort to get there on time.

'I thoroughly enjoy the football, and the matches and training sessions give me something to do,' I replied.

'I have been ordered to form a branch of the Hitler Youth in this suburb of Lubeck, and you are the type of young man I have been told to recruit into the group. Your time keeping is excellent and you try hard to win every match. What is also tremendously important is that you look the part. You have the blue eyes, the square jaw and the high cheek bones that we have been told to look for in a typical German male. You are also quite tall for your age, and your sandy coloured hair is also what we have been told to look out for.'

'In school we have been told that Hitler wants to develop a 'Master Race', is this what he was referring to? I asked.

'Yes, he believes that the Aryan male is the ideal German and if we fill our sports teams and army with these people we will attain world domination.'

'Can Walter Peters join with me as he stays in my house?' I didn't want to have to leave Walter sitting at home while I attended the meetings.

'Yes he can come along if he wants. Will you ask him and tell me?'

'I am sure that he will want to come with me, but I will ask him.'

The following week Walter and I attended our first Hitler Youth meeting at the stadium. My mother had tried to dissuade me as she said that she had heard so many terrible stories about the movement. I just told her that it was a Youth Club and was the same as the Football Club which she had encouraged me to join. Little did I know what my membership of the Hitler Youth would lead to and where my country was headed?

Chapter 2

My life had a regular and disciplined pattern to it. During school terms, I got out of bed at 7:00 every morning and then tried to get Walter up. Yesterday's bread was our breakfast as my mother brought the fresh bread with her when she returned from work at 3:00 pm. There was still no butter around, so we used to spread some lard or just jam on the bread.

School started at 8:30 and I preferred to get in a bit early to play marbles with my friends. On many a day, I left Walter still getting ready at home and I went to school ahead of him. He preferred his bed to getting to school early just to play games. I hated to be delayed and possibly late.

School for the day finished at 3:30 pm, and I was glad to get home as my mother would have cooked dinner for us and we always ate our main meal for the day at 4:30 pm. There was never any shortage of bread and the bread that we ate at our dinner was fresh from the bakery, so even more welcome.

On a Tuesday, Thursday and Friday evening, we went to the Club at the local stadium. Tuesday and Thursday evenings were for football training, and Friday was for the Hitler Youth. Usually we would have a football match against another youth team on the Saturday afternoon at our stadium, or we travelled to other teams' grounds in the Lubeck area.

During the school holidays our Hitler Youth leader, Stefan Mulder, organized events during the day at the stadium to give us something to do. We only commenced at 11:00 am, giving us a chance for a lie in, and we stayed there until 5:00 pm. I don't know where Herr Mulder got the food from, but we always had lunch at the stadium, and there didn't seem to be any shortages where the Hitler Youth was concerned. When the other children in our area heard about the food they all came along to join and our group grew during the holidays until it was about a hundred strong.

The Hitler Youth meetings were not like normal youth clubs but focused on physical exercise and group activities like marching. They built obstacles around the outside of the pitch as an assault course which we had to train on. The first time that I tried it, I barely got around, and I had a massive problem with the high wall and what they called the monkey swing, where we had to swing from rung to rung on an overhead ladder for about ten metres. When we first started using the course, I used to go home with a lot of bruises and scrapes to my skin. As I got older and got taller, I got better, and my times came down. Walter genuinely struggled as his arms to weight ratio was all wrong. It was an effort to persuade him to attend when he knew that the obstacle course would be on the agenda.

Herr Mulder explained to us that we were doing the exercises to harden us for roles in the German army. He said that Hitler visualised a generation of "victorious, active, daring youth, immune to pain". Hitler demanded that we be "quick like greyhounds, tough like leather and hard like Krupp steel". After an intense training session, I was so sore sometimes that I found a place, out of the sight of everybody, where I wept tears of pain and frustration. Walter wasn't able to keep up, and he suffered even more than me. He finally gave up the unequal struggle and dropped out altogether.

One day I went to the stadium, and there were a pile of snare drums and drum sticks in the changing rooms.

'Sir, what are these drums for, are we going to have a marching band?' I asked Herr Mulder.

'Yes, we are going to do all our marching and exercises to the roll of drums from now on,' he replied.

'Who is going to play the drums, will there be new people specially coming to our meetings to play them?'

'No Markus, we will have to choose people from our current membership to be trained.'

I had a brain wave. 'Sir, do you remember that Walter decided to stop coming to the Hitler Youth meetings because he couldn't do the assault course.'

'Yes I remember Markus. He isn't old enough or fit enough to keep up.

'Is it alright if I ask him to come and learn to be a drummer. He then can re-join the group. At the moment, he is sitting at home, on his own, doing nothing when I am at the meetings.'

'Tell him to come in and see me tomorrow, and I'll consider him.'

I ran home that evening to tell Walter.

'Walter I have some good news for you,' I shouted out as I burst in through the door into the kitchen.

'Steady on Markus,' my mother scolded. 'You're like a whirlwind. What good news have you got for Walter?'

'There is going to be a separate group of boys that will be taught the drums. They will then play while everybody else does the exercises. I asked Herr Mulder if he would consider Walter. He told me to tell you to go along and talk to him tomorrow, that is, if you are interested,' I said triumphantly.

'Does that mean that I wouldn't have to do the assault course Markus?'

'Yes, from what he told me, you would be playing the drum all the time.'

'I'll definitely go and see him then. Thanks for suggesting me Markus, you are a true brother.' Walter gave me a beaming smile that made me feel good.

Walter was selected as a drummer, and he started to learn immediately. We now had the sound from the snare drums accompanying all our activities which gave an orderly feeling to everything we did. Our marching improved immensely, and it was a lot more fun keeping time to the beat of the drums. They even played while we did the obstacle course which seemed a bit stupid as we couldn't match our efforts to the drum beat. Walter picked up the skill of drumming remarkably quickly and became one of the star members of the new group. The Hitler Youth members started to march around Lubeck with the drummers split between the back and the front of the group which amounted to as many as fifty boys at a time, or more on special occasions.

Once the weather started to get warmer we went camping at the weekends in fields lent to the Hitler Youth by local farmers. The tents and equipment were dropped off by a truck so as we wouldn't have to carry them, then all the members used to march to the field. I was one of the tallest in my age group, so I was given a leadership role during these camps. I wouldn't be fourteen, and able to join the older group, until February 1931, but because of my size they made an exception for me on certain occasions. My preferred activity was the wrestling where we were carried on the shoulders of one of the bigger boys. I was lighter to carry around but quite strong for my age, so my partner and I won the majority of our contests.

In the evening, we lit fires and had sing songs around the fire. The songs we sang were flavoured with Nazi propaganda. The words spelt out the need for additional lands to cater for Germany's growth, and the need for more and more soldiers to fight against those who were opposed to German ideals. At every camp, we were also spoken to about the great aims of our leader Hitler and how we could help the party to achieve its aims. It was emphasised to us how the Jews were destroying our nation and that all the suffering in Germany, as a result of the great depression, was due to the Jews. We even had mock burial ceremonies to honour a comrade who had fallen bravely in battle. The talks we received on a regular basis emphasised the noble fate that lay ahead for Hitler Youth members when they died for Hitler and for the Third Reich. I fully believed what we were being told and was convinced that Germany was heading for greatness. My whole life was wrapped up in the ideology that we were being filled with.

I returned home from these camps energised and willing to do anything for Germany. Right and wrong never entered into the equation. If Hitler wanted us to do something, we would do it and not ask questions.

About once every two months we were driven in an army truck to a firing range. We started off firing low calibre rifles, and then graduated to regular infantry pieces. The better shots, of which I was certainly not one, were selected for special training as snipers.

The Hitler Youth was my whole life and was instrumental in making an exceptional physical specimen out of me and also in expanding my mind. We would do anything for the party and often went out and distributed leaflets, signing propaganda songs as we went. I had grown up with zero confidence due to my grandpa shouting at me all the time and having to keep a very low profile at home just to survive. In school, I had been picked on as I consciously avoided situations where I might get into trouble. My class mates called me a goody goody, I had even developed a stammer when asked to read or speak in class. My role in the Hitler Youth developed a lot more confidence in me and my size gave me much greater courage. I was starting to believe that I had a future where my mother would be proud of me.

Everything was going well until one week in summer when I was fourteen, and we were away at camp.

'Markus, will you please come and see me after the sing song this evening,' Herr Mulder, our leader, asked me as we were queuing up for our meal on the final evening of the camp.

'Where will you be sir?' I asked him, not having any idea as to what it was all about.

'I'll be at my tent, and the regional director Herr Schmidt will be with me.'

'What is it about Sir?'

'We just want to talk to you Markus; there is nothing to be afraid of.'

Despite what he said I was scared, and I didn't enjoy the sing song that night as I was extremely apprehensive as to why the leader and the regional director would want to see me. I couldn't recall doing anything wrong that would justify being called before the leader and regional director. I was quite mature and tall for my age, but I was still only a fourteen year old and a very junior member of the Hitler Youth.

At around 10 o'clock, when the evening's activities were over, and it was getting pretty dark, I went over to his tent with dread in every part of my body and anxiety like I have never felt before. I coughed outside to let them know that I was there. There was nowhere to knock, and I didn't want to call out.

Herr Mulder put his head out of the tent and asked me to enter.

'Ah Markus, thank you for coming,' he said as he pushed the canvas flap back to allow me to go in.

I assumed that the man sitting on the end of the bed was the regional director. He looked to be aged about thirty which seemed surprisingly young for his exalted position in the Hitler Youth. He was dressed in a very smart uniform, his black hair was smeared across his head, in the fashion of Hitler, and he sneered at me.

'Markus, this is Kommandant Schmidt who is the regional director of the Hitler Youth for this area,' Herr Mulder said introducing the director.

'Do you like chocolate Markus?' Herr Schmidt rather surprisingly asked me.

'I like it a lot sir, but it's a luxury that we can't afford at home.'

'Well I have a bar of chocolate for you Markus, which you can take away with you.' Herr Schmidt said, giving me the bar of Swiss chocolate.

I started to relax a bit as obviously it wasn't because I had done something wrong that they wanted to see me. They wouldn't offer chocolate to someone who they were about to chastise.

'Markus we have an extremely important role that we believe you would be particularly suitable for, but we don't know if you are up to it,' Herr Mulder said, sitting down on a wooden box against the side of the tent.

It was now totally dark outside, but there was a lantern in the centre of the tent which gave off a gentle glow that relieved the darkness. The tent was filled with the overcoming smell of paraffin from the burning lamp.

'What do you want me to do sir?' I asked. I was feeling quite anxious again as it was quite spooky in the semi-darkness and the 'chocolate bribe' was giving me a horrible thought as to what this meeting could be all about.

'Will you please take off your top and your shorts as we want to see how well developed you are? The project we have in mind for you will need a strong physical specimen, so we need to check out your whole body?' Herr Schmidt said to me. I did as he asked and stood there very self-consciously. It was quite a small tent; big enough to stand up in, but the confined space pushed me quite close to the two men and I now only had my underpants on.

'Come closer to me Markus,' Herr Schmidt said, beckoning me towards him.

He put his right hand up and felt my shoulders and then moved his hands down to my chest where he tweaked my chest muscles and my nipples. He then felt my stomach muscles. His hands were quite sensuous as he slowly moved them over my body making me have strong feelings that I hadn't had before.

'Turn around and face Herr Mulder,' he directed.

I turned around, and he felt the muscles at the top of my back, and my shoulders and then he ran his hands down my spine. I felt his hands move onto my bottom and, slipping his hands under the fabric of my underpants, he felt and squeezed each cheek. By now I was thoroughly aroused by the gentle and calculated touch of his hands on my body. I tried to control my feelings, but I was unable to prevent my penis hardening and bulging my underpants. The more I tried to stop my erection the stiffer it became. I was extremely self-conscious and embarrassed by what was happening. I watched Herr Mulder's interest in me increase as the bulge in my underpants grew.

I had never felt such embarrassment as I now felt, exposing myself to these two men. I was also dreading what they would do to me next.

My embarrassment increased considerably when Herr Schmidt gripped the band of my underpants and forced them to the ground. I was now totally naked. I tried to grab them as he was moving them down, but I wasn't fast enough. My shame was so great now that I felt physically sick which had the effect of reducing the blood flow to my nether regions and my erection started to decrease.

'You have a beautiful body Markus and are remarkably mature for your age. You will make a fantastic leader in the Hitler Youth when your time comes,' he said as he fondled me.

I wasn't enjoying this, but what was I supposed to do. I couldn't make a dash for it in my naked state. I was also in the presence of the two most powerful men in the local Hitler Youth movement, and I felt that it was imperative that I didn't do anything to upset them. There were plenty of stories of members who had crossed the leadership of the Hitler Youth and had been handed over for interrogation to the SS.

'You can put your clothes on now Markus?' Stefan Mulder suddenly said in a not particularly convincing voice.

'But I haven't finished with him Herr Mulder?' Herr Schmidt said decidedly tetchily, still fondling me.

'It is very cold in here, and he will become ill,' Herr Mulder said sympathetically but forcefully.

'OK Markus, you had better get dressed and go,' Herr Schmidt said, letting go of the part of me he had been holding.

I didn't wait any longer. I pulled my clothes on and got ready to leave.

'Thank you Markus for being so compliant and co-operative. We will remember what you have done for us tonight when your name comes up for a leadership role,' Herr Schmidt said.

'You mustn't tell anybody what happened in this tent tonight Markus,' Herr Mulder said to me as he undid the tent flap to let me out. 'If you do talk to your friends we will hear about it, and you will be in really serious trouble. So remember that.'

I went back to the tent that I was sharing with five others in a total state of shock with tears of shame in my eyes. All I had for my horrible experience was a bar of chocolate.

'Where have you been Markus,' Walter asked me when I got back.

Luckily he couldn't see my face as there was no light in the tent. I was sure that my face must be reflecting the disgust and shame that I was feeling.

'I had to go and see Stefan Mulder after the sing song finished and he gave me a bar of chocolate. Would you like some?'

'He gave you chocolate,' one of the others piped up; all questions as to what I had been doing were banished from their minds at the thought of the chocolate.

I shared the chocolate bar and lay down on the ground to sleep. I felt dirty and abused after the treatment I had received. I had always looked up to Herr Mulder as my father figure; he had always been there for me as I was growing up. My whole life centred on the Football Club and the Hitler Youth, and he was the leader of both. How could he have let Herr Schmidt do that to me tonight? The trust that there had been between us had been irrevocably broken. I cried myself to sleep.

Chapter 3

I seemed to have just gone to sleep when the whistles were being blown at 6:30 am to get us up. We had to have breakfast and pack up the camp. Going towards the breakfast area anxiety gripped me as I dreaded bumping into either Herr Mulder or Herr Schmidt.

I was careful to stay away from the areas where it was likely the leaders would be, and I didn't meet either of them before we left to return to Lubeck.

All the Hitler Youth members, from the different areas of Lubeck, marched back together. It was only as we entered the city itself that we split off to go to our own stadium. There were about forty drummers divided evenly between the front and the rear of the three hundred members, and they rasped out a steady beat as we marched along. It was an impressive sight as we marched along on that beautiful summer's morning. There was even a smell of summer in the air from all the wild flowers in the hedge rows that bordered the road.

At about the halfway point, the beat of the drums suddenly stopped, and we were given a break. I slumped down on the grass bank at the side of the road with the events of last night retreating into the back of my mind. One of the older members of our section, a rather unpleasant individual named Boris, came over to talk to me.

'What were you up to last night BEKER?' he asked me with a smirk on his face.

'What do you mean what was I up to,' I replied not too politely. Suddenly anxiety filled my heart again, and my stomach tightened. I was startled by his question.

'I saw you go into Stefan Mulder's tent last night, and you were in there for quite a long time,' he added poking me in the shoulder.

'He asked to see me with the regional director, and they then discussed a job that they wanted me to do for them,' I replied as innocently as I was able.

'I saw what happened, BEKER. I could see your silhouette through the canvas; the light in the tent illuminated what you were up you and I saw you strip,' he poked me on the shoulder again.

'Well I don't know what you thought that you saw, but I was just talking to them and trying on some pieces of uniform that they gave me. When I was finished, they gave me a bar of chocolate to take back to share with my mates in my tent. You can ask Walter if you like.' I decided to try and talk as casually as possible, in the hope that he couldn't have seen much as the light had been very dim and the tent had been double skinned.

'Well what is the project they discussed with you?' he asked quite aggressively.

I was stuck now as I couldn't think up an answer quickly enough..... Slightly desperate I said, 'they ordered me not to discuss it with anyone so I can't tell you.'

'That's a good one BEKER. Why did you take off your clothes?'

'I took my shirt off; because they wanted me try on another one.'

'And your shorts?'

'Yes I also tried on a pair of shorts, and I obviously couldn't wear the new ones over the old could I?'

I could see that there was now doubt in his eyes, and he didn't appear to be as sure of himself as he had been. I decided to go on the attack.

'What do you think that I was doing in their tent?' I asked him.

'It looked as if you were giving them a bit of a show as you seemed to take off all your clothes and then one of them fondled you. I couldn't quite make out what happened at the end. Then you dressed again and left.'

'Well I did take off my shirt and my shorts and then I modelled the new outfits for them, and the regional director touched me as he straightened out the creases. That's probably what you saw. You have far too vivid an imagination.'

'I know what I saw Bakker. Why are you defending what they did?' I could now see from his attitude that he wasn't 100% convinced of his facts, and there was an expression of doubt appearing on his face.

'You don't think that they would do anything when the Nazi party is so against any dubious activities. Would you like me to arrange for you to have a meeting with Herr Schmidt and Herr Mulder?' I thought that this last bit was a masterstroke on my part.

'No, that's alright I don't need to talk to them.'

He turned around and went back to join his mates, leaving me alone to dwell on what he had just accused me of. I reckoned that I had done a very good job of getting him off my back, but I was still worried about what Boris might say to the other members of our group.

When we returned to the Stadium and were putting the tents and other equipment away, Stefan Mulder called me over to him.

'How are you today Markus?' he asked me.

'I am good thank you sir,' I said, avoiding his eyes.

'I saw Boris talking to you when we had our break on the way back from the camp. What did he want?'

'He said he had seen me go into your tent and that he was able to see what was going on through the tent wall. He said that the lamp illuminated my profile and actions.'

'What did you tell him?' Stefan Mulder had become quite tense and was looking anxious.

'I told him that his imagination had run away with him, and all I was doing was talking and modelling some pieces of a new uniform.'

'Did that seem to satisfy him Markus?'

'It planted seeds of doubt in his mind and made him question what he thought he had seen. I am just worried at what he will tell the rest of the group.'

'Well done Markus, I think that you have done extremely well, and I will talk to him.'

He left me and went over to where Boris was putting away some of the heavier items. I could see him take Boris over to the side where he talked to him with a good deal of finger wagging.

I was more upset by this latest incident than I had been by the actual event the night before. By denying Boris's allegation, I was now lying to cover up the whole horrible action of the night before. I was now in much deeper into the deceit, and I felt there was a possibility that Stefan Mulder could use it to make me do a sexual act with him again. The only way for me to step cleanly out of the situation would be to remove myself from the Hitler Youth and the Football practices.

As I was standing there trying to work out what was the best action to take, Walter came over to me.

'Come on Markus let's go home. I am starving, and your mother will have cooked us our dinner.'

'OK Walter, I just have to get my bag and then we can leave.'
On the way home, I decided to tell Walter of my decision.

'Walter, I am strongly thinking of leaving the HJ and the Football team as I am finding it is taking up too much of my time and my mother wants me to help at home.'

'You can't do that Markus. They are talking about making membership of the Hitler Youth compulsory so you will have to stay.'

'They haven't made that law yet so I can leave if I want.'

'But Markus, what about me? You got me back into the Hitler Youth as a drummer, and now you are leaving. I can't stay on my own without my brother to back me up.'

'I am afraid I am going to have to Walter, and I have made up my mind. I am sorry for letting you down.'

'There is something else Markus isn't there. What did Stefan Mulder and the Regional Director say to you last night?' Walter stopped walking and looked straight into my face.

'Nothing serious; they were only asking me to try on a new uniform. My leaving is not as a result of what they discussed with me.'

'OK Markus, but why do you have to leave the HJ and the football club. I will miss you.'

'You'll be alright Walter, and I will be with you at home anyhow.' I gave him a brotherly punch on his shoulder.

We walked on home in silence. I loved the Hitler Youth and all that it stood for, and I also loved my football, so it was going to be a terrible wrench to give it all up. I had nothing else in my life to replace it.

Chapter 4

My mother gave me a hug as I went into the kitchen where the welcoming smells of her cooking assaulted our nostrils. Usually I resisted hugs as it embarrassed me in front of Walter, but in my current fragile state I welcomed her affection

'How did it go boys?' she asked us.

'It was good except for the food, so I am looking forward to a home cooked meal,' I replied. 'I'll just go and put my stuff in my room and have a quick wash.'

'Well your food will be ready in five minutes so don't be long. How are you Walter did you have a good time?'

'I am totally knackered. We had to play the drums the whole way back to the stadium other than a short break at the halfway mark.'

'You poor thing; anyway go and wash and be back here chop chop.'

We were both a bit longer than five minutes, so the food was on the table by the time we sat down.

'Markus is leaving the Hitler Youth and the Football Club Frau BEKER,' Walter blurted out just as we started eating.

My mother put her knife and fork down and looked at me aghast.

'You are doing what Markus?'

I gave Walter my best withering scowl, and he immediately saw that he had blundered by telling her.

'I am spending far too much of my time at the stadium, and I want to be at home when you are here mum.'

'What an extraordinary thing to say Markus. Why have you suddenly decided that you want to be at home when I am here?'

'I spend half my life at the Stadium, and the training sessions and meetings go on longer and longer. I have no time to do anything else after school.'

'Well Markus I am finding all of this very strange; however if that is what you want then go ahead and do it,' she said resigned to the fact that I had made up my mind. I was already proving to be an extremely stubborn teenager.

I found it extremely difficult to spend my leisure time at home or with my granddad at the bakery. I was used to being out all the time and had only been at home in the past between getting home from school and leaving for the Stadium at 5:30 pm. My mother noted my restlessness.

One Monday, about two weeks after I had taken my decision to leave the HJ, there was a knock at the door. My mother went to see who it was. I froze, and my stomach hit my boots when I recognized Stefan Mulder's voice.

'Good evening Frau BEKER. I am worried about Markus as he hasn't been to the Hitler Youth meetings or the Football. Is he sick or what is wrong?'

'No he is not sick. He decided, for reasons best known to himself that he needed a break from both the activities you run at the stadium for the time being. He said that he was spending all his out of school time at the stadium.'

'Can I talk to him Frau BEKER?' he asked my mother.

'Come in and I will get him for you Herr Mulder.' My mother ushered him into the front room and came to get me.

'I don't want to see him Mum,' I said to her when she joined me in the kitchen.

'I don't know what this is all about Markus, but you will have to talk him after he has come to the house to see you.'

'I won't see him.'

'I am sorry Markus, but you are going to have to. It won't kill you just to meet with him for a few minutes.'

I was almost in tears, and there was no way that I could tell my mother the real reason that I didn't want to see him. I just stood there looking thoroughly miserable.

She put her arm around me. 'Markus, I can see how upset you are, but please talk to him, and we can discuss the whole thing when he has gone.'

She brought me to the door into the sitting room, opened it and coaxed me through the doorway until I was in the room. She then calmly turned around, closed the door, leaving me alone with Herr Mulder.

'Are you alright Markus?' Stefan Mulder said to me as he stood up to face me.

I wasn't able to answer but just looked at him with tear filled eyes.

'Is this as a result of the encounter with Herr Schmidt at the camp Markus?'

I nodded my head; still unable to speak.

'It's because you are such a strong and resilient character that I chose you Markus. I also felt that you would be able to deal with whatever he might do to you. I stupidly thought that it would be beneficial for you to be in the director's good books. I didn't mean to upset you.'

He put his hand on my shoulder and guided me to sit down opposite him.

'Why are you not coming to the meetings Markus?'

'I am afraid of it happening again and the rest of the group labelling me as a homosexual and ostracising me,' I finally managed to say.

'They don't know anything about what happened in that tent,' he said in a comforting voice.

'Yes they do, and I suspect even Walter has heard things about me. Don't forget that Boris saw what happened.'

'I have talked to Boris and backed up the story you told him about the modelling of the new uniform,' he added.

'Yes; but as you know there is no new uniform sir. They are not idiots.' I was starting to cry again.

'Stand up Markus I need to clarify something for you.'

I stood up, and he embraced me so as I was now weeping on his shoulder.

"Markus I am so sorry for what happened at the camp. Kurt Schmidt ordered me to get one of my troop to come to my tent, and the only person I thought that I could trust was you. I now realize that I was totally wrong for giving in to him. I should have stood up to him.'

'I felt so humiliated standing in front of both of you with no clothes on,' I sobbed.

'I didn't think that he would go that far Markus. I had heard rumours about him, but I was hoping for the best.'

'But you even watched me sir and saw me naked.'

'I can never apologise enough for what happened; I only stayed to try and protect you from him as he was clearly getting carried away.'

'And why did you encourage him?'

'I didn't encourage him, in fact, I was horrified at the way he was handling and touching you. Don't forget that I was the one who told you to get dressed. After you left us, he was extremely angry with me for spoiling his fun.'

'I wish that I could believe you sir. From where I was it looked as if the two of you had decided on how you were going to embarrass and humiliate me.'

'Markus I am sorry that things turned out the way they did, but I can give you a guarantee that nothing like this will ever happen again. You have been coming to football, and the Hitler Youth, for a number of years, so a lot of trust has built up between us. It would be a disaster if I lost one of my better members over this.'

I almost said to him that he should have thought of that before they sexually abused me in their tent.

'I will think about it sir and go back if I feel that I can.'

'Well Markus I want you back for highly personal reasons. I am particularly fond of you and miss having you around. He gave me another hug. I showed him to the door and let him out.

I went straight back into the sitting room to avoid facing my mother until I had the story that I was going to tell her worked out. She must have been waiting for me to let Stefan Mulder out for she immediately came into the room.

27

'Markus I think that you and I need to have a chat because there is something going on that I am not happy about.

'Everything is alright Mum. Something happened at camp and Herr Mulder was sorting it out. That is why he came around.'

'Everything is not alright Markus. I have seen what you have been like since you came back from camp. You won't even go to the meetings and your football practice which you love.'

'It's all sorted Mum, and I will probably start going back to the HJ and playing for the football team again.'

'I am going to get to the bottom of this whole matter, no matter what you say. Something happened to upset you, and I want to know what it was.' I could see that she wasn't going to give up on this and wanted answers.

It had been traumatic enough exposing my private parts in front of the two men at the camp, but what was I going to tell my mother. I had never talked about sexual things to her before in my life and would be highly embarrassed in discussing the incident with her.

'It's nothing Mum and something that I don't want to talk about,' I said as casually as possible, looking past her at a picture of Jesus that hung on the wall.

'Markus I talked to Walter the other day as I was worried about you, and he told me that there is a story going around the group that you were sexually abused at the camp by Stefan Mulder and the Regional Director Kurt Schmidt. Is that what happened?'

I couldn't stop the tears coming and found it impossible to answer my mother. The deep shame of the incident just overwhelmed me, and I sobbed uncontrollably.

'So the rumour is right Markus. I can see by your reaction, that what they are saying did actually happen,' my mother said as she came over to sit on the arm of my chair and put an arm around me. 'I am not going to ask you any more about it as it must be terribly embarrassing for you, but I will report it and get those men thrown out of their positions. I wish that you had a father around to sort this out.'

'Mum, I don't want anything done about it as I am fearful of what they will do to me in retaliation for having told on them. I am especially fearful of Herr Schmidt.'

'I'm sorry, but I can't just ignore what has happened Markus. It is far too serious to allow it to go unchallenged.'

'But Stefan Mulder has been like a father to me over the years. He mustn't lose his position as coach of the football team and leader of the Hitler Youth because of this. It wasn't his idea, and he was ordered to do it by the director.'

As I talked to my mother, it became very clear to me why I had been so upset by what had happened. Growing up had been tough without having a father around and Stefan Mulder had been the only father figure that I had known. I believed him when he said that he had a soft spot for me and that he had been forced to invite me to his tent by Kurt Schmidt. I didn't want to lose Stefan Mulder as my father figure as he had been such an influential person in my life. I was willing to forgive him for what happened in the tent, provided a similar situation never happened again.

'I will go and see your leader Stefan Mulder tomorrow Markus and get the whole thing sorted out. I have to do something about what happened; otherwise more children are going to be abused.'

I could see our little chat was at an end. She gave me a hug and then returned to the kitchen, leaving me in a decidedly confused emotional state. I never thought that Walter would have told her what he knew. My mother could be remarkably persistent at times, and he obviously hadn't been able to avoid her direct questioning.

I felt immensely relieved that it was all out in the open now and that my mother knew. I had been very apprehensive about what she would do if she heard about it and also if I had to tell her the details of what exactly had happened.

Chapter 5

My mother went over to the stadium the following day after she got off from work and was home by 5:00 pm looking extremely pleased with herself.

Walter and I had got home from school, starving as usual, only to find that the smells of dinner didn't hit us as we came through the door. My mother wasn't even at home.

'Sorry boys,' she said as she came into the house. 'I did that job that we talked about last night Markus on my way home, and it took a bit longer than expected. We will talk about it later.'

She cooked the dinner and about two hours later she invited me to join her in the sitting room.

'Well Markus let me tell you how I got on. It went a lot better than expected, and I am quite pleased with what I have agreed with Herr Mulder.'

'You actually talked to him Mum.'

'Yes Markus I certainly did.'

'Did he take it seriously as he must have been quite surprised?'

'If you give me a minute Markus I'll tell you. Stop interrupting,' my mother replied irritably. 'To summarise what was agreed between us; he is going to report Kurt Schmidt for what he did and make sure that it never happens again. In exchange, I said that we would support his story that he was made to do it and didn't participate in any of the abuse.'

'How did you get him to agree to that?' I asked.

'I told him that if he didn't do what I asked then we would implicate him in the abuse, and that would be the end of his job working with the youth. That seemed to focus his attention on what I was saying.'

'Will I have to give evidence mum?' I was anxious that I would have to stand up in a court of law and give my account of what happened which would be highly embarrassing.'

'I have checked on the procedure Markus, and, because you are under age, the judge would hear your evidence in private and not in an open court.'

'Thanks Mum; you have done a terrific job in sorting it out.'

'I surprised myself Markus, and I am confident that Stefan Mulder will stick to his word.' She got up, terminating our little meeting.

I went up to my bedroom to consider the implications of what she had told me. I was very relieved that Stefan Mulder hadn't been implicated, and, in fact, my mother had been clever in using him to expose the real villain in the piece, Kurt Schmidt. My father figure was still in place and I felt confident in returning to the stadium now without the risk of being sexually abused again. It still would be difficult being in Stefan Mulder's presence as he had seen me naked and suffering something that I was highly embarrassed about, but I suppose that I would get over that in time.

I returned to the Hitler Youth the following day and also started attending the football practices. Two weeks later I was called into the office during training to see a very intimidating man who was wearing an SS uniform. The SS had a reputation for being unscrupulous and very aggressive, so I feared the worst.

'I am told that you are Markus BEKER, is that correct?' he asked me.

'Yes sir.'

I want to ask you some questions about what happened at your recent camp?'

My heart dropped to my boots, and I suddenly felt extremely nervous.

'Markus, I don't want you to feel anxious as it sounds as if you have been put through enough drama recently,' he said in a friendly voice. I was surprised by his casual tone. 'I will try and make it as easy as possible for you and I can also tell you that I am reasonably certain that you won't have to appear in court.'

'I don't want to give details in case they take revenge on me.'

'Don't worry about that, the culprit won't be around to harm you. We have had a report from your Hitler Youth leader that he was forced to invite you to his tent where you were subject to sexual abuse. Can you confirm that?'

'I was asked to go to my leader's tent after the evening sing song and Herr Schmidt asked me to undress and then he touched me sexually and fondled me.'

'Did Herr Mulder participate at all in what was going on?'

'No; he just sat there watching and I saw that he was quite upset by what Herr Schmidt was doing.'

'Was that the only time you have been sexually abused by these two men or either of them on their own?'

'Yes, it has never happened before or since.'

'Have you ever been involved in sexual activity with the other boys in the group?'

'No, I have never even heard of something like that happening in our group or in the football team,' I truthfully replied.

'How well do you know Herr Mulder and do you trust him?'

'Herr Mulder has been a father figure for me as I have been growing up. He has always been in charge of the football club, and he then took over the role of Hitler Youth leader when that started. My father was killed in France in 1916, so I have never known a father at home. I totally trust Herr Mulder and know that he wouldn't do anything like this if he hadn't been forced.'

'Markus you have answered my questions extremely well and I believe all that you have told me. It will not be necessary to question you again or for you to attend court. I have enough evidence now to put Herr Schmidt away for a very long time and make sure that he doesn't abuse any more HJ members. The party is trying its hardest to get rid of all homosexuals out of society. They are the scum of the earth. We will not tolerate any leaders who exhibit homosexual tendencies. You can go back and join your friends now.'

And that was it. Stefan Mulder called me into his office a few days later and said that Kurt Schmidt had been arrested and imprisoned based on the evidence that had been collected by the SS officer, and that was the end of the matter. My life returned to normal, and all the gossiping stopped. Boris had also been interviewed by the SS and had been told, in no uncertain terms that he must stop spreading malicious rumours, or they would arrest him and lock him up far away from Lubeck.

'Mum, that whole matter with the regional director of the Hitler Youth has been sorted out,' I told her when I got home that evening. He has been arrested and put in prison. I have also been told that I won't have to give evidence at his trial.'

'Is Herr Mulder still the leader of your group?'

'Yes it was him who told me what happened. So he is still around.'

'Do you still trust him Markus after what happened?'

'Yes Mum and I am sure that it will never happen again while he is around. I still look up to him as my leader. It's also terrific that I am now back at the stadium like before. In fact, there is a stronger bond between us now than there was before this whole unpleasant event took place.'

'Just be careful the next time that you go to a camp Markus, and don't go to late meetings in the leaders' tents.'

'Yes Mum I have learnt my lesson, but there is not much that I can do if they order me to attend.'

Chapter 6

Life settled down again in Lubeck and my week resumed its usual pattern. The only difference was that I lost my non-blood brother. Walter moved out of our house and went to live with his parents in Munich. His father's job had worked out well, and he had managed to secure an apartment that would accommodate Walter and his sister, so he left us in September of 1931. I missed him as there was now nobody with me going to and from school every day and when I went to the stadium. His chatter and constant questions had been irritating at times, but, now that he wasn't around, the silence was hard to endure. He had been a true brother to me, and a strong bond had formed between us. Little did I know at the time that Walter would prove to me, later in my life, what a true brother he was.

As the thirties progressed, the Nazi party increased its control of the country, and a law was passed making it mandatory for all young people to join the Hitler Youth. The numbers coming to the meetings increased significantly, and it became a lot less personal. Because of the large numbers all we did most of the time was parade around the town singing Nazi propaganda songs with the drums playing. It became quite tiresome, and there were a lot of disgruntled members unhappy with having to attend.

The meetings moved from Friday evening to Saturday displacing our football matches, and they lasted most of the day. On a Friday evening, smaller groups used to meet in people's houses and the leaders used to go around giving propaganda talks. Our heads were filled with what the Nazi authorities felt we should know.

The members of the Hitler Youth were also used to carry out certain tasks for the party such as distribute leaflets on the street or push them through people's mail boxes. It was also compulsory to go to the annual mass meeting and celebration in Nuremberg where Hitler used to address us with his spine tingling rhetoric. We would have done anything for Hitler; he was our idol.

In 1935, when I was eighteen, I decided to join the Flieger-HJ which was the flying section of the Hitler Youth. I left the mainstream Hitler Youth, which still met at the local stadium, and joined another group that met in a large field beside the aerodrome just outside the town. It was an extremely sad day leaving Stefan Mulder and the group I had been part of for so many years, but doing the same old routine every day wasn't keeping me interested.

The Flieger-HJ was much better fun and actually involved learning to fly in gliders. Under the conditions the allies had imposed following the First World War, Germany was limited in the number of aircraft the Luftwaffe was allowed to have. Hitler got around the restrictions by having masses of gliders built. These were not classified as aircraft and were the best method of training pilots.

The first task that we had to do when we joined was make model gliders, and these had to be able to fly. By making the gliders, we started to understand the principals of flight. At every meeting, there were competitions between the members to see whose glider could fly furthest. If we lost, we would go away and make modifications to our glider to make it stay up longer and fly further.

After a few months, we were told to buy the materials to make a full sized glider capable of being flown by the builder or in my case builders. A number of us didn't have enough money to pay for all the materials required to make a glider, so three of us clubbed together to raise the money to buy the necessary materials. We then took it turns to be taught how to fly our glider.

It was only the older members of the Flieger-HJ who were allowed to pilot the gliders, the younger members, and those without gliders, manned the catapults that were used to launch them. I loved the flying, and, after a few months training, was classified as a competent glider pilot and ear marked for the Luftwaffe, if and when war came.

As yet there weren't the motorised planes available to teach us in, but one day they took the better pilots from our group across to the other side of the airfield where we were taken up in a proper plane for a twenty minute flight. I loved everything about flying; the roar of the engines, the sudden calm when we left the ground, the overwhelming smell of fuel and hot oil, the bird's eye view of the ground. I was totally hooked, and I decided that when war came, I would fly for Germany. This was appearing more and more likely as the rhetoric from Hitler became increasingly warlike.

In April 1936, when I was nineteen years of age, I applied to the Engineering School at Christian-Albrechts-University in Kiel, and I was extremely excited when I passed all the examinations required to be accepted for the semester that would commence in September of that year. Unknown to me, Walter had also been accepted by the university in Kiel to study the Sciences. When we realised that we were both going to be in Kiel, we agreed to share digs together when we commenced our courses in late September. Before term started, we both travelled to Kiel to look around the University and to find suitable accommodation close to the University that was in our price range.

One of the strict conditions we had to follow in being allowed to attend University was to remain an active member in one of the sections of the Hitler Youth, which in my case was the Flieger-HJ. In fact, because it was a mandatory condition for all students, there were branches of all the different sections of the Hitler Youth available on the University Campus. Walter joined the section that was associated with the SS.

To give us something else to do Walter and I joined the University rowing club where we both became competent oarsmen.

One outcome of all the physical training and development that we had done in the Hitler Youth was we both had considerable strength in our upper body. This now aided our rowing. I was a few centimetres under 2 meters, with broad shoulders and well developed biceps, and had no difficulty in being included in the University racing crews.

I settled into University life surprisingly quickly and found myself fully occupied in my studies and social activities. Walter and I attended the same lectures for six hours per week in our first year, so that helped in the settling in process. I had to study Mathematics and Physics as part of my engineering course while he also had to study these subjects as part of his Science course. The other twenty eight hours a week of my time table were spent in the Engineering Block studying subjects such as engineering drawing and mechanical skills. I loved it, and every day proved to me that I had chosen the correct discipline. I also made a whole new group of friends.

Partying and socialising was also an essential part of the curriculum and one that I enjoyed more than Walter did. At a social event to celebrate the start of the year, I met a very intelligent and attractive female student called Susie Rothenburger who was studying Modern Languages. She lived at home in Kiel with her parents as her father was a naval officer based at the dockyards in Kiel.

The first love of my life swept me off my feet and gave me an education in relationships with the female of the species. In Lubeck, I hadn't had the opportunity of getting to know the fairer sex as I had been so tied up with my activities, and looking after my mother. Walter, who was very shy and kept away from women, wasn't too impressed, but we tried to include him in our activities on as many occasions as it was feasible. Life was good, and I grew in confidence on a daily basis, thoroughly enjoying life as a University student.

In March of 1937 I saw a notice on the Rowing Club notice board:

THE CLUB IS SENDING TWO CREWS TO THE
HENLEY ROYAL REGATTA

VENUE: THE RIVER THAMES JUST OUTSIDE LONDON,

DATE: 20th. - 27th. JULY

ANY MEMBERS INTERESTED PLEASE CONTACT
THE SECRETARY etc.......

'What do you think of that Walter,' I asked him as we stopped to read the notice.

'That would be an exciting trip, but it probably would be too expensive?' He didn't look as enthusiastic as I felt.

'I imagine that the Club will provide some financial help to the crews that go, so it may be affordable.'

'I would love to go Markus. Let's find out more about it.'

After various negotiations with the Club and our parents, we managed to get the money together and set off by train for England in the middle of July. Walter and I were selected in a crew that was entered in the Visitors Challenge Cup which was an event for coxless fours. The College had arranged to borrow boats when we got to Henley, so we didn't have to go through the drama of taking them with us. The train took us as far as the port of Rotterdam from where we caught a boat to Harwich on the east coast of England. After a rough voyage across the North Sea on an ancient ferry, we disembarked at a very grey and misty Harwich, feeling the worse for wear. From there, we travelled by train to Liverpool Street station in London where we transferred by underground to the University of London residences in Bloomsbury where we were staying.

Chapter 7

To the approval of all in our group, we discovered that the student residences for London University, where we were staying for the duration of the regatta, were within walking distance of all the main tourist attractions and restaurants. On the evening of the day we arrived, we searched locally for a low cost place to eat that was within our students' budget. Exhausted from the long journey by boat and train we decided to leave the tourist sites for another day.

The following morning we had to travel out to Henley-on-Thames so as we could try out our borrowed boats and become acquainted with the river. It was warm and clammy with the smell of sweaty bodies pervading the air in the tube that we caught from Russel Square underground station to Paddington where we had to take a suburban train to Henley-on-Thames. Just over an hour later we were getting off the train at Henley station, very close to the area of the riverbank used for the regatta. As we came out of the station, we saw rows of large white tents lined up in the fields that bordered the river. The green grass, the white tents and the colour of the river made a truly impressive picture. The dank, heavy air of the city had been replaced by the fresh air of the countryside. We followed the signs to the boating park, and a short time later both the Kiel crews were muscling their oars on the river. Our club house in Kiel was situated on the edge of the large harbour, an inlet of the Baltic Sea. We rowed in the shallower waters of the harbour well away from the main shipping; however, the water often was quite rough which endangered the boats. Of course, it was also salt water and icy cold being so far north. There were many times during the winter when it was too cold to take the boats out as the harbour was frozen. At such times, we had to do all our training in the club house. Henley was heaven compared to what we were used to. The biggest advantage was that the Thames was a fresh water river, and the course was also well protected from the wind and calm as a duck pond. Another plus for us was that the sun was out, so it was lovely and warm. My crew got used to our boat remarkably quickly. Looking around we saw a lot of other crews out on the river getting in their practice for the races which were due to start the following day. Most of the crews we saw seemed to exceptionally talented and fast.

After an hour on the river, we left our 'four' in the boat park and went to have lunch in one of the marquees that we had seen dotted along the river bank. I was able to practise some of my English on the people serving and found that I could get on extremely well. The biggest problem I had in understanding was when they talked too fast. I also had difficulty in picking up the words because of their accents. All through my schooling my mother insisted that I learn English as one of my subjects. She said that I would need to be able to read the language when I qualified as an engineer. Being in England I was now able to practice what I had learnt on real English speakers.

In the afternoon, we went out for another test row, and we did a lot better. The problem with borrowing a boat was that every shell has its own idiosyncrasies, and we had to get used to this one extremely quickly if we wanted to be competitive. Near the end of the time given to us for acclimatisation, our Coach was happy that the shell was going as fast or even faster than we had gone in Kiel, and he terminated training for the day. We packed up and caught the train back to Paddington and from there we returned in the cauldron of the tube to the hostel. Nerves started to hit me as I thought about tomorrow's race. It wasn't just the fact that we were up against crews that we had never met before, it was also that it was such a grand occasion and so different to the scene back in Kiel. I was starting to realise how large the world was and how different it was to the places I was familiar with, my home town of Lubeck and the university town of Kiel. The people that we had met so far in London seemed to be so much more relaxed and there was a lot of colour around which added to the splendour of everything. My eyes had been opened.

'What do you think of London Walter?' I asked him as we walked down Tottenham Court Road towards Leicester Square. We were looking for a restaurant we could afford for dinner.

'I love it here Markus. There is such a bustle about the place, and there are all these cars, buses and taxis around.'

'The people look happier here than in Germany for some reason. Back home everything is a dark grey and people are going around with long faces. They are also dressed in an old fashioned way compared to London.'

'I could get used to it here,' Walter said looking around him, taking in all that was going on in the street.

'I would love to have the money to go to a theatre. There are so many fabulous shows advertised outside the theatres that we walk past,' I said as we passed the Lyric Theatre in Shaftsbury Avenue.

'Would your English be good enough to understand what was going on Markus?' Walter asked me.

'I think that I would follow what was going on, provided it was a musical or something like that, and it was not too deep.'

'We are only here for a few days so we won't have time. Keep your money for beer as we will need plenty of that after our races.'

We had a delicious meal and then walked back to the hostel to spend the night. The following day we left at just after 11:30 am and made our way to Henley-on-Thames on the train. Our event wasn't until 3:15 pm, so we didn't want to get there too early and have to spend a lot of time hanging around.

We excelled ourselves and won our race by half a length which meant that we would be racing the following day, which was the Thursday, against a crew from Oxford University. We had a couple of beers in a tent set up as a bar before catching the train back to the hostel. After bathing and relaxing, the members of our victorious crew, went out together to celebrate our win with a meal, and not with more beers. The other Kiel crew had lost, so they were drowning their sorrows. Our coach came along too to keep an eye on us and make sure that we didn't break his rule on drink.

Our race on the Thursday was against Oriel College, Oxford, one of the better crews in our section of the regatta. The assessment of Oriel proved to be correct as they beat us very easily, coming in a full boat length ahead of us. That was the end of our participation in the Visitors Challenge Cup. Rather than 'celebratory' beers, we went for some 'forget the race' beers. In fact, we were invited by our victors, the members of the Oriel crew, to join them in the Watney's beer tent.

Chapter 8

That invitation unexpectedly changed the rest of my life.

I was sitting having a quiet drink in the group which now contained members of the Oriel crew that had beaten us. Walter poked me in the ribs and pointed to one of the Oriel crew sitting three away from me.

'That's your twin over there Markus. Look at him; he actually looks your double.'

'There is a strong resemblance I must admit,' I replied, looking more closely at him.

'If he didn't come from England and you from Germany, I would suggest that you were the offspring of the same window cleaner,' Walter added.

'Don't be obscene Walter, but I must agree that he looks remarkably like me.'

Walter had got my curiosity aroused as I had never seen anybody that looked exactly like the image that I saw in the mirror every day. I got up and went over to talk to my double.

'Hi. My name is Markus BEKER,' I put out my hand to shake his as I leant towards him.

'Hi Markus, my name is Chris Becker,' he replied, giving me a funny look.

Now it was getting weird. He had the same surname as me.

'How do you spell your surname?' I asked, wedging myself onto the bench beside him.

'B E C K E R,' he spelt it out for me. 'And what about you?'

'B E K E R - it's the German way of spelling it.'

'That is unbelievable we look like peas out of the same pod, and our names are the same,' Chris added. 'I am almost afraid to ask for your date of birth.'

'If we happen to have the same birth date then that certainly makes it interesting,' I said, joking but still fascinated by this development. 'How does the 5th. February 1917 sound.'

Chris looked totally shocked and couldn't answer for a minute........

'Markus it is the same, which is just far too much of a coincidence. In some extraordinary way, you may be my twin brother.'

As an automatic reaction, we grabbed hold of each other and embraced. I didn't care who watched us; I had possibly found an unknown brother and there were tears in my eyes.

'The neighbours back home in Lubeck used to tell me that they thought I had a twin brother, but my mother used to deny it when I confronted her,' I said.

'Markus, my father is coming to watch me row tomorrow, and I have already made a plan to meet him after our race. Why don't you come and meet him with me and give him a surprise,' Chris said as he broke away from my embrace.

'But my father was killed at the Somme in 1916 Markus,' I stuttered. 'If we are brothers then how can he still be alive?'

'No, he wasn't killed Markus. He was captured by the British at the battle of the Somme and interred in a POW camp, in the north of England, until the end of the war,' Chris replied.

'My mother and grandparents have always told me that he was killed. I can't believe that I still have a father, and I will see him tomorrow.'

'No doubt he will explain it all to you when he meets you Markus. I knew he came from Lubeck in Germany, but I didn't know that I had a twin brother and a mother still living.'

'Do you think that it is a good idea to confront him Chris? Should you not warn him first?'

'No I want to see his face when he sees the two of us together.'

'How strong is his heart, will he be able to take the shock?'

'Oh he's as strong as an ox, and don't forget that it won't be a surprise for him as if we are correct in our assumptions, he knows about us already,' Chris said, now extremely excited about the prospect of confronting his Dad.

'I don't know how to express how I feel Chris, but it just feels right.'

'I would love to meet you this evening Markus. Where are you staying?'

'I am at a hostel in London, are you able to come in this evening?'

"I am afraid that we have a bus organized to take us back to Oxford at 6:00 pm, so I can't divert by London. How about meeting in the morning? I can get the train from Oxford to Paddington station and meet you there around 10:00 am. We can have an early lunch, and then we can travel together to Henley.'

'That sounds perfect Chris. I'll see you in the morning.'

I took ages to go to sleep that night after the amazing experience of discovering that I had a twin brother. It was also going to be a highly emotional experience to meet my father who, up until now, I had been led to believe had died in the last war.

The following morning, being as tall as I was, and he being of a similar height, I had no trouble in spotting Chris when he got off the Oxford train.

He came through the ticket barrier, and we embraced again just as if we had known each other all our lives. It just seemed to be the right thing to do. We then found a restaurant close to the station that we could afford.

'Who is going to be first to tell their story?' I asked when we had sat down with our plates of food.

'Perhaps you could start telling me about my mother as I don't know her and I haven't even seen a picture of her.'

'Well, her name is Anelie and she is quite tall relative to the other women in our neighbourhood, being around 1.60 meters. She has dark brown hair flecked with a bit of grey, she is far too thin, and she has a kind face. She works in the bakery run by my granddad; he is our father's father.' I had considerable difficulty in describing my mother. I had always just taken her for granted as she had been a permanent fixture for the whole of my life and not somebody that I had ever had to describe.

'Is she in good health?' He butted in.

'I have never known her to be sick and miss a day at the bakery.'

'Are her parents, who would be my grandparents, still alive?'

'No, they both died in 1926. They lived with Mum and I until their deaths. Grandpa was a permanent invalid as a result of being gassed at Ypres in the First World War. They died within a few months of each other during the winter of 1926.'

'What else can you tell me about Lubeck?

I went on to give him as many details as I felt were relevant and would give him a picture of my childhood and of the area where we lived. He was particularly interested in hearing about my involvement in the Hitler Youth organization and my flying experience. I obviously didn't tell him about my exposure and humiliation with Herr Mulder and Herr Schmidt at the camp.

'What happens if there is another war Markus?' Chris suddenly asked me.

'I hope it won't come to that, especially now that I know I have a brother in England.'

'Our newspapers are full of it at the moment, and some of the commentators are convinced that Hitler wants to go to war,' Chris said with considerable feeling.

'We are told all the time at our meetings that we are going to be soldiers and airmen fighting for the glory of Germany. I hope that it doesn't end up in war as I want to become an engineer.'

'I am sure that all the leaders will see sense and will avoid war.' Chris added.

'I hope that you are correct. It's your turn now to tell me all about my father and Yorkshire,' I said, leaning towards him over the table.

He leant back in his chair and looked at his watch.

'We had better go and catch the train to Henley-on-Thames now Markus as I need to be there by 1:30 pm. I will tell you about Yorkshire on the way'

He collected his bag, and we paid our bill and left for Paddington station. On the way, he told me about his life with his father in Harrogate and how he helped his Dad out in the bakery. It sounded just like the bakery in Lubeck where I helped out. He also talked about his schooling, his experience playing rugby and cricket and getting in to Oxford University. By the time that we got to Henley I knew a lot more about him, and I also felt that I knew Helmut, my father.

I watched from the bank as the Oxford four, with Chris at number two, lost to a very good American University crew. I commiserated with Chris after the race, but he didn't seem too upset about it. He seemed to be now fully focused on the meeting with our father.

We located him in the Watney's beer tent where Chris had arranged to meet him. Luckily he had his back to us, so he didn't see us approach. Even amongst rowing men it was easy to spot him as he was 1.8 meters in his socks and still had a back that was ramrod straight.

Chris tapped him on the shoulder, 'Dad we are here.'

'Whose we?' he said cheerfully as he turned around.

His face froze, and some of his beer slopped onto the ground.

'Markus, how do you happen to be here?' he gasped, saying my name without any hesitancy.

'So it's true. He is my twin,' Chris blurted out. The look on my father's face told us everything.

'Yes Chris, you have a twin brother. Let's go and find somewhere quiet where I can tell you all about the secret I have had to hide from you for the whole of your life.'

My Dad bought each of us a beer and we wandered outside until we found a quiet place where we wouldn't be disturbed. My father started off:

'It all started in 1916 when there was a lull in the fighting, and I was given leave to go home for a week from the trenches in France. The weather had been dreadful, and the Spring offensives wouldn't start for a while, so a lot of us were given home leave to strengthen us for the battles to come. You two were the result of that little break.'

'But that doesn't explain why my mother is in Germany while you are here in England?' Chris said.

'After my leave I went back to the front to my regiment and was one of the rare and fortunate ones to be taken prisoner by the British in the battle of the Somme in July 1916. I was taken to England and ended up in a POW camp in Richmond, North Yorkshire, where I was interred for the remainder of the war. I did receive letters from home and was aware that I was the father of twin boys.'

'So you were in the POW camp for around two years, was that a terrible experience?' I asked.

'It was extremely cold in the winter, but they allowed us out to work on the farms which helped to pass the time, and we also were fed well by the farmers. We had no desire to return to the war and the trenches, so there were no attempts to escape. We were quite happy to stay where we were.'

'What happened when the war finished Dad?' I asked.

'There were terrible stories coming back from Germany about the Communists taking over the main cities and lots of criminal activity on the streets. There were also major food shortages, so I wasn't in any great hurry to return to Germany. I had been doing a lot of work for a local landowner, who was a very pleasant old boy, and he kindly offered to sponsor me in opening a German style bakery in Harrogate if I wanted to stay.'

'Did many other internees not return home Dad,' Chris asked

'Oh I suppose not more than ten stayed in the end.'

'What happened next? I asked

'I wrote to your mother and asked her to join me in Harrogate with both of you. She replied that she couldn't leave Lubeck as her father was suffering terribly and she needed to remain there to look after him and her mother.

'I travelled to her parent's home in St. Lorenz Sud in Lubeck to try and change your mother's mind. She still refused to move to England, but said that she would come later if circumstances changed. Because of the continuing severe food shortages in Germany we decided to split you up for the time being or until her parents passed on. So Kristoff, I brought you back to the UK, and you stayed with your mother in Lubeck, Markus.'

'Why are our surnames spelt differently?' Chris asked.

'I decided that it would make it easier for us to be assimilated into the community in Yorkshire if I changed our name to Becker, spelt with a C K and not two K's. Also, I changed your name to Christopher from the German Kristoff.'

'Why have we never been told about this? Why have I had to grow up on my own when, in fact, I had a brother?' I was now very upset if not a little angry.

'You're mother, for one reason or another, never came to England and one year passed to the next until we felt that it would upset you too much to move, especially as you were both getting on so well where you were.'

'So our housekeeper Gwen, who has been around all my life, isn't my mother?' Chris asked his father.

'No, you now understand the reason why I could never marry Gwen, and why I have called her my housekeeper,' my father explained.

'Should I tell my mother that I have met you and Chris? I asked.

'I think that she will be relieved that she doesn't have to conceal the truth any longer. You can tell her that you have a father who is alive and that your twin brother is also flourishing.'

'Can I come and visit you and Chris soon? I asked.

'You can come over next year during the summer holidays and spend some time with us. Perhaps Chris can return to Lubeck with you and meet his mother.'

'I'll look forward to that, and in the meantime maybe we can write letters to each other,' I replied.

My father then suggested that Chris and I go off and watch the rowing and leave him to adjust to the miracle of having his two sons in England. I could see that meeting me after all these years had affected him and he had withdrawn into himself. Over the next two hours, I glanced back at him a number of times to check that he was still happy to be on his own, and he had the look of someone who was doing a lot of remembering.

Chapter 9

What the father remembered:

The train pulled into Lubeck station after an exceptionally long and tortuous journey from the German front lines at Arras. The date was May 1916, and Unteroffizier Helmut BEKER had been given leave to escape the horrors of war for ten days. The German army was firmly entrenched opposite the British and French forces at Arras in Eastern France. The First World War had been grinding along for over eighteen months, and Helmut, having been a part of it from the beginning in 1914, was mentally and physically exhausted. The winter had been a particularly tough one, and Helmut's little troop had been reduced to a state where they were barely able to survive let alone fight valiantly for the Emperor. With the rain, hail and snow continuing, and the Spring offensives postponed, the German commanders decided to give the longer serving men two weeks leave.

The journey had started off with a long trudge through the night along a potholed muddy road from the town of Arras to a small station ten kilometres away where a train had managed to get to. The smell of the mud was reinforced by the smell of death. Arras station itself wasn't considered to be safe as shells from the enemy batteries were able to reach that far and they had a habit of arriving at inconvenient times. Hence the reason for the long march through the dark, wet and stormy night.

By the time they reached the safety of the train Helmut was soaked through and caked with mud, but in good spirits for once as there was no danger here. The smell of death had been replaced by the smell of the steam engine waiting to take him away from the fighting. He would wake up in the morning knowing that he hadn't lost another good friend and colleague during the night.

The train had finally departed and had chugged all through what was left of the night. Dawn saw them crossing the border into Germany. Looking out the window that he was leaning against, he thought how ironic it was that the countryside here was untouched by war and yet, not so far away, there was still a deadly war going on involving millions of soldiers. The people lucky enough to be still living in Germany had no idea as to the suffering their husbands and sons were going through at the front.

The journey continued throughout the day and into the following night, with a number of long delays in cold stations waiting for yet another train to bring him closer to Lubeck. One thing that kept his spirits at a high level was the thought of spending time with his beloved wife Anelie, who he had married in a rushed ceremony just before he set off for war in 1914. He hadn't been able to let her know that he was on his way home, so his arrival would be a massive surprise.

Helmut had been born in Lubeck, Northern Germany, in March 1894. He was the son of a baker who was the proud owner of his own Backhaus. Leaving the local school when he was fifteen, he had been apprenticed in the same trade as his father. He was just twenty one when he had been called up to the German army and plucked from his job in the bakery to fight on the Western front. He was still only twenty two, but he looked like an old man and he felt like a hundred and two.

Much taller than the average German male at nearly 1.8 meters, he was unusually gentle in nature and called, by his mates, 'the Gentle Giant'. Prior to going off to the war he had played for the local football team as the goalkeeper. He was given that position, much to his disgust because he was the tallest and, therefore, the biggest barrier on the team. In the trenches, his friends were convinced that his height would be the death of him as he was considerably taller than the other members of his troop, and there was always the possibility of his head popping up above the parapet of the trench, especially when they were digging a new trench.

Even though it was 4:30 am when he arrived in Lubeck, he decided to walk to his wife's parents' house. Hopefully she would be still staying there. Not knowing that he was coming home they would be very surprised; however, he was confident the joy soon would dispel the anxiety of someone banging on the door at such an early hour.

He banged on the front door. No answer. He banged again and called out her name. An upstairs window opened in the house opposite, and an old woman stuck her head out.

'What's all the noise at this hour of the morning,' she called out.

'It's Helmut BEKER, Frau Muller. I am trying to wake my wife,

'Be a bit more quiet about it will you. You'll wake the dead with the noise you are making,' she added as she slammed down the window.

Helmut heard a noise inside the house which sounded as if someone was coming down the stairs.

'Whose there?' he heard his wife's voice.

'It's Helmut, Anelie.'

The next sound was of the bolts being drawn back on the door and the lock being turned. The door was thrown open. His wife rushed out and threw her arms around him.

'Are you going to let me into the house Anelie?' Helmut gasped. 'It is cold out here in the street, and Frau Muller is probably going to yell at me again.

'Come in, come in, come in, Helmut. I am just so surprised to see you.' She kept touching his face, checking whether it was actually him or some extraordinary dream.

He went through the passageway to the rear of the house and entered the kitchen. His mother in law had got up as a result of his knocking and was now vigorously poking the range cooker to get the fire going.

'This is a surprise Helmut,' Frau Schreiber commented.

'I had no time to write to you as they only told us that we could take leave at the last minute.'

'Anyway it is nice to see you after so long, even though you are looking as if you could do with a good meal,' Frau Schreiber added.

'I only have to return to the Front in eight days' time, so I have plenty of time to recover and get used to sleeping in a bed again.'

'Oh Helmut, I can't believe that it is you. It's a year and a half since I have seen you and I have missed you,' Anelie said, giving him another massive hug.

'Well, I have got the fire going now, so I am going back to your father, Anelie. You should give Helmut something to eat before you go to work. I'll leave you two to it.' With that she left them to return upstairs to her husband.

'So your Father is also here, Anelie?' Helmut asked.

'Yes, he was gassed at the second battle of Ypres in April last year. He then spent six months in hospital before being invalided out of the army. He has been here ever since.'

'Has he fully recovered?'

'No, he will never get better as his lungs were so badly damaged. He is sadly not the same person as he used to be as he has trouble breathing and is continually having coughing fits. I sympathise with my mother for what she has to put up with, and it has taken its toll on her health.'

'This bloody war Anelie, it has a lot to answer for. I have lost so many good friends. They have been chatting to me one minute, and blown to pieces the next.'

'It's even worse than that Helmut.' Anelie looked into his eyes. 'You probably haven't heard that your twin brother Markus was killed last year at the Battle of Bolimov. He was buried close to Warsaw. Your poor father was devastated.'

'I did hear that news and it hit me particularly hard as I couldn't even get to his funeral. I'll talk to my Dad about the situation tomorrow when, hopefully, I will feel stronger.'

'I must go to work at 6:00 Helmut so you can sleep until I get back after 3:00 pm. I guess that you need a lot of sleep and rest.'

'I'll be fine Anelie. The thing that I crave the most is to be warm.'

'You can make yourself some coffee and have something to eat. I must get dressed and get off to work. The customers will be coming into the bakery at 6:30 as usual. Unfortunately, they don't know that you have returned for a few days from the war, and they get terribly grumpy if they have to wait.'

When Anelie returned from the bakery at 3:30 pm he was still in bed, having slept the sleep of the dead.

She leant over to give him a kiss, and he sensed her presence. He grabbed her and pulled her to him and managed to get her under the covers. That started an evening of love making the like of which neither had experienced before. The months of being apart had bred a new greed in both of them, and they just wanted to spend time locked in each other's embrace.

That established the pattern of the next eight days. Anelie managed to take some days off from the bakery and they spent an enjoyable time rediscovering the picturesque old city of Lubeck. Little did they know that this was the last time they would be able to spend time together as the war would intervene dramatically in their relationship.

Once Helmut had caught up on his sleep he was able to help his father in the bakery, and it was just like old times. The heat from the ovens was superb and drove all the raw cold of the trenches out of his bones, and the smell of the freshly baked bread made him feel extremely secure.

The time flew by, and all too soon there was the very sad scene at Lubeck train station of Anelie and Helmut locked in a final embrace. It was with immense difficulty that he had to tear himself away from her and get on the train before it left without him. As the train chugged its way out of the station, he waved to her through the space at the window he had fought to gain. For once his size had helped in winning his space.

Chapter 10

The Father's story continues:

The train was packed with many of his fellow travellers being uniformed clad members of the Wehrmacht returning to the front in France. Helmut managed to squeeze himself into a seat which certainly wasn't large enough for his large frame, but meant that he didn't have to stand for the entire journey.

He thought to himself: *I must be out of my mind to be returning voluntarily to the hell of the trenches? Could I not slip away somewhere with Anelie until this dreadful war is over? I can't endure what I experienced in France, and I will most likely be killed in the next attack. I won't have the lovely comforting smell of freshly baked bread in my life for a long time if ever again.*

Dread invaded Helmut's heart and a fear that he hadn't experienced before took over his whole thought process. Sadness enveloped him, and he put his head down to hide the tears that were welling in his eyes.

Arriving at the station near Arras, where he had left with hope in his heart two weeks previously, he had to trudge through the deep mud and puddles in order to re-join his men in the support trenches. Shortly after arriving he was called to a briefing where he was told that his regiment was being relocated to the Somme area to strengthen the German lines there. A major offensive was expected as the enemy was massing their troops against them in that area.

Helmut's hope that he might be going to a region where the conditions would be better were quickly dispelled. They were given two days to familiarise themselves with the geography of the new trench layout before being moved up into the front line. More deep mud and the stench of death. Information from enemy soldiers, taken prisoner in forays that took place at night, confirmed that the British and French forces were preparing a massive attack which would involve hundreds of thousands of soldiers across an unusually wide front.

On the 1st. July all hell broke loose. Just before dawn a massive bombardment on the German advanced trenches commenced. Masses of the enemy came over the top of their trenches and started moving towards the German positions like ants. The bombardment suddenly stopped, and an eerie silence hung over no-man's land. The enemy troops kept approaching in a line about two kilometres long. The order to fire wasn't given until the enemy were well within range, and then every gun, on the German side, opened fire. It was a massacre and the British and French soldiers dropped like flies in front of the German lines. Amazingly enough the occasional brave soul got through and started firing into the trenches. Relief parties were immediately sent to the areas under attack, and they were quickly expelled back into no-man's land.

War had been easier to handle emotionally when the opposing armies were just confronting each other from the safety of their respective trenches. The enemy had seemed just a faceless foe. A wounded Tommy fell into the trench that Helmut and his men were occupying. They gave him whatever help they could, under the circumstances, but he died right beside them. War had become highly personal.

The Battle of the Somme was a long affair and ground on and on, day after day. There was no respite for the defenders as the enemy continued to launch attack after attack against all areas of the front. Survival was the key and Helmut thanked God for every day that he survived. He hadn't been religious before he arrived at the trenches, but he now believed that there was somebody up there protecting him. He and his men were moved around the defensive area on a daily basis, providing reinforcements wherever they were required. His commanders had continually to determine where the next threat was likely to come from and move troops to strengthen that area.

It was on the 16th. July that Helmut's war came to an end. His small detachment had been moved to defensive positions in a small town called Ovillers in anticipation of an attack. Unlike most of the other defensive positions that he had been in over the past two weeks, he was on a back slope, and forward vision was extremely limited.

Suddenly a mass of enemy troops appeared about a hundred meters away, and from the other flank another attack commenced. The outer defences were overwhelmed and the enemy kept coming. Helmut's position was quickly surrounded, and he gave the orders to his troop to lay down their arms and surrender. In the confusion the Tommies kept firing, killing a lot of his men. Seeing how large and strong a man he was one of the approaching soldiers gave an order just as he was about to be shot.

'Don't shoot him Norm, we can use him to take the Captain back,' the Corporal shouted.

'Who; this one Corp?' he said pointing at Helmut.

'Yes him'

The Corporal waved his rifle at Helmut, indicating that he should follow him back down the trench the way they had come. Just around the corner there was an officer lying on the ground holding a badly damaged knee. Another soldier was kneeling in front of him fixing a tourniquet around the upper part of the leg to lessen the bleeding.

'Captain, we have just captured this powerful guy, and we will make him carry you back to our lines,' the corporal shouted down to the Captain. 'Norm here will go with you, and he will make sure that you get to our trenches. He has orders to shoot the Kraut if he tries to escape.'

'Thank you Corporal. There is no way that I can go back on my own.'

Helmut bent down and grabbed the officer under his armpits, putting him across his shoulders. The small rescue party then set off at a trot across no-man's land to the British trenches.

Bullets were still flying around them as they ran across the 200 meters or so of intervening territory. Helmut had to be careful where he placed his feet as there were so many bodies scattered across the ground that he was in danger of tripping on one and falling.

Just as he got to the British trenches, the soldier, who had been called Norm, staggered and fell. He had been hit and killed instantly by a stray bullet. Helmut stopped momentarily, but then ran the last twenty meters and jumped over the parapet into the trench with the officer. He was immediately surrounded by enemy soldiers.

'Don't shoot the Captain called out. This man has just carried me back from the German trenches where I was injured. Get help for me organized and take him to join the rest of the prisoners.

Helmut put the Captain down on an ammunition box. The officer put out his hand to shake Helmut's hand.

'What's your name soldier,' he asked.

'Helmut BEKER.'

'Well Helmut BEKER, thank you for saving my life and getting me back to my own lines safely.'

Helmut, terrified at what might happen to him now his job of carrying the officer had finished, nodded politely and shook the officer's hand.

Two soldiers plus an NCO had assembled while the pleasantries were going on, and Helmut was now marched away along the connecting trenches from the front towards the rear of the British positions. He joined a group of about fifty other Germans who had been captured that day. Shortly afterwards they were marched under guard further away from the scene of the battle.

Helmut thought to himself: *My war is over and I am alive. This morning I woke up thinking that this could be my last day on earth, and now the battle is behind me. Carrying that officer saved my life and got me behind the British front line and now I am going into captivity for the duration of the war.*

Helmut smiled, and his whole body relaxed. He certainly had no intention of trying to escape. As a captive, life might be difficult, but at least he would be alive.

They gradually made their way to the coast and on to Dunkirk where they met up with more prisoners and were loaded onto a boat. They were made to sit on the deck in groups which were covered by sentries with rifles. It started to rain and spray blew over the prisoners as the boat ploughed through rough seas. Helmut let the spray wash over his face, welcoming the salt taste of the water. The rain and the spray were bearable as there wasn't the smell of death and mud any more. Helmut said a short prayer thanking God for his deliverance.

On arriving at Folkstone in the South of England, they were all put on to a train, and, in various stages, brought to the North of England. What surprised Helmut was that they were actually given food at regular intervals, and there was no animosity towards them.

Finally, they arrived at a place called Catterick, which Helmut was told, was in Yorkshire. They were then marched to the internment camp a short distance away where Helmut was destined to spend the next few years of his life.

Just less than a year later, Helmut received a letter from home delivered to the camp by the Red Cross. To his amazement he read that he was now the father of twin boys who had been born in Lubeck on the 5th. February 1917. His wife had named them Kristoff and Markus.

Chapter 11

Back with Markus:

Too soon it was time for me re-join my fellow rowers from Kiel as we had to return home, so I had to make my farewells to my father and Chris. I didn't want to leave them. Lubeck seemed so terribly far away from Yorkshire where Chris and my Dad lived. I had arrived in London only a few days before as a German student who had lost his father in the First World War and whose life centred on his mother and granddad in Lubeck and his university life in Kiel. I had seen another better side of life in England and unbelievably I had found out that my father wasn't dead, and I also had a twin brother who was very English. My whole existence had been shaken to the core.

We had worked out a plan for keeping in touch and getting to know each other better. Provided war didn't break out in the meantime, I would come to England the following summer and Chris would visit Germany.

They came to see me off at Henley-on-Thames station, and we hugged until the train departed. I had never known such heart ache, and, if the truth be known, I didn't want to leave them and return to Germany.

When I had set out from Germany, just over a week before, I had no idea that I would be such a different person on the return journey. My whole world had changed, and my heart was now with my brother and father in England. I tried to explain my feelings to Walter, but he couldn't possible know what was going on in my head. I think that he was more concerned that he had a lost a valued friend, and I now was pre-occupied with thoughts about my family rather than with him.

Arriving back in Kiel, I couldn't wait to dump all my rowing gear and catch a train back to Lubeck to tell my mother about the encounter with my father and Chris. Early the next morning Walter and I headed for the train station from where he would set off for Munich and his home, and I would get the train to Lubeck. I didn't envy him his seven hour plus trip as I would be home in ninety minutes.

I was like an overwound clock spring. I was dying to bring my mother up to date on what had happened, but wasn't too sure how she would take the fact that her secret about my father and brother was now no longer a secret. I practically ran home to drop off my bag before going to the bakery where she worked.

The bakery was full of customers and my mother was flat out serving them. She smiled as she spotted me waiting to talk to her. I went over and gave her a hug,

'Mum, is there any chance of me talking to you,' I said in her ear as she continued to serve the customers.

'I can't leave now as we are extremely busy. Go and see if your granddad will relieve me for a few minutes.'

I went further into the bakery to see if I could find my granddad. He was speaking on the telephone in the office.

When he put the phone down I approached him.

'Granddad, please can you go and take over the counter while I talk to my mother. I have just arrived home from England and have something important to tell her,' I said in my best pleading voice.

'OK Markus, I will go out there for a bit, but please don't be too long as I am very busy. You wait in the office here, and I will send your mother through to you.'

A few minutes later my mother came rushing in and gave me another hug and an affectionate kiss.

'What do you want to tell me that is so urgent that it can't wait till later Markus?'

'When I was in England, something extraordinary occurred, Mum.'

'What do you mean extraordinary Markus?'

'Well I had an unexpected meeting with someone that I didn't know existed.'

'I think I know what is coming Markus as in the back of my mind I was afraid that something like this would happen if you went to England.'

'I met my twin brother Chris and my father.' I felt tears coming to my eyes and I felt intensely emotional.

'Oh Markus, how did you feel?

'I was extremely happy, but also extremely upset for some reason. Dad was able to explain what happened all those years ago, and I understand why you kept me and gave Chris to Dad to live in England.'

I then explained to my mother how Chris and I had come to meet each other and how that had resulted in the encounter with our father.

'Listen Markus I must go back to the counter and let granddad get back to his work. He hates looking after the customers as he can't resist talking to them and people, still in the queue, get annoyed at being kept waiting.

'I'll remain here and talk to granddad for a while and then I'll go home and catch up on my sleep. When you get home from work, I will fill you in on the details.'

A little while later granddad came back into the office.

'You're looking good Markus. Did your trip to London go off well?' he asked me as he entered the office.

'Yes, it was fantastic and I brought you this to put on your desk.' I handed him the miniature red London bus I had brought for him.

'Do they have this type of bus in London, Markus? It is extremely colourful.'

'The streets are full of red buses like this one and also black taxis. The best thing about London is the underground railway system which we used a lot.'

'Did you get lost on the underground system?' my granddad asked.

'No, because we only went from the hostel to Paddington station and back again, so we didn't experiment more than that.'

'What else did you get up to then Markus?'

I decided that I had better tell him about bumping into Chris and my father. He would be terribly upset if he heard later from someone else about it.

'I had an incredible encounter with your son who is of course my father. I also met my twin brother Chris,' I said as matter-of-factly as I could

'You met Helmut and Kristoff? My granddad spluttered out, becoming much more animated than I had seen him for years.

'He is not called Kristoff now but is called Chris. He was a member of one of the crews that we raced against, and we got talking when we met for a beer after the race. I met my father the following day when he came to watch Chris rowing.'

'How is my son, Markus?

'He is remarkably well, and his bakery seems to be thriving. I was amazed to find that he has a bakery just like you. Like father like son, as they say.'

'They never should have split the two of you up Markus. You should have grown up with your brother and not on your own, without your father around, especially as your mother was working for me all the time. When her parents died in 1926 you were only nine, so you both could have gone to live in England then.'

I had never heard my granddad talk this way before. He wasn't someone who I had ever heard give his opinions freely, but he had obviously been upset for quite a few years.

'Chris will be coming to visit Lubeck next year in the summer holidays, so you will see him when he comes. I will be going to Yorkshire to stay with them for a few weeks.'

'I am so pleased for you that you have finally found out you have a father who is alive and that you also have a twin brother. You will have a lot of catching up to do over the next few years.'

'I just hope that Germany doesn't go to war with anybody in the next year or so and spoil all my plans.'

'Let's just hope that Hitler doesn't get involved in anything stupid. I must get back to my work now Markus, so you must go home and leave us in peace to make some money.'

'I'll see you later granddad.' He picked up the telephone to make a call, and I excused myself and left the shop to go home.

The summer holidays flew by as I was kept fully occupied. I went to stay in Munich for a week with Walter and I also was invited to spend ten days with Susie Rothenburger with her parents in Kiel. During my remaining time in Lubeck, I helped in the bakery giving my mother a break from the continual serving of customers and lifting the heavy sacks of flour for my granddad. My good intentions of writing to Chris went the same way as a lot of my other good intentions, and I was back at University before I put pen to paper.

1937 turned into 1938, and it wasn't long before it was time to organize our long planned re-union. There was still a lot of talk of war, and in the Anschluss, Germany had sent troops into Austria and had taken over control of the country. It looked as if all borders with the countries that surrounded Germany would remain open, and it would be possible for Chris to come to Germany and for me to return with him to England. We were so keen to see each other that we decided to take a chance on nothing serious happening.

Chris's year in Oxford ended before mine, so we decided that he should come to see me first and then I would travel to England with him. He could spend a few days bunked down in my digs with Walter and me, before we travelled on to Lubeck. It was with considerable excitement that I went to meet his train.

Chapter 12

It turned out to be not the brightest of ideas to have my twin brother staying while I was finishing off my projects for the year. I had three days to get a mountain of work done which meant that I had to work well into the night. Luckily Walter, who had been like a brother to me for most of my life, was under less pressure. He took Chris under his wing and showed him the sights of Kiel. The other students who knew us were amazed when Walter told them that this was Chris Becker and not Markus. He looked so like me that they all just assumed that it was the two of us as usual. When he opened his mouth to speak, he gave himself away as, even after a year's hard work on his German, he was not very fluent.

He was amazed to see that I still had to attend the HJ meetings; despite the pressure I was under to get my term work completed. He found it hard to understand that if I missed a lot of the HJ meetings, I would be thrown out of University for a poor attendance record.

I finally finished all my work and could relax. We had a mind blowing party in one of the bars near the University to celebrate the end of the academic year. It was two exceedingly hung over brothers who caught the 11.00 am train to Lubeck the following morning.

'I wish that I was feeling in better shape Markus. I hadn't planned on meeting my mother and granddad feeling like this,' Chris said in a melancholic voice.

'By the time we arrive in Lubeck, you will have had another hour and a half to recover, so cheer up.'

'I have been looking forward so much to this day, and then I go and get blitzed the night before,' Chris added.

'When we finally get to Lubeck we will drop our bags at home and then we will go to the bakery and see Mum and granddad. You can then have another sleep or come with me around the city to see all my own haunts. I'll even take you to the stadium to meet Stefan Mulder who was like a father to me as I was growing up.'

'I am going to catch up on my sleep until we get there if you don't mind and I'll then decide how I feel.' Chris rolled up his jacket, put it between his head and the corner of the window, and closed his eyes.

Once we got to Lubeck events took over, and we didn't have time to remember our hang overs. Granddad had given my mother the afternoon off, so she was able to join us for lunch at a restaurant overlooking the river. I had never seen my mother looking so well. She had bought a new outfit to greet her long lost son and looked years younger. She even had her hair done for the occasion.

Chris just sat there with a big grin on his face looking at her and absorbing the atmosphere. He obviously was emotionally touched by the meeting.

By the time that the ten days had gone by, and it was time for me to return with Chris to England, he was a fully-fledged member of the family. I had to work in the bakery from 5.30 am every morning. Chris used to join me when I went to the bakery, making the rigours of getting up at that time of the day more pleasurable. The fact that he had experience of working in my Dad's bakery in Harrogate made him a particularly valuable part of the team, and we got the work done a lot quicker. My granddad also was delighted to have his two grandsons in his bakery. He could be seen walking around the bakery with a prideful smile on his face. On many occasions, he talked to customers in the queue telling them all about his new grandson from England.

On the few occasions that I had to go to the Flieger-HJ meetings at the aerodrome Chris amused himself around the city or worked in the bakery.

'I can't believe that you spend so much time at your Hitler Youth meetings Markus,' Chris commented one evening near the end of his stay.

'I don't have any choice as my log book must be signed and there must be two entries in it for every week.'

'What happens if you miss some meetings?'

'I will have to go before the Kommandant and explain myself.'

'And, what can he do to you?' Chris asked.

'He can refer you to the SS, and they will stop you attending University and also probably make you to join the regular army as a Private.'

'I can't believe what you are telling me Markus. It's like a police state. How do you put up with it?'

'It is what I have grown up with and what I am used to. It is the same for everybody.'

'I don't think that I could live in a country like this, but then you do, so I suppose that it can't be that bad.' Chris gave me a tolerant smile.

'I love my flying and by being a member of the Flieger-HJ I am able to fly for nothing even if it is just gliders.'

'I belong to the Oxford University flying school, and I have trained as a pilot too. They want to have a supply of pilots just in case war breaks out, and we have to defend ourselves,' Chris said.

'Do you actually fly fully fledged planes?' I asked him.

'Yes, we have been flying the De Havilland Tiger Moth which is a bi-plane trainer. It is ideal for learning in as it is extremely forgiving.'

'Have you pranged a plane yet Chris?'

'I have had one unfortunate landing which damaged the undercarriage, but other than that I have been OK.'

'I have heard that when the University term resumes at the end of September, we will have some real planes to train on in Kiel,' I added. 'Evidently Hitler has decided to ignore the treaty of Versailles and provide lots of war planes to the Luftwaffe as a matter of urgency. Rumour has it that the planes we are getting will be Messerschmitt Bf 109's which proved so effective in the Spanish Civil War.'

'I envy you Markus. They won't let us near a Hurricane which is the equivalent of your ME109.'

'It's your last night in Lubeck Chris, so let's go down to the harbour area and drink a beer or two,' I suggested.

After our experience in Kiel, we just had two steins of beer and then left to spend the rest of the evening with our mother.

That was our intention; however, it didn't work out as we planned. As we were coming up a street that led from the centre of town to our house, we heard a sound like a football crowd makes when their team has just scored a goal. We also heard the sound of many feet running towards us. We pulled back to the side of the street to give them plenty of room to get by. A high percentage of the participants were wearing Hitler Youth uniforms, and there was one of the older boys shouting instructions at them.

Just before they reached us, they stopped and faced a shop. They all started to chant 'Juden, Juden, Juden……' and they worked themselves up into a frenzy. Some of the crowd had pots of white paint with them. They went to the front walls of the shop they had stopped outside, and painted the Star of David in a number of places and also daubed on anti-Semitic slogans.

The leader of the group moved over closer to the shop, and I recognized him. It was Boris, who I had known since my days in the HJ in Lubeck, and who had tormented me after that night with the two leaders in the tent. He turned around to yell at the crowd.

'Come on guys, let's break every window in this shop, and set it on fire.'

He came over to where we were standing to get some stones. He spotted me standing there with Chris and came over to confront me.

'Well if it isn't the leaders' pet. Are you not going to join in with us?' he sneered as he spoke the words.

'I'm on my way home with my brother, so I don't want to get involved,' I said in as strong a voice as I could muster.

'Oh come on goodie goodie, dirty your hands and get involved like a true Hitler Youth member.'

Just then there was a tremendous crash and the main window of the shop splintered into a thousand pieces, this drew the attention of Boris away from us, and he rushed back to the gaping hole in the front of the shop. We beat a hasty retreat as he lit a rag and threw it with some petrol into the shop. There was a whoosh and the whole shop went up in flames. Thankfully the assembled mob, with their job done, took off at a run. Chris and I took the opportunity to run off and get well away from the mob and the taunts of Boris.

When we went through the door into the house, we weren't able to speak for a few minutes as we were out of breath. I could see the anxious face on my mother as she waited for us to provide an explanation.

'What have you two been up to,' she asked when she saw that we were able to speak.

'We got caught up in a group of youths burning down a shop owned by a Jew,' I explained.

'It was genuinely scary as the leader tried to make Markus participate,' Chris added.

'Who tried to get you involved Markus?' Mother asked.

'Do you remember Boris who used to be in the Hitler Youth when I was in the Lubeck branch and who used to pick on me.'

'That is the guy you said was a bully.'

'Yes him. He seemed to be leading the mob tonight, and he saw me and told me to get involved. Luckily he was distracted by the smashing of the window and we escaped,' I added.

'How can they burn down a shop like that without the police getting involved? Would someone not have told the police what was going on?' Chris had a look of disbelief on his face that something like this could happen.

'Oh the police were told alright, but they won't come out to protect the Jews. Basically, Hitler wants all Jews driven out of the country.'

I was highly embarrassed by what had happened and could imagine what Chris was thinking. In his place, I would not have been very impressed, and I was upset that I had accepted what had been going on as 'the norm'.

'Is there nothing that you can do about it? How has it come to a point where someone's shop can just be burnt to the ground?' Chris obviously was still extremely angry.

'We elected the Nazi party into power and they are now so much in control of everything that we can do nothing but agree with them,' my mother explained.

'In some ways I am glad that I am going home in the morning. I was extremely frightened on the street tonight with that crowd shouting 'Juden' and then burning down the shop.

"I will make you both a hot drink to calm you down and then you must get to bed as you have an early start in the morning and then a long journey ahead of you.

Chapter 13

The following morning, after a very tearful goodbye to my mother, Chris and I started our marathon journey by train and ferry to Yorkshire. We caught the train at 6.30 am from Lubeck to Hamburg where we transferred to a train to Rotterdam. A special boat train took us to the Hook of Holland where we caught the same ancient ferry to Harwich that I had taken the year before with the rowing crew. We took yet another train to Liverpool Street station in London, transferred by the underground to King's Cross station, and finally caught a train to cover the last leg of our journey to Harrogate. We finally arrived at our destination just after midnight in a near comatose state, totally 'journeyed out'. Needless to say, our father wasn't there to meet us, and we had to struggle with our bags to the accommodation above the bakery. I was shown to the bed I was sleeping in, and that was the last anyone saw of the BEKER twins until just after noon the following day.

After brunch, we joined our father in the bakery, and I met Gwen, who had acted as a mother for Chris while he was growing up. I could see that they were quite close, and it must have been strange for him when he learnt that he had a natural mother in Germany.

The two weeks flew by far too quickly, and it was soon time for me to return home to Lubeck.

On the last evening, we went as a family to the local pub, to have our final beers together.

"Well Markus, have you enjoyed your time in Harrogate?' my father asked me.

'I have never been able to relax like I have over the past two weeks, Dad. I hadn't realised how oppressive living in Germany has become. It was only seeing how you live your lives in Yorkshire, without the police watching everything you do that my eyes have been opened.'

'You do know Markus that you can stay here if you want. Chris and I would love to have you here with us, and if you stayed your mother might come as well.' I hadn't anticipated this offer from my father, and I was very tempted to accept. 'I want you here Markus,' Chris added. 'If it does end up that there is a war between Germany and England, I don't want you to be on the other side.'

"I'm sure that there won't be a war. Everyone is still suffering from the last major conflict and common sense must prevail,' I said hopefully, although, having seen the preparations in Germany, I didn't honestly believe what I was saying.

'I am also concerned for your safety after what happened on our last night together in Lubeck,' Chris said. 'That encounter with the Hitler Youth mob was really frightening.'

'I will be going back to University soon, and life is decidedly different there.'

'Anyway Markus, you know that you can always come here, provided of course that the borders are still open, and we aren't at war,' my Dad said.

'If things get any worse back in Lubeck I will certainly talk to Mum about coming here, but I do want to finish my engineering degree which will give me a passport to anywhere in the world.'

'We had better go home now as you will have to be up early in the morning and I have to be at the bakery by five o'clock,' my father said, getting up to leave.

I couldn't get to sleep that night thinking about my situation: *Up to meeting Chris and my father, I had accepted the events in Germany as being necessary to make Germany great again. My eyes had been opened, and I was now starting to question the ideals that Hitler was indoctrinating the nation with. How had it evolved that we accepted that Jews could be burnt out of their shops that they had operated for years. I knew a lot of the Jewish shopkeepers in Lubeck, and they were decent people. Should I stay in Harrogate with my father and Chris? The answer was 'No'; I had to go home to my mother and granddad. I was all that they had, and I would just have to get on with life. Although I had an English father and an English brother, I was a born and bred German.*

In the morning, Chris came to the station to see me onto the 6:15 am train to London and I started my journey home. This time I didn't have company as Chris wasn't coming with me, it would be a long and lonely trip on my own.

When we had come from Germany to England, Chris and I had managed to catch all our connections. Due to exceptionally severe weather in the North Sea the ancient ferry was delayed, and I missed the Hamburg train in Rotterdam which meant that I had to wait until the evening train which left at 8:30 pm and arrived in Hamburg the following morning at 6.30 am. I managed to find a seat in a corner of a crowded carriage where I made myself a nest to fall asleep in. By the time that I arrived, I was cold, tired and hungry and not a little grumpy. The train for Lubeck didn't leave until 10:00 am, so I had time to go into the town to find a café where I could purchase breakfast. I digested the contents of a newspaper as I consumed my breakfast. After seeing the world, from an English point of view during my time in Yorkshire, I wanted to update myself on the current political situation and the recent dramatic events in Austria. Not only was I exhausted from the long journey, I was also extremely sad as I read through the articles. The newspaper was full of rhetoric about expanding the country and making Germany great again, and how Hitler would ensure that the German people got what was theirs' by right. It was pretty obvious to me that the only way Hitler could deliver on his promises was by making war on neighbouring countries. I felt like getting back on the train to Rotterdam and returning to Yorkshire. If didn't have my close family in Lubeck, it would have been a simple decision.

I arrived back in Lubeck at lunchtime, and, after visiting my mother and granddad in the bakery, went home, grabbed some food and collapsed into bed. I didn't wake up until the following morning.

'Did you have a good rest?' my mother asked me as I arrived in the bakery.

'I slept the sleep of the dead Mum and feel more normal this morning.'

'Take a fresh loaf of bread and go and join your granddad in the back of the shop for your breakfast. He has just made some coffee which I am sure that he will share with you.'

'Thanks Mum I will talk to you later.' I left her to the customers and went into the back to my granddad.

'Welcome back Markus. How did your trip to Yorkshire go?' my granddad asked me.

'If I can have some of your coffee I will tell you all about it,' I replied as I poured a cup of strong coffee.

I spent the next half an hour telling him all about the time I had spent with my father and Chris.

'My Dad asked me to think of moving from Germany and stay with him. He told me to convince my mother to come with me so as we all could be together as a family.'

'You can't leave me all on my own here,' my granddad said plaintively. My grandma had died eight years ago in 1930, so he relied a lot on us for company.

'I told him that I couldn't leave Germany until I had finished my engineering degree in Kiel and also that my Mum wouldn't leave you on your own,' I said putting my arm around him.

'If you left with your Mum, I would close this place down and retire. It probably would be a good idea if I took it easier anyway. You never know, I might go with you as I don't like the new Germany and all this Hitler mania.'

'Don't let anybody hear you say what you have just said. People have been arrested for less, and you never know who is in your queue waiting for bread,' I suggested.

'I'll try to remember that Markus. Now I think that it is time to get some work done back here. I haven't been able to move the heavier sacks while you have been away, so you had better lend me your muscles for a while.' He smiled as he got up and went out to the store at the rear of the building.

I went to a Flieger-HJ meeting the following day and was told that I would have to attend for training at the Lubeck Blankensee aerodrome every day until the end of my holidays from University. They had received some training planes and the older members of the Flieger-HJ would be getting flying lessons. My granddad wasn't too impressed, but I had no choice in the matter. I would be picked up from the local stadium at 8:00 in the morning, being dropped back there shortly after 8:00 at night.

This was the fulfilment of my dream and my 'raison d'etre' for joining the Flieger-HJ in the first place. As an experienced glider pilot and twenty one years of age, I was included in the most senior group of trainee pilots. We spent the mornings doing theory on topics such as navigation and the afternoon actually flying the planes. The instructor that I was put under had been flying Stuka dive bombers in the Spanish Civil War, so he had lots of experience of combat flying. The first time that I tried to sit in the pilot's seat I didn't fit. At nearly two meters tall and with a physique to match, I was too big for the cockpit. The mechanic had to make some adjustments to a spare seat they had in the workshop and then exchange the regular seat before I could fly. It was named the "Big BEKER" seat.

The planes we flew in had the trainee in the front seat and the instructor behind at a duplicate set of controls. Occasionally my instructor took over with loud curses as I did something stupid. All in all, I did exceptionally well and after three weeks was selected to fly solo.

My flight was scheduled for Wednesday afternoon at around 3.00 pm, so I had the whole day to wait around anxiously. There were three other solo flights planned for the same day and disaster struck the second one of the morning.

I had made friends with a guy my own age called Horst van Tinden and he had been selected to make his solo flight the same day as mine. In fact, we had planned to go out in Lubeck together for a few beers that evening to celebrate what we hoped would be our successful solo flights.

I was watching his flight from a platform on the roof of the control tower together with the other trainee pilots. It was the best place to keep an eye on what was going on as there was an uninterrupted 360 degree view.

'Horst is doing well isn't he,' one of the others said to me.

'He looks to be very much in control and his take off was extremely professional' I replied.

'He has to make one more circuit and then he will have to land,' one of the instructors said.

About ten minutes later he was on his approach to the airstrip to land.

'Should that other aircraft be taxiing towards the runway?' I asked, alarmed at seeing a dangerous situation developing.

'He mustn't have seen that there is an aircraft coming in to land,' another voice piped up also alarmed by the situation.

Horst, now extremely close to landing, panicked and pulled the plane up, but without increasing his speed. The plane rapidly lost altitude, and bellied into the ground, hitting the fencing that surrounded the airfield. The plane flipped, landing on its back, and it burst into flames. The fire-truck rushed to where the plane came to a halt, but there was no hope of saving my friend Horst. We all stood in a state of shock with our eyes riveted on the terrifying scene. We had lost a colleague in distressing circumstances.

The rest of the solo flights, due to take place that day, were postponed to the following day, so I had to remain in a extremely anxious state for an additional twenty four hours. I was already extremely nervous at the thought of making my solo flight, and my condition was made considerably worse, by Horst's accident.

The Kommandant in charge of the school called us all into the meeting room to talk to us.

'An extremely tragic event happened today, and we lost one of our trainee pilots, Horst van Tinden. I have called you to this meeting because I want you all to know that Horst's reaction when he saw a plane crossing his path was correct, and an experienced pilot would have done exactly the same. He took the decision to climb, but the engine didn't react quickly enough as he had reached a critical point in his descent. A similar accident will not happen again. We have already taken steps to make sure that no other planes will be flying or manoeuvring while you make your solo flights. So go home now, relax and come back tomorrow ready for your flight.'

I went home but didn't tell my mother what had happened at the aerodrome. She would have done her nut and tried to stop me from flying. The following evening, I went home triumphantly, having successfully completed my solo flight. I even had the Pilot's Badge for my mother to sew on my uniform to prove it.

When I arrived at the first Flieger-HJ meeting after I returned to University at the end of September, I got a lot of envious comments from the other members of the troop when they saw my badge. Lubeck had been the only city where pilot training had taken place, so I was only one of two who had obtained their Pilot's Badge. We were still meeting at the Kiel-Holtenau airport, and the two planes we had been promised had been delivered. Obviously I had completed my training and was allowed to fly when the others were at their theory sessions. They had to make another 'BEKER' seat for me so as I could fit into the cockpit.

During September, there was the Munich conference where there was agreement between Hitler and the British Prime Minister Neville Chamberlain that Germany could take control of the areas of Czechoslovakia where German was the spoken language. I was so busy at University, and my other activities, including my relationship with Susie that I didn't have time to fully appreciate what was going on, but it did appear to us students that there was not going to be a war. The first term of my year at university flew by, and I soon was back in Lubeck for Christmas with my mother and granddad.

Chapter 14

It was unusually cold weather at Christmas, and the inlet of the Baltic, on which Lubeck stands, was frozen to a greater thickness than normal. We were able to skate and have fun on the ice making it a particularly enjoyable holiday.

I was lying in bed one morning, in fact, it was the 6th January 1939, the first Friday of the New Year, when my mother knocked on my bedroom door and brought me in an official looking letter.

'This looks important Markus, and it has the stamp of the Third Reich on it, so I thought that I would bring it up to you,' she said as she handed it to me. I suspect that she was also curious as to the contents.

'I hope that I am not in trouble for something that I have done,' I said as I sat up in bed.

I opened the letter with trepidation dreading what I might read.

So much for thinking that there wasn't going to be war. The letter was my call up instructions. The letter asked me to report for duty on Monday 16th January to join a new squadron being formed at Lubeck Blankensee airfield. It also told me that I now held the rank of Leutnant which was the lowest level of pilot in the Luftwaffe.

'Mum, I don't believe it. I have been called up to the Luftwaffe so will have to abandon my studies. I won't be able to get my degree in July.'

There was a look of shock on my mother's face. She sat down on the side of my bed.

'Do you think they have made a mistake, Markus? Surely they will allow you to complete your degree before they take you into the Luftwaffe. You are so close to finishing.'

'There was speculation in Kiel before I came home for the Christmas holidays that they were going to call up all the pilots in the Flieger-HJ early in the New Year, so I don't think it is an error.' I had never felt so depressed in my life. When would I be able to get back to University to finish my degree? 'We've struggled to find the money to send you to University and now that you're close to the finishing line they have done this to you. It's not fair.' My mother was clearly as disappointed as I was. 'I will go downstairs and get your breakfast ready.'

'I have to go out to the aerodrome on Monday so I will ask at the office if they might have made a mistake,' I said more in hope than belief.

I lay in bed for a few minutes just considering the impact the letter I had just received would have on my life. The fact that I was being called up must mean that Germany was going to become involved in another war and it would include me. As I lay thinking, I was invaded by thoughts that were increased in their intensity by fear:

My comfortable life as a student was about to be turned upside down. I would enter a life where my every move would be planned, in advance, by someone else. What about Chris; were we going to go to war against England and would I end up fighting against him? How long was I going to have to serve in the Luftwaffe? Disturbed by my thoughts I decided that I had better get up and face the new day.

Chris was so much on my mind that I sat down after lunch and wrote him a long letter. I poured out my heart to him about how I was feeling at having to give up my University studies and how upset my mother was about the situation. I felt that I wasn't breaking any confidences by telling him that I was about to become a Leutnant in a squadron flying Messerschmitt Bf 109's and based at the Lubeck Blankensee aerodrome. If war broke out, I might have to be more careful about the information I sent to him.

I queued up with a number of other concerned students on Monday at the offices at the aerodrome. They informed us that they had no other information, and there was nobody there who could help us. We were told to wait while they called someone in authority. Eventually, an officer came into the area where we were waiting. He told us that there was no mistake, and we must report the following Monday as instructed in the letters we had received. We were also told that we didn't need to attend for the remainder of the week.

They gave us a kit bag, a uniform and dropped us off in Lubeck. I walked home to drop my stuff off and then went to the bakery to talk to my mother.

'I assume that it is terrible news from the look on your face, Markus,' she said as I joined her at the back of the counter.

'Yes, I am afraid that I have to report next Monday and can't go back to University. There were a lot of other disgruntled students there with me, and they addressed us all together.'

'Do you have to go in this week or can you help us here?' she asked me.

'We have been given the rest of the week off, so I can help you and granddad. I would also like to go and visit Susie for a few days to bring her up to date with what is going on.'

'Don't worry about us Markus; we will have to manage when you have gone anyway, so you just enjoy yourself for your last week of freedom.'

I arranged to travel to Kiel on Thursday to see Susie, and also pick up my stuff from my digs. I needed to cancel my student accommodation and let Walter know that I wouldn't be going back when the term started at the end of January. Susie understood when I told her that I wasn't coming back to Kiel for the new university term. She fully appreciated that orders were orders as her father was a senior naval man. I joined her family on the Friday evening, and, in conversation over dinner, her father explained that the navy was also mobilising.

'There must be something significant coming up as we are bringing the ships up to their full complement and have called in a lot of the reserves,' he told me.

'Do you know what is happening or about to happen?' I asked him.

'They haven't told us yet, but we have been told to increase the amount of supplies we have in stock and also to step up the ordering of ammunition.'

'It sounds serious that they have asked us to increase our stocks of ammunition as that can only mean one thing. They expect that the ammunition will be used,' I added.

'There is another intriguing development. They have given instructions that fuel must be conserved and not wasted, and a lot of manoeuvres have been cancelled to protect the fuel supplies,' Susie's father explained.

'I wonder if that is why they cancelled our flying this week. I suppose that on-going fuel supplies must be a worry for the powers that be.'

The discussions continued as we ate our dinner. After the meal, Susie and I went into the City of Kiel to find our friends, and have a few drinks.

She helped me take all my bits and pieces from my digs to the train station on Saturday afternoon, and finally saw me onto the train to Lubeck. We had no idea when we would be able to see each other again. With me going off to war, anything could happen, and I might not even return, so it was a very emotional farewell.

The weekend flew by, and Monday morning saw me at the local stadium waiting for the bus to take me to the aerodrome, dressed up in my new uniform and carrying my kitbag. My life as a Leutnant had begun for better or for worse.

Chapter 15

A bus didn't arrive, but a truck with benches in the back did and the seven of us who had assembled at the stadium, kitted out for our new lives in the Luftwaffe, climbed into the back. I recognized the three pilots but had never seen the others. They turned out to be aircrew who would be involved in the servicing of the planes.

In the week between my last visit and today, the aerodrome had changed dramatically. The fence around the airfield had been strengthened considerably, and there was now a guard on the main gate. As we entered, our papers were checked. This had the effect of making me feel that I was losing my freedom and was no longer in control of my own destiny. Although I was twenty one, I felt like a naughty schoolboy.

A lot of temporary accommodation units had been added to the site, and the pilots were housed in the two units that were closest to the airfield. We were lucky enough to have single cubicles and didn't have to share with others, or that was the theory as the walls were extremely thin and there really was no privacy. The officers' mess, where we would eat our meals and socialise, was in the main building. I was amazed to see how organized everything was, and it certainly exceeded my expectations.

Lined up on the edge of the airfield, waiting for their pilots, were twenty five Bf109, series E, Messerschmitt fighters looking spectacular in the winter sun. After we located the specific cubicle allocated to us, and dumped our kit bags, we all wandered over to take a look at the dark grey fighting machines.

'Do you see the difference between these planes and the ones that we trained in Markus?' one of the other pilots who had trained with me in Lubeck asked me.

I thought for a moment as I closely examined the Me109.......
'Ah, I have spotted it. These are equipped with guns,' I said triumphantly.

'It looks as if they are equipped with two machine guns on the engine cowling. They must be synchronised to fire between the blades of the propeller,' he added.

'I wonder will we notice the difference when we fly the plane as there will be a lot of extra weight,' I commented.

'We won't have to wait long as I expect that we will be flying fairly soon,' he said as we turned around and headed back to the mess for lunch.

During the rest of the day, more and more young men arrived at the aerodrome, and by evening there was a full complement of pilots gathered in the mess getting acquainted with one another. It was a bit like being at University as we were all roughly the same age except for a few of the officers who had been in the Luftwaffe for a few years, but even they were not much older than twenty five.

On the Tuesday, we were all called into the briefing room and were told what was going to happen during the period of bringing the squadron to a level where we could be signed off as a fully operational unit. We had been given six weeks to reach full operational capability.

It didn't take us long to realise the level of difficulty of the task facing us. During the afternoon of the first day, we had our first fatality. The Me109's were much more unstable with the extra weight of the machine guns, and it was considerably harder to maintain control of the aircraft on take-off and landing.

We were taking off in threes, and the right hand aircraft started to yaw and swing from side to side. The young pilot over compensated and the aircraft slewed off to the right and crashed into a watch tower, bursting into flames. Black smoke enveloped the airfield and the smell of burning fuel and oil was everywhere. The Me109 was totally destroyed, and the pilot killed.

There was an air of gloom in the mess that evening at dinner and a number of the pilots drowned their sorrows at the bar afterwards to try and get rid of the memory. It was only our first day together as a squadron, and we had already had a fatality.

The thought going through my head was: *How many of this group of enthusiastic and eager pilots would be killed before this period of service was over, and we weren't even at war yet?*

Before our six weeks training was over, we had lost two more pilots through landing and take-off errors. In fact, the Me109 started to get a poor reputation for its instability when the wheels were down, and we heard of similar accidents from other airfields. My greater upper body strength, from my rowing training, gave me the extra strength I needed to control the plane at the critical moments.

At the start of March 1939, we were signed off as being fully operational, and the squadron was transferred to an airfield about eleven kilometres from Dresden. On the 15th March, we were woken before dawn and at a briefing told that Germany was invading Czechoslovakia and our role would be assist the land forces by strafing the Czechoslovakian army and their supply lines. Other squadrons would be responsible for putting the opposition planes out of action and neutralising their air force.

We took off to begin our war, but had a very disappointing time as we couldn't locate any targets before we had return to base. Refuelled we returned to the theatre of operations, but I still wasn't able to fire a single shot in anger. We did see our own troops, and I waggled my wings as I swooped in over an armoured column. The troops on the ground were moving fast and weren't encountering any stiff opposition. It was a very disconsolate group who met later that evening to discuss the events of the day. One pilot was missing from the second mission. He got lost and run out of fuel; however, he had been seen safely landing his plane in a field, so had survived.

Czechoslovakia capitulated in a day, so there were no further sorties for our squadron. A week later we were transferred back to our base at Lubeck, and I was able to get home for my first spot of leave to see my family. When I got to my room, there was a letter from Chris sitting on my bed. I lounged back against the pillows and read it.

Dear Brother,

Many thanks for your long letter which you sent to me after you heard that you were being called up. I don't know when you will receive this letter as you will obviously not be living at home and I don't have any other address for you to send this to.

It must have been terrible for you to find out that you can't complete your degree this year, especially as you were so close to the finishing line. You also have no idea when you will be able to do your final six months which must be extremely frustrating. From what I read in the newspapers it looks as if I will be luckier than you and will finish my degree this year. I won't have to join the RAF until later in the year. I have been selected as a member of the Oxford University eight for this year's Boat Race to be held in a few weeks' time, and am spending a lot of my time rowing. Great news as I have trained hard to be selected. I am having difficulty spending a sufficient amount of time at my studies, due to the fact that I also have to put in more hours flying.

Last September the 'papers were convinced that there wouldn't be a war and that Hitler's aspirations could be controlled. I am afraid that it now appears that the Munich Agreement between Hitler and Chamberlain was a load of hot air, and Hitler is just continuing to grab land from surrounding countries. All the 'papers here are now saying that Britain and her allies are eventually going to have to go to war against Germany and probably Italy to bring Hitler under control.

Markus why don't you come here and live with us and get well away from Germany? I know that you have been called up and are now in the Luftwaffe, and it would be deserting if you left and came to us here, but I am very apprehensive as to what will happen to you. I also don't want to end up fighting against you. It would be just our luck to confront each other when the RAF fights against the Luftwaffe. Please seriously consider joining us here.

I will write to you again if I get the chance.

Your brother

Chris

I read the letter again and then just lay back thinking of the difficult situation I was in: *I had a father and brother who would be on the other side in any conflict, but they would welcome me with open arms if I could get there. On the other hand I was a German, and I was now a member of the Luftwaffe, something that I had trained towards for many years. I was now committed to the other members of my squadron and couldn't let them down. I had to put such thoughts out of my mind and focus on becoming an outstanding pilot. My survival depended on it.*

Chapter 16

One month passed to another as winter turned to summer and there were no further attempts to invade any other countries by Germany. We actually became quite bored with life at our base at Lubeck Blankensee airdrome. Great efforts were being made by the powers that be to conserve fuel, so our flying was limited. We just sat around on the ground.

All this changed near the end of August when the squadron was transferred to Gatow airport, close to Berlin. There had been a lot of talk in the newspapers about Germany invading Poland in a copycat operation to the invasion of Czechoslovakia. We assumed that our relocation to Berlin indicated that we were going to be involved in a similar role to our previous attack that year, in March. Gatow was normally an airfield used for training pilots, but all the trainees had been sent home, and the facilities placed at the disposal of the two squadrons who had been relocated there.

On the 1st September we were woken up at 5:00 am to be greeted by the staccato sound of extremely heavy rain battering the tin roofs of our billet. A gale accompanied the rain. Not a day particularly suitable for flying. We were all called to a briefing where the Kommandant addressed us.

'I want to inform you that German armed forces are attacking Poland this morning, and you are supposed to have a supporting role in the invasion.' You could have heard a pin drop in the room, and there were a lot of worried looking faces among the gathered pilots.

'Unfortunately, as you can see for yourselves, the weather is too bad at the moment for you to get airborne; however, you will be required to remain in a state of readiness until instructed to the contrary. As soon as there is any let up in the weather, you will take off. Is that clear?'

We were already wearing our flying suits and had all our other gear with us, so we just stayed where we were to wait for any easing of the storm. The leader of our particular squadron, Major von Stanstedt, called us together to talk to us.

'Right guys you have heard what the Kommandant said at the meeting and the fact that we are going into action as soon as the weather eases. I want to emphasise to you that Poland has a well-trained air force, with good planes, and they can be expected to resist,' he said.

'Are we going to be going after their air force,' one of the younger pilots asked.

'No, our role is to support the ground troops by strafing the enemies supply lines and also by firing on any enemy troops that we come across. Other squadrons of Stukas and fighters have been allocated to wipe out the enemies planes and to bomb their airports. Please remember that you can expect to be attacked until their planes have been knocked out. Keep your eyes open and stay in your formations.'

The Major then displayed a map on an easel and showed us where our operational area would be, and he told us what we could expect to see in the countryside below. He also told us how long we would have to carry out our mission once we got there as we obviously had to have enough fuel to get home.

I then had to endure a day of extreme anxiousness as we sat around in full flying gear for the rest of the day listening to the storm raging outside. Finally, at 5:00 pm, we were stood down and allowed to go to our quarters.

The following morning we were roused about an hour before dawn to find that the weather had improved considerably, and we would be able to fly. As dawn rose in the eastern sky, the engines roared and we took off heading for Poland. As we crossed the border, the action started. We were attacked by a group of Polish pilots in their PZL P11 fighters who had obviously been waiting for us. They ran rings around us as we struggled to come to grips with our first dog fight. We dispersed in a bid to survive which is exactly what we shouldn't have done.

I got involved in my own fight for survival when a Polish pilot latched on to me. My mind went back to the lessons I had learnt from my instructor when I had learnt how to fly in Lubeck. He had been an experienced pilot from the Spanish Civil War, and, although it wasn't included in his brief, he had taught me the tricks of the trade. One thing that he had emphasised was always to remain calm and in control. I mustn't panic. My Me109 outperformed his plane in the turns and climbing, and I managed to get underneath him, train my sights on his fuselage, and push the button. I had my first victim. Much to my relief I saw him force his canopy open and parachute out, so at least I hadn't killed him. I headed for home as I had used up a lot of fuel in the dog fight.

Having left Berlin Gatow airfield full of confidence that morning, a very sorry and bruised squadron limped back. Three of my colleagues didn't return, and one of those missing was Major von Stanstedt. Another pilot had been seriously injured when his plane was riddled with machine gun fire, but he had managed to fly his damaged plane back to base and land it safely. Luckily he survived.

There were no more sorties that day as the senior officers came to terms with the losses. We weren't the only squadron to have been badly mauled, and, the Polish air force, had turned out to be a worthy foe. Prior to leaving that morning we had been told that most of their planes had been destroyed by Stuka bombing of their airfields. It appeared that the Poles had managed to move their planes and conceal them elsewhere.

That evening I was called in by the Kommandant and received some good news. I had been promoted to be Oberleutnant as part of the restructuring resulting from the death of the Major.

The campaign in Poland lasted for a further twenty one days, and we tragically continued to lose men and machines. Gradually we got the upper hand over the Polish air force, largely due to the work of the army on the ground and their capture of the enemy's airfields. As the army progressed, the

Poles gradually ran out of places to refuel and fly from. By the time the mini-war was over, we had lost nine men out of the twenty eight who had originally arrived at Gatow, and it was a very weary, but a much wiser squadron that returned to Lubeck at the end of September. A lot of lessons had been learnt the hard way.

'You look exhausted Markus,' my mother said to me, when I dropped into the bakery to see her on my return. 'You look as if you haven't slept for a week.'

'It's been an extremely tough time for the squadron, and we didn't get any rest for the entire month we were away,' I replied. 'We also lost nine of our squadron and they were all friends of mine.'

'That's terrible Markus; you wouldn't have expected all those deaths after what happened in Czechoslovakia.'

'The Poles fought back and resisted with everything that they had. Their pilots were highly skilled and matched us despite having inferior aircraft.'

'How long are you home for?' she asked me.

'I have a week off to recover as they are re-supplying us with planes and new pilots.'

'Why don't you go to Kiel and see Susie? I'm sure she would love to see you.'

'I might just do that. First I am going to go home and catch up on my sleep.'

I left my mother in the bakery and went home to unwind and enjoy a lot of 'anxious free' sleep.

As a result of the invasion of Poland, France and England had declared war on Germany. What people were calling, The Second World War had commenced. The only good news was that Hitler and Stalin had signed a non-aggression pact in August, and they were now dividing up Poland between them.

While I had been in Berlin and involved in the operations in Poland I hadn't had much time to consider the implications of the declaration of war on my life, but my week's leave gave me plenty of time to think. I obviously couldn't write to Chris as the borders were now closed and there was no mail service to Yorkshire. Presumably, now that war was declared, he had been called up to fly Hurricanes in the RAF.

I was able to get hold of Susie and travelled to Kiel by train to see her. She was working in the offices associated with the docks but could see me in the evening

'You're looking so tired Markus,' she said when I arrived at her house.

'That's a lovely way to greet me Susie,' I replied, not impressed with her opening remark.

'Sorry, come in while I get my coat, I presume that you want to go for a drink in the city.'

'I actually have some money so we can have a meal at a restaurant. I am no longer a penniless student.' I said with some pride.

She got her coat, and we walked into the city and found a restaurant that was open. A lot of places seemed to have closed even though Kiel was now packed with service personnel.

'How has it been Markus,' she asked me after our order had been taken

'It's been very difficult. Our squadron lost nine men fighting in Poland, and I knew them all exceptionally well. We were told that we would meet no opposition, but we had to deal with the entire Polish air force. They were very competent fliers, and we suffered.'

'I thought that you had the best planes, and it would have been easy for you,' she added.

'Our equipment was a lot better than theirs, and we had superior numbers, but they still did a lot of damage. They were remarkably brave and defended their country with great passion,' I said with a lot of feeling.

'You sound depressed Markus,' Susie said, putting an arm around me.

'The biggest problem is that I can't sleep. I wake up in the middle of the night with my brain racing as if I am the middle of a dog fight. I am actually scared of what I am involved in, and there is no end in sight.'

'Have you any idea what is going to happen now that war has been declared by England and France?' she asked me.

'We are being supplied with new planes and also have replacement pilots joining us, so we are going to have to work up to full operational capability before we take on anybody else. I don't think that England or France will attack us as they are not really ready'

'I hope that you get some rest and are able to sleep Markus. This war really is terrible, and there now seems to be no end in sight. I hate to think what will happen next.'

We finished our meal and had a couple more drinks before I walked her home. Her father had returned by the time we got back and we sat up talking until quite late. The following morning Susie went off to work, and I went to the train station to take the train back to Lubeck.

The rest of my leave was uneventful, and I was able to relax. By the time I returned to the squadron I was also sleeping a lot better.

Chapter 17

That was my last leave during the year 1939. There were all sorts of rumours as to what was going to happen next and obviously we were looking to the West for the next phase of Germany's break out. The airfield and facilities at Lubeck were expanded, and, by the end of the year, a second squadron was located there. It was a particularly harsh winter which limited the number of days that we were able to operate. In addition, our flying hours were severely curtailed on the days when it was suitable to fly, to conserve fuel. The available fuel was used for training flights for the new pilots and to develop better tactics. After the debacle in Poland, it was decided that improved tactics were required to protect the pilots and aircraft. As an Oberleutnant, I was a member of the group who was responsible for developing the tactics and for training the pilots which meant I got more flying time than most.

We had to learn rapidly before we met the enemy again, and by December, we were much better prepared for the next stage of the war. Clearly 1940 was going to be a year full of action as we were aware that the British expeditionary force had landed in France and were consolidating their positions. We also heard that Hurricane and Spitfire squadrons had been moved to French airfields. By the end of 1939, there were a considerable number of modern and well equipped fighters facing us.

The unfavourable weather conditions continued into the first few months of 1940, and we spent most of our time in a state of boredom on the ground. There was obviously something significant coming as, on the days that we were able to fly in clear skies; we did spot a lot of our own troops being deployed to forward positions.

On the 7th April, the brakes were taken off, and we went into action.

We were called to a briefing on the evening of the 6th April. The room was packed with all the members of the two squadrons, including most of the ground crew. As the Kommandant strode to the front of the room accompanied by the other senior officers, a hush fell over the assembled masses. I felt particularly nervous and for some reason had a strong sense of foreboding.

'You will be glad to hear that the waiting is over, and our illustrious leader Hitler has declared we are ready to attack the enemies who have declared war against Germany. Tomorrow the forces of the Third Reich will launch an attack on Denmark and will also invade Norway. Your role will be to eliminate the Danish air force, and, having completed that task, you will be responsible for protecting the landings in Norway. More detailed instructions will be given to you by your squadron leaders. Good hunting. Heil Hitler.' He saluted and left the room.

We were then organized into our squadrons where we received specific instructions for the operations to be carried out the following day.

As the sun rose, ushering in a fine day in Lubeck, there was a cacophony of noise as more than fifty powerful engines rumbled into life, and roared as the planes took-off.

I recalled the day last March when we had taken off from near Berlin full of enthusiasm and bravado and how we had returned after our mission totally deflated. Certain of our colleagues hadn't returned, and the realisation had hit us that war was tough. When we had set out all the pilots were full of pride, but we knew remarkably little about the stark facts of war. I looked around me at my colleagues sitting anxiously in the cockpits of their Me109's waiting to take-off. There were a lot of them who hadn't seen action in Poland, and I wondered which ones wouldn't be coming back.

The flight in front of mine took off. I indicated to my flight it was time to go, pushing the throttle forward at the same time. I raced across the grass of the airfield and my war resumed.

Denmark was overcome fairly quickly, and there was only one fatality in the squadron. Two days later the whole squadron was relocated to a captured airfield, close to Viborg in northern Denmark. This would reduce the flying time to the operational areas of Norway. We encountered only minor opposition as the planes put up against us were no match for our technology and our well trained pilots. We had learnt a lot of lessons from Poland and had put them into practice.

On the 20th April, with most of our objectives achieved in the Norwegian theatre of operations, the squadron returned to Lubeck to regroup and get ready for the attack on Western Europe. We had only lost three planes in the operations over Denmark and Norway, largely because both air forces had been destroyed on the ground. We had encountered the RAF for the first time in Norway, but our squadron had only met one or two and they hadn't been a threat.

That all changed on the 10th May when the German invasion of Holland, Belgium and France commenced. All restrictions on the use of fuel were cancelled, and we were in the air as long as there was daylight. As soon as my flight landed back at base, the planes were serviced, ammunition was replenished, and we were ready to go again. We hardly had time to eat and had to make do with a breakfast before dawn and a meal in the evening after it got dark.

We even had a continual supply of spare planes to replace any that were mechanically unfit to take-off. Losses were high, and we lost about twenty five percent of our strength. We rapidly ran out of back-up 109's and also of pilots. New pilots and planes were arriving all the time to replace our losses, and one of my roles was to ensure that the new arrivals to my flight, received the basic skills to enable them to survive.

Every morning, when I opened my tired eyes, I was hopeful that I would hear the welcome sound of rain and wind. The only days that I had a chance to recover from the unrelenting pressure were the ones that we couldn't fly due to the bad weather.

I didn't escape the carnage but was extremely lucky to survive when my luck ran out. My flight was flying over Holland, protecting a group of Stuka dive bombers, whose mission was to attack Dutch defences near Amsterdam. There was a lot of flak being thrown up from anti-aircraft batteries, and I was unlucky to receive a hit from some shrapnel. Fuel started to leak, and I soon realised that I wouldn't have enough to make it back to Lubeck.

I headed towards Germany, and, once over friendly territory, I looked for a field that I might be able to land in without killing myself. My first attempt was a disaster, and I overshot the field I had selected, but on the second attempt, I managed to make a pretty decent landing suffering only minimal damage to the undercarriage. At least I survived. I found a farmhouse that luckily had a telephone. I was put through to the airfield at Lubeck, and was able to arrange for a recovery crew to come and collect me and my Me109.

That evening I celebrated my survival in the mess. I had been reported missing along with two others, but they sadly turned out to have been killed. They readied another plane for me overnight, fitting my 'BEKER seat' to the new plane. At dawn, I took off leading my flight back into the action.

Progress of the army in the countries that were being attacked was rapid, and by the 24th May the British army was pinned back in Dunkirk. Shortly afterwards, the Belgium army surrendered, along with the Dutch, so all our air resources now could be focused over the defeated enemy at Dunkirk.

We then witnessed an extraordinary sight. Thousands of ships came across the Channel and started to pick up the British, French and other members of the defeated army, bringing them back to the south coast of England. Our role was to strafe the beaches where the defeated army was collecting and also attack the Hurricanes and Spitfires who were trying to protect them. It was our first real encounter with a mass of enemy fighters, and we suffered a lot of casualties.

What I had dreaded was happening. We were now fighting the air force that my twin brother Chris was a member of, and the possibility of fighting against my brother was becoming a reality.

I was intelligent enough to realise that my thoughts about Chris were endangering my life. I was actually looking at every enemy Hurricane, to see if I could recognise Chris. This resulted in a split seconds delay in firing. Realistically that might be the difference between survival and death. I was able to convince myself that the chances of encountering Chris would be infinitesimal, and I had better ignore the possibility if I wanted to stay alive.

Looking at what was going on below me in the seas off Dunkirk, I was actually quite surprised at how relieved I felt that so many men were escaping. I learnt afterwards that over three hundred thousand managed to escape back to England.

It was shortly afterwards that France surrendered, and the newspapers were full of pictures of Hitler in Paris celebrating the German victory. I was so tired that celebrations were beyond me, and I felt extremely lucky to have survived so far.

Chapter 18

We had a few days out of the firing line. We had been in action, with no rest days, for almost a month. Being a resident of Lubeck, I was allowed to go home for a few days. All I did was sleep.

Shortly after my return to the Squadron, all the Oberleutnants and officers above that rank were called to a briefing.

'I want to pass on to you the directions that the Fuehrer has issued, and it concerns the next phase of the war against Great Britain.' The Kommandant sounded full of confidence as he addressed us. 'There is going to be an all-out air attack on England, and this will involve every fighter and bomber squadron in the Luftwaffe. The squadrons based here in Lubeck are being relocated to airfields in the north of France. This will put them closer to the south coast of England and will enable you to spend more time over the operational areas. Our objective will be to defeat the RAF and destroy their airfields making it impossible for them to operate, which will cause the British Government to capitulate and seek peace. Heil Hitler.'

'When will we be moving,' one of the officers asked.

'We will be moving in two days from now. The ground crews will leave on Tuesday, and the squadron will fly to France on Friday, by which time the airfield will have been set up to receive you. '

'Can you tell us where we are going?' another officer asked.

'Not at the moment as we don't want any information to get out prior to the move. There will be a party in the mess tonight to celebrate the successful invasion of France and the Low Countries. You can let your hair down, but we want you fully recovered by the time that you have to move.'

With that, he terminated the meeting, and we all retired to the mess to start the party.

The conditions that we found at our new location when we flew there on the Friday were extremely primitive as there had been no time to set up proper accommodation. The pilots were housed in whatever buildings were available while the ground crews were housed in tents. Field kitchens provided the food, so it was very basic and was often cold.

The Battle for Britain was launched on the 10th July with our squadron's role being to escort bombers as they went in wave after wave across the French coast and the south coast of England. Needless to say, we met heavy resistance as the RAF's Spitfires and Hurricanes came up in their swarms against us. We lost a lot of bombers and quite a few fighters, so the mood back at our base was not a happy one. From my own personal point of view, the chances of me bumping into Chris had increased considerably as every fighter plane in the RAF was being thrown up against the Luftwaffe hordes.

On 23rd July, I was escorting a large flight of bombers across Kent just before sunset. We were jumped on by RAF fighter planes which we didn't spot early enough as they came out of the low setting sun in the west. I dived to avoid a fighter that had latched on to me, but I was too late and my engine received a direct hit and went on fire. Luckily I was unhurt and had avoided serious injury, but my Messerschmitt 109 was going nowhere.

As the fighter that had just disabled me flashed past, I just caught sight of the pilot. It was unquestionably my twin brother Chris. It registered in my brain, but at that moment all I was concerned about, was getting out of my damaged aircraft.

I was now diving, out of control, towards the ground. My large frame was wedged into my special 'BEKER' seat. If I was to survive, I needed to exit the plane, without hitting the tail. I eased myself out of the seat, threw the rudder over, and with all the strength that I possessed, pushed myself upwards. I exited the cockpit and just managed to miss the tail, pulled on the rip cord of my parachute, and, to my great relief, it opened successfully.

Chris must have recognized who he had shot down, and he circled in his Hurricane making sure that I was OK. Taking my eyes off Chris and looking down at the ground, I could see that there were electricity pylons in the area that I was heading for. It now was getting quite dark, so I had considerable difficulty in picking out the cables. By pulling frantically on the lines of my parachute, I managed to avoid both pylons and cables, and I landed safely.

Chris was still circling, keeping an eye on me and checking to make sure that I came to no harm. He then made a fatal mistake. He came to a very low height to verify that I had landed safely. Despite the canopy of his cockpit being fully open to give him better visibility, he didn't see the cables. His plane collided with the cables and did an instant somersault. He was ejected through the open canopy when his Hurricane somersaulted. I stood there in horror as I saw my brother fly through the air and land in a hay rick which was situated in a corner of the field that I had landed in. His Hurricane hit the ground and became a blazing inferno. I ran over to the hay rick in a total panic. I was stunned. It was bad enough going through the trauma of being shot down, but I had also seen my twin brother killed in front of me.

What did I do now? I heard the sound of a tractor coming down a lane towards the field. I had to do something quick and get away from there. I decided to switch tunics with my brother and also to switch our dog tags. Whoever found him would assume that he was Markus BEKER of the Luftwaffe, and there was no way that Chris Becker would have survived the inferno that the Hurricane had become.

With great difficulty, I took off his RAF tunic and somehow managed to dress him in my Luftwaffe tunic. I was in such shock that I did it all in a dream. I ended up leaving the scene as an RAF officer but with Luftwaffe trousers. Hopefully, no one would look too closely below my waist.

I slid off the hay rick and climbed over the fence behind the hay rick just as the tractor was entering through the gate at the other end of the field. I skirted around the field behind a tall hedge, keeping well out of sight of whoever was on the tractor. I found the lane that the tractor had come along, and headed away from the tragedy.

Chapter 19

It was now quite dark, and I was having considerable difficulty finding my way as there was a total blackout in operation. I decided that the best option would be to find somewhere to hide for the night. I then would set off at first light.

As I walked along the lane, there was the dark outline of quite a large building beside me, so I investigated further and found a barn. Rather than stumble around in the dark, I went into the barn, and curled up on some hay to sleep. Hunger was my next problem. I hadn't eaten for about sixteen hours, which was a problem as my large frame needed plenty of fodder to maintain its energy levels. Eventually, I managed to fall asleep and got some rest before I had to leave my sanctuary when the darkness receded at around 5:30 am the following morning.

At least I could see where I was going now although all the signposts had been taken down. I was conscious that I didn't have any flying cap and my head was bare. Chris had been wearing his flying helmet, and I obviously couldn't wear that and had left it with him. I hoped my hatless state wouldn't give me away.

I came to a town, but had no idea where I was because of the absence of signs. As I was progressing through the town I heard a steam train in the distance, so there must be a station where hopefully I could get a train to London. I duly found the station and was able to find out that I was in Swanley as the name plate hadn't been removed. I purchased a ticket from the rather sleepy looking clerk in the ticket office, and boarded the next train for London that arrived. Forty minutes later the train puffed into Victoria station and came to a grinding halt. I had survived the first part of my journey, and nobody had asked me a question or tried to talk to me. There were so many people travelling around in uniform that I fitted in a lot better than if I had been in casual clothes or a suit. The only people not in uniform were too young or too old to be serving their country.

I knew from my previous train trip to Yorkshire in 1938 that the train left from Kings Cross station. I now had to transport myself across London on the underground.

I arrived at Kings Cross at 9:30 am only to find that the next train to Harrogate would not leave until 11:15 am. With time to kill, I decided to risk buying some food as by this time I was weak with the hunger. As food rationing had been introduced earlier in the year the menu was extremely limited, but I was able to purchase a large portion of bully-beef pie with some bread and a cup of tea.

Feeling much better and gaining in confidence I caught the 11:15 train.

I hadn't had a chance to have a proper look in Chris's wallet, so, once the train was under way, I took it out and went through all the items in it. There was only one piece of paper that was vital, his service papers, which gave his rank, squadron, and personal details. An hour later the conductor came around checking tickets and with him was a policeman who was checking papers. I handed my ticket to the conductor and the service papers to the policemen. They both nodded at me and moved on. I didn't have to say a word which of course would have been a possible giveaway with my pronounced German accent.

It was a hugely relieved Markus that got off the train in Harrogate. The next difficult task would be to tell my father about Chris's accident and probable death.

It was with a lot of trepidation that I pushed open the door and entered the bakery. The lady behind the counter looked up and waved to me obviously believing that it was Chris. I moved past her and saw my father in the rear of the bakery with his back to me.

'Dad, it's me Markus.'

He turned around with a look of surprise on his face which turned to alarm when he saw me standing there in an RAF uniform.

'Markus, what is going on? Why are you dressed in an RAF uniform?'

'Chris is dead Dad.' I collapsed into his arms and started to weep like a baby. He held onto me and helped me into the small office.

I hugged him, the last fifteen hours pouring out of me, and I felt like a small boy again.

Eventually, I started to get control of myself. He pulled a bottle of whiskey and a glass out of a cupboard at the side of the room and poured me a measure.

'Drink this lad and tell me all about it,' he said, sitting down in the chair behind his desk.

'Chris shot me down and then came to see if I had survived. He mustn't have seen the electricity cables as he hit them with his undercarriage, his plane flipped, and he was thrown out and landed on a haystack. It was terrible Dad, and there was nothing that I could do to help him.'

There were now tears in both our eyes.

'OK Markus, just tell me nice and calmly what happened and how you ended coming through the door into my bakery.'

I drew a deep breath and told him the full story. As the story flowed out of me, so I came to terms with what had happened and I started to relax.

'The most crucial thing we have to decide Markus is what we are going to do with you now. You can obviously stay here with me, but long term the truth is going to come out. We also have to do something about Chris as they will find his body and his plane. They will also be looking for you as someone will have seen you parachute down. He will have to get a decent burial.'

'I can't go back to my squadron now after what happened to Chris. I have had enough of this killing and want out.' I was sobbing again.

'It's Wednesday evening, so we'll give it few days and take a decision on Saturday. In the meantime, you can help me in the shop. Chris always leaves some of his clothes here so you will be able to wear those around the bakery.'

Over the next few days, I got to know what it was like being a fugitive. The two of us were on edge all the time, jumping at every knock on the door. With the Battle of Britain still very much in the news, questions were undoubtedly being asked as to why Chris was home on leave when they needed every available pilot to repel the German raiders.

I read the newspaper every day and was amazed to see that the battle for the skies over Britain was still going on. On the German side, we had been told it would be over in a week. They gave casualty figures showing that the Luftwaffe was losing two planes for every one RAF aircraft lost. The number of brave pilots being killed on both sides was horrendous.

'I am feeling terribly guilty about Chris,' my Dad said on the Thursday afternoon as we finished work for the day.

'I have also been thinking about it Dad,' I replied. 'I just left him there in the field in my tunic lying on that hay stack. I don't know what they will do with him. My Squadron will report me as missing, presumed dead, and that is what they will tell my mother and granddad. It's a gigantic mess.'

'I don't want you interred Markus. If we only could find some satisfactory way out of this situation, I would be a lot happier.'

'Perhaps I should just go to the authorities and hand myself over. That would sort everything out.'

'I said that I would decide on Saturday, so let's just leave it till then.'

In fact, the decision was taken for us. On Friday, just after lunch, four men dressed in uniform came in to the bakery.

My father saw them enter and went to greet them.

'Are you Mr Becker, the owner of this bakery?' the senior officer asked.

'That's correct. How can I help you?'

I was in the back of the bakery where the ovens were, but could see and hear what was happening in the shop. I had a feeling of dread in the pit of my stomach.

'Mr Becker, my name is Captain Adlington, and I would like to talk to your son please,' the Captain asked my Dad.

'What do you want him for?'

'We just need to talk to him. He has been reported missing by his squadron, and the local police station has been notified that he has been seen at your bakery. Is he here?' the Captain asked.

Yes, he is over there,' my Dad said pointing to where I was standing.

'Can we use your office as it would be better talking to him in private?"

'Better still, you can go through to the living quarters and talk to him in the sitting room,' my Dad suggested.

'That sounds perfect. Will you lead the way please?' The Captain seemed to be relieved to get out of the shop where there were customers looking on.

My father showed them the way, and they made sure that I stayed between them as we went into the house which was connected with the shop by a corridor.

I felt that my world was crashing down around me. I was terrified. If this had happened in Germany, I would probably be shot as would my father and anybody else working in the bakery. So far it had been remarkably civilised.

When we arrived in the living room, my father approached the Captain.

'May I have a quick word with my son Captain Adlington,' my father asked.

'Anything you have to say to him must be in our hearing,' he replied.

'That's fine. It's nothing confidential.'

My father turned to me. 'Markus I think you should tell the Captain the whole truth, as Chris's death has to be respected.'

He put his hand on my shoulder and gave it a squeeze and left the room.

Once the door was closed, the Captain asked me, 'What was that all about and who are you? I thought that your name was Chris Becker.'

'No, I am afraid that I am his twin brother. My name is Markus BEKER, and I am a member of the Luftwaffe.'

'Perhaps you had better take a seat and start at the beginning. I want you to tell me everything,' the Captain said, sitting down opposite me. The others stood between me and the door

I described in detail what had occurred in the field in Kent. How my brother had managed to shoot up my Messerschmitt and had then destroyed his own aircraft when he hit the electricity cables. I then described how I had switched tunics with him and travelled to my Dad in Harrogate. I filled him in on our background and how I was flying for the German air force while he was flying for the RAF.

The Captain sat patiently while I related my story, and he didn't even ask a question. The others also stood listening to what to them must have been an unbelievable story.

"I am sorry, but even though your father is an English citizen, you are a pilot flying for a country that we are at war with. I will have to take you into custody,' the Captain explained, almost apologetically.

'I understand the situation,' I muttered, feeling extremely relieved. 'Can I just go and say goodbye to my father.'

'Yes, but I'll come with you just to make sure that you don't run away; although you don't look the sort to scarper.'

My father, in fact, was waiting in the passage and hadn't returned to the bakery.

'Mr Becker, I am taking your son Markus with me. He will be held in a house just outside Harrogate where he will be interrogated. What happens to him after that depends on the information he gives us and whether the story he has told us is true.'

'I am quite thankful that this whole thing has come out in the open. I can now get in touch with Chris's squadron and sort out his burial. It is a tremendous weight off my mind,' my father said.

I gave my Dad a hug as I passed him. There were tears in his eyes. He had lost one son, and the other was being interred. War had a lot to answer for.

He let us out the side door of the house which meant that we didn't have to go back through the shop in front of all the customers.

I turned around to wave to him, but he had closed the door.

Chapter 20

There was a small military Bedford truck parked in the street in front of the bakery. I was put in the back with two of the men who had come to collect me while the Captain rode in the front with the driver. I was quite content to go along with them and had no intention of trying to escape. Once the officer had vanished out of sight sit in the cab, the two soldiers lit up and smoked a quiet cigarette.

About half an hour later we slowed down and then entered through some large gates into what appeared from my rear view to a country estate.

'Nearly there now,' one of my guards said. 'You'll be alright here as there are not many other internees held in this house.'

'Is this where I am going to be held then,' I asked them.

'They usually keep people here for about two weeks, and they are all officers. If you were an ordinary 'Joe Soap' like us, they would take you to the camp over near Catterick which is a lot more basic.' The other soldier chipped in.

'I am just grateful to have survived,' I added.

Shortly afterwards we went through another gate before pulling up in front of an enormous old mansion. When I descended from the back of the truck, I looked in awe at the magnificent building.

'We requisitioned this house about three months ago as a temporary holding centre for captured officers,' Captain Adlington said as I was looking at the building. 'You will be held here for a while as we check out your story and interrogate you. After that, we will decide where to inter you on a long term basis.'

As we went into the large entrance hall, I was taken off to the side to an office. There a sergeant entered my name in a register, plus some of my details and he then took all my personal possessions, filing them away in a box. I still had Chris's wallet on me including his RAF papers. They studied these in some detail but didn't place them in the box with the rest of my personal effects.

'You will now be taken to a room where you will be locked in. Your meals will be brought to you and you will be taken to the toilet when you need to use it.' The sergeant read out the list of rules to me. 'There will be a 'pee pot' in the room which you can empty every morning. The interrogation sessions will commence tomorrow morning,' he continued.

I was taken up the stairs and down a passage which had rooms opening off it on either side. The guard stopped outside one of the rooms, opened the door and ushered me inside. The door closed behind me and I heard the key turn, locking me in.

There were very few pieces of furniture in the room; a bed and one chair, but at least there was a carpet on the floor, so it was quite homely. I tested the bed and was agreeably surprised how comfy it was. I could survive this. I opened the wardrobe and was greeted by an overpowering smell of moth balls, but it was empty.

The following morning, after my breakfast, I was taken by an armed guard to a room on the ground floor where two uniformed officers were waiting for me.

'Good morning Oberleutnant BEKER, I am Major Martin, and this is Captain Dobbs. We will be interrogating you, and, amongst other things, trying to verify how you were staying in a house, in Harrogate. If you make our task as straightforward as possible, then your stay here is going to be comfortable if you don't then we will have to take a different approach. Do you understand?'

'I have no reason to hide anything from you and intend to answer as many of your questions as I can,' I replied.

'It sounds as if we aren't going to have any problems Markus. Let's get going,' the Major said, relaxing and leaning back in his chair.

Quite a few days of questioning then commenced and I was totally amazed at the level of detail that they wanted. The friendly atmosphere probably loosened my tongue, and I told them rather more than I originally intended, but then there was nothing that I knew that could be classified as 'Top Secret'

It was exceedingly strange and surprisingly civilised, being imprisoned by the British, and I was starting to see why my father had decided to stay in England when he was released in 1918. If I had been arrested in Germany by the Gestapo, I probably would have vanished without a trace by now. Sitting here in an English country mansion gave me a totally different view of the workings of the Third Reich. I was now looking in with a totally different perspective from the outside. The SS operated on the basis of fear while the British treated you with respect and got your trust. I knew which way I preferred.

For five consecutive days, I was interrogated for three hours in the morning and another two hours in the afternoon. I was mentally exhausted as it was a long time since I had to use my brain for so long. It was a totally different type of exhaustion than I had experienced from non-stop flying.

Without any notice, they didn't come for me on the sixth day. The food still kept coming, but the guard, who usually took me downstairs, didn't.

'Are they not sending for me today?' I asked the guard when he brought my food.

'They don't tell me things like that Sir. You'll find out soon enough,' he replied.

Three weeks passed, and I was getting quite bored just lying in my room all day with no entertainment other than my meals. They had provided me with a few English novels which I was struggling to read

Finally, in the fourth week, the guard came to my room during the afternoon to conduct me downstairs again.

As I entered the interview room, I noticed that Major Martin and Captain Dobbs had been replaced by an officer who I hadn't seen before. He was sitting there puffing on a pipe, and the room was filled with smoke and the aroma of tobacco.

I sat down opposite him in my usual chair.

'Oberleutnant BEKER, I have read your file and appreciate that you have talked to us very frankly during your sessions with Major Martin and Captain Dobbs. My name is Major Richards, and I come from a totally different part of the British Army. I am based in Surrey, in the South of England.' He stopped talking to take a puff on his pipe.

'What do you want from me Sir?' I asked him, not too sure where this was going.

'I have a proposition for you Markus, which, if you agree to it, will give you your freedom.'

'What is a proposition; it is a very big word, and I don't like the sound of it?' I said, not expecting the meeting to begin that way. Major Richards seemed unusually relaxed and friendly.

'Well a proposition is actually just a question, and I want to ask you to help us.'

'I will listen to what you have to say to me, but I am not promising you anything,' I was highly suspicious of the direction things were going. I sat forward in my chair so as I could hear him better.

'We know that the Luftwaffe is developing a plane with jet engines and we are extremely worried about the damage it will do to our bombers and our fighter planes. We, unfortunately, don't know how successful they have been in the development, or when the jet engined fighters are likely to be ready to enter active service. I am asking you to honour your brother's death and work for us in finding out the details of when it will be ready.'

'But I know nothing about the jet fighter Sir, and how would I find out,' I interjected.

'We would need to find a way of returning you to Europe and you would then need to transfer into the squadron that would be flying the jet fighters,' he replied.

'But they are aware that I was shot down and that I landed in England and have been captured,' I reasoned.

'We would find a way to get you back to France so as you could say that you escaped from custody here and crossed the Channel to return to your unit. Let's not go into the detail now as that will require a lot of work, I just need an answer from you as to whether you will consider my proposition.'

'When do you need my response Major Richards?'

'I would like to get your answer as soon as possible, so as we can proceed with the arrangements. One thing you should know Oberleutnant is that while you have been in custody the RAF have won the Battle of Britain and Hitler has transferred his planes to take part in the invasion of Russia. Your squadron is now active on the Eastern front with all that entails. Hitler has made an enormous mistake, and it is likely that you will now lose the war. I am offering you a chance to help in beating him,' Major Richards said this last bit in a serious tone tapping the stem of his pipe on the table between us..

This last news had hit me hard and made me feel tremendously sad. All that I had grown up with and the pride that I had in the Third Reich and Hitler was now starting to crumble.

'Can you get my father to come and see me so I can get his advice?' I asked him.

'I will go out and phone him now and see if he can come in today or tomorrow.'

'What is the alternative if I say No?'

'You will be transferred to a Prisoner of War camp in Canada where you will stay until the end of the war. This transfer will entail you having to travel across the Atlantic, and you will have the added risk of getting sunk by a German U Boat.'

'I'll give you your answer tomorrow when I have seen my father.'

'I understand; I'll have you taken back to your room now and go and phone your father.'

The meeting terminated, and I was able to escape the smoke and return to my bedroom.

They came to get me the following morning, and I thought that it was to talk to my father, but, in fact, they allowed me to walk around outside in the grounds of the estate that surrounded the house. It was a pleasant surprise even though I felt that it was a softening up process. It was so good to feel the breeze on my face and hear the sounds of the countryside.

In the afternoon, they came for me again and brought me to the interview room, where my father was sitting waiting for me. He got up as I entered and gave me a fatherly hug. There were tears in his eyes as he embraced me.

'How are you Markus? Are they looking after you alright?' he asked me once we were sitting opposite each other.

'Yes it is not too bad. I am a bit lonely as I am on my own, but they have treated me well, certainly a lot better than I would have expected.'

'The Major said that you wanted to talk to me about something, but he didn't tell me what it was about.'

'It's a long story, but I have been asked to go back to Europe and work for the British as a spy, finding out about the jet engined fighters that are being developed for the Luftwaffe. They say that I owe it to the memory of my brother.' I explained.

'How can I help you in your decision,' my father inquired, defensively.

'Well you fought for Germany in the First World War and then stayed in England when you were released from the POW camp. Why did you do that?'

'I was luckily captured by some English Tommies, and I found them to be extremely fair. They were only fighting because Germany had created a situation where they had to defend themselves. Despite the horrors that the army was enduring I was treated like a human being and given respect, even as a prisoner. On top of all that, life in Germany was impossible after being defeated and German ended up fighting

German in all the towns right across the country. I wanted a better life, and I got it in England.'

'I am starting to realise the same thing Dad. If I had been captured in Germany, I would probably be dead by now. All the people here have treated me fairly.'

'So what are you going to do Markus?' he asked me, looking into my eyes.

'When Chris visited me in Germany before the war and when I came here to see you and Chris, I began to realise the level of indoctrination that I had been subjected to in the Hitler Youth. Chris was a lot freer and had a much better life here. I started to have doubts.'

'But becoming a spy is a gigantic step Markus; are you sure that you will be able to cope?' I had never seen my father look so serious. .

'I feel that if Chris was still alive, he would want me to go and get the information on the jet engines and the new fighter, and give it to the RAF. He would like me to do anything that would help defeat Germany. I have decided to do it for Chris and not for myself because I am still totally confused.'

My father stood up and came around the table, and I got up top meet him. He took me into his arms, and I wept on his shoulder for quite some time.

Seeing that we had finished talking the army sergeant, who had been keeping an eye on us, came in and let my father out. He then told me that he was going off to get the Major who came into the room a few minutes later.

'Well, have you made up your mind what you are going to do?' he asked me.

'I have decided to go along with your request, but I want to you know that it is for my brother Chris and for no other reason.'

'I appreciate how difficult it must have been to come to your decision, but I am extremely thankful that you have agreed to help us.'

I was mentally drained. I had just taken the hardest decision of my life. In the battle that had gone on inside my head, two forces had been fighting for control of my life:

I had been brought up in the belief that Germany had been wronged and that I must join with my fellow countrymen, to fight against the enemies who were trying to control and destroy Germany. I had discovered that I had a father and a twin brother who lived in one of the countries considered an enemy of Germany and, therefore, an enemy of mine. My love for my brother had triumphed, and I had to change sides because of what I had done to him. I could never bring him back to life, but I could make him proud of me.

'What happens now?' I asked the Major.

'You will relocate to another house in Surrey where you will undergo extensive training and be fully briefed on your new role. You will of course also be released from custody and will be free to move around as you please. It is vital that you stay within confines of the house you will be moving to. We don't want any chance of you being spotted and identified by someone you might casually meet, prior to you arriving back in France.'

'I would appreciate getting some more clothes as I only have the ones that I was wearing when I was picked up.'

'We'll sort all that out for you when we get to Surrey. We will leave from Harrogate train station first thing tomorrow morning, so if you like you can go and stay with your father this evening. Perhaps you can get some clothes and a bag from him. I asked your father to wait outside for you as I thought that you would like to go with him. Welcome aboard.' He took his pipe out of his right hand and shook my hand, sealing the deal. What a difference to what I was used to back home; the Heil Hitlers and the clicking of heels.

Chapter 21

'Dad, do you think that I am doing the right thing,' I asked my father. We were sitting in the back of a khaki coloured car that had been assigned to take us to the bakery in Harrogate.

'In war it is very difficult to know what the right thing is Markus. You are living in an age where your choices are limited because of the war going on around you. You have been flying in the Luftwaffe, and, if you were still in your squadron, would probably be fighting against the Russians on the Eastern Front. By all accounts, the losses are horrendous, and you probably would be dead by now. You, in fact, are fortunate that you were shot down over Kent.'

'But I can't get rid of a feeling of guilt for changing sides and agreeing to work for the British,' I replied.

'If it wasn't for the fact that you feel responsible for Chris's death, would you have agreed to change sides?'

'That certainly is a factor, but I was already questioning whether Hitler was right in what he was saying and I don't agree with where Germany is heading. Living in a police dictatorship is not particularly pleasant and the Nazi party rules by fear. If you don't do what you are told, they simply shoot you.'

'Anyway now you have made your decision, so your days of choosing are over. Don't forget that you can pull out at any time Markus, although the alternative is to be shipped to Canada to an internment camp where you will be held for as long as the war lasts.'

'I am doing it for Chris, Dad, and I won't back out of what I have committed to, no matter what happens.'

'I am tremendously proud of you and the decision that you have taken. I hate this war just as much as the last World War which I was actively involved in. Families are being destroyed by it.'

'Thanks Dad, I hope that I continue to make you proud.'

We continued to talk after we got back to the house, and it was quite late when I finally got to bed. Before I lay down, I went through Chris's clothes and managed to find a few that fitted me and looked reasonable. I packed these away into a small suitcase that my father managed to find in the attic.

I was woken at 5:00 am. I dressed, breakfasted and went to the station to meet Major Richards. My Dad had the baking to do, to stock the shelves ready for the customers, so he couldn't come to the station to see me off. We had a very tearful embrace before I left.

Major Richards had bought the tickets, and we boarded the 6:50 am train to London. Thankfully we were travelling in a first class carriage, and there was less chance of people asking me questions. The only problem I had to put up with was the smell of tobacco smoke from the Major's pipe.

'Any early morning regrets, Markus?' the Major asked me.

'Not yet. I haven't fully woken up yet.' I smiled.

'Did you have a late night then?' he added.

'Yes, I was talking to my father well into the night and, afterwards, I had to sort through Chris's clothes.'

'We have a three hour journey ahead of us so you can have a nap if you like. I promise not to talk to you and disturb you'

It wasn't long before my eyes closed, and I slept most of the way to London.

We took the underground from Kings Cross to Victoria station and then caught an overland train to Witley in Surrey. Major Richards informed me that the estate that I would be billeted at was only five minutes' drive from Witley station.

As soon as the train arrived and we descended to the platform, the Major went into the ticket office, to make a phone call to his office to let them know that we had arrived and needed transport. Ten minutes later an army vehicle arrived to pick us up.

I had never seen anything like the house that we arrived at. It wasn't a house it was a mansion.

Security was extremely tight, and we had to pass through two security check points before we pulled up at the main entrance.

'Welcome to Witley Park, Markus. This is where you will spend the next few months of your life,' Major Richards said as we got out of the car.

I looked in awe at the magnificent edifice and the surrounding grounds. About fifty meters away, in front of the house, there was an artificial lake with castellated buildings surrounding it.

'There is a ballroom under the largest of the lakes,' Major Richards commented. 'It was constructed in the late nineteenth century when the house was built.'

'Will I be able to have a look at it, Major?'

'Yes you will be able to go anywhere on the grounds in your free time.'

The army driver grabbed my suitcase out of the boot of the car, and we went through the entrance door into the hallway.

'He is in room B4 Corporal Kane,' the Major told the driver. 'Come back down Markus in half an hour and I will introduce you to the others. The Corporal will show you to your room.'

'Thank you Major I will see you in thirty minutes.'

We went up the stairs and along a corridor towards the right hand side of the building. The Corporal stopped outside room B4.

'This is it Sir,' he offered. 'If you like to go in, I will follow with your case.'

I opened the door and entered the room. I got a surprise as there was a middle aged man lounging back on a bed close to the window.

'Oh I am sorry, I would have knocked if I knew you were in here,' I stuttered out.

'You must be Flight Lieutenant Becker; I was told that you were coming. My name is Captain Vic Biddlecome,' he said, getting up off his bed and coming towards me.

I took his outstretched hand and shook it.

'Please call me Markus, Vic. It looks as if we are going to be roommates.'

'I'll leave you now Sir if there is nothing else,' the Corporal said, obviously uncomfortable in the presence of officers. He left the room closing the door behind him.

I hadn't expected to have to share a room, but, in fact, it was quite a welcome development as I had been on my own for over a month and it would be nice to have someone to talk to. It was only a welcome development, provided of course that we got on together.

I put away the few clothes that I had brought with me and chatted to Vic until it was time to go downstairs to meet the others.

There were only five of us in total and that included Major Richards and his commanding officer Colonel Trevor Thorpe. The only person undergoing training, other than Vic and I, was a naval officer called Captain Brian Wilkinson.

Major Richards did the introductions before we grabbed a plate each and helped ourselves from the buffet.

I sat down at the large dining table beside the naval Captain.

'Welcome to our school Markus, we will probably get to know each other very well over the training period as there are only three trainees here at the moment.'

'Have you been here long, Brian?'

'I came here just over two months ago, so I have been here about nine weeks,' he replied.

'Do you know how long the rest of your training is going to take?'

'No, I haven't been given a finishing date. They have told me that I will have to remain here until I have no weaknesses and am fully trained. They have also said that I can only leave here when conditions for the mission I am being trained for are perfect.'

'Are you allowed to tell me what mission you are preparing for?' I asked, not expecting a positive answer.

'No, I can't tell you anything other than my name and the same will apply to you. There were three other guys here up to two days ago, and then they left on a mission. I have no idea where they went or what they were going to do. All I can tell you is that everybody who passes through this house is going to operate in enemy territory'

'It all seems very strange to me as I am not used to this level of secrecy.' I applied myself to eating my lunch and not asking any further questions.

On his way out of the dining room, Major Richards came over to me.

'Will you join Colonel Thorpe and I in his office at 2.00pm please Markus?'

'Yes Sir. I'll see you then.' I wasn't looking forward to an afternoon of tobacco smoke

At 2:00 sharp I knocked on the door of the room I had been told was Colonel Thorpe's office.

'Come in Lieutenant,' a voice called out.

When I entered I found the Colonel and the Major seated at a round table that had four chairs around it. To my great relief the Major wasn't smoking his pipe.

'Take a seat with us here Markus,' the Colonel instructed.

I sat down on the opposite side of the table.

'Are you settled into your room?'

'Yes, I have unpacked and everything is fine,' I replied.

'Wherever possible we try and pair you up with another trainee, and there is a reason for this. It is essential that you never tell anybody about any aspect of the mission that you will be undertaking. Vic will never tell you about what he is up to, and, if he does, you must report the fact to us immediately. In the same way if you disclose anything to Vic he has been instructed to report back to us.'

'Are we put together because you want us to spy on each other?' I inquired, rather alarmed at what they were suggesting.

'In a way yes, but the main reason is to teach you the importance of secrecy. One casual word said out of place could mean you blow your cover resulting in your capture and death.'

'I understand now what you are telling me,' I replied, better appreciating the hazardous role I was about to be trained for.

I spent another two hours with them. They outlined the training programme I would have to go through and the rules applicable to a trainee in the house. They also told me that if I needed to speak to them or had any problems that I should make an appointment with their admin assistant Corporal Elizabeth Walters who was to be found in an office next door to the Colonel's.

It was a much wiser and mature Markus that left the office and re-joined Vic in room B4.

Chapter 22

The following day my training started.

All the trainees were woken up at 6:30 am and immediately got stuck into a work out under a fearsome physical training instructor. This lasted an hour and a half. Showered and shaved we then went for breakfast at 9:00. Colonel Thorpe and Major Richards gave us a rest from their presence at breakfast, so there were just the three of us.

The mornings we spent together being trained in general skills that applied to everyone, such as using a radio, communication skills and living off the land if we had to make our way back to England through Spain or Switzerland. The afternoons, for the most part, were spent learning about our individual projects. The weekends they gave us off to revise what we had learnt during the week as the first thing that they did on Monday morning was to test us on what we had covered the previous week. They didn't expect just fifty or sixty percent, they expected us to achieve in the high nineties and they kept the pressure on.

The third day I was there I received an unpleasant surprise. I went up to my bedroom at lunchtime to hang my jacket up as the weather was getting quite warm. I opened my wardrobe, and as I was hanging it up, I noticed a piece of paper pinned to the back of the wardrobe with a knife. I pulled out the knife releasing the paper and read what had been written:

GO HOME KRAUT BACK TO YOUR MURDERERS.
WE DON'T NEED YOUR HELP.
WE'LL GET YOU WHEN YOU ARE OUTSIDE.

My heart sank to my boots. I was stunned. I thought that I was amongst friends, but clearly there was someone that was upset at me being there. It could be any of the support staff, although they had all seemed genuinely friendly when I encountered them around the house. I doubted very much if it could be the Colonel or the Major or even Vic. I folded the paper and stuck it in my back pocket.

What did I do now? I would think about it over lunch and try and see if I could come up with an action plan.

Lunch over I sought out Major Richards as he was the person that I knew the best.

'Major Richards, can I talk to you about something?' I leant towards him so as he would be the only person who heard my request.

'You can come with me now as I have finished my lunch and was just leaving.'

We left the dining room and went to his office on the ground floor.

'What's this all about Markus?' He asked as soon as the door was shut and he had lit up.

I took the piece of paper out of my back pocket and handed it to him.

Having read the contents, he looked up at me.

'When did you get this Markus?'

'I found it on the back of my wardrobe just before lunch. It was pinned to the back with a knife.'

'I need to get to the bottom of this immediately. The person who put this on your wardrobe could leak information about you to the outside world which would be a disaster. I will get the guards to seal off the house and grounds, and we will find the culprit this afternoon. Leave it with me.'

He left his office at the same time as I did and knocked on the Colonel's door as we passed. I went back upstairs to my bedroom.

About five minutes later we were all called downstairs to the bigger of the two reception rooms, where the Colonel addressed us.

'I am cancelling all activities planned for this afternoon as an emergency has arisen which needs to be resolved. Both the entrances have been sealed off, and the guards have instructions to allow nobody in or out. I would be obliged if you would stay in your rooms.'

'Are you able to tell us what the emergency is all about?' the naval Captain asked.

'I will be able to tell you all about it once the situation has been resolved,' the Colonel answered. 'You are now all dismissed.'

As I was leaving the room, Major Richards called me over.

'Please join us in the Colonel's office, Markus.'

When we were all seated the Colonel addressed me.

'I have seen the message that was pinned to your wardrobe, and I would like to suggest a possible way of resolving the issue, but it will need your co-operation. Are you willing to help?'

'Of course I am willing to help, but what will be involved?'

'We would like to set you up as a target to see if we can flush out the person who sent you this note. They have stated that you must 'watch out' if you go outside, so we want you to go for a walk outside this afternoon. It should be easy to spot anybody if they follow you,' Major Richards explained.

'What happens if he shoots at me from the house?' I asked, not too impressed with their suggestion.

'We will give you a route to follow and we will have sharp shooters placed, at strategic points, to cover where you will be walking. We have already called in extra guards. They will cover every possible place the culprit might hide in,' the Colonel explained.

'I don't like the sound of it, but if you think it will work I am game.'

'That's settled then; let's work out the finer details of the plan to ensure that we don't lose one of our agents.' The Colonel smiled at me. 'You can look upon this as a training exercise.'

On a plan of the estate, we worked out the route that I should take, and they established where they would need to place their sharp shooters.

An hour later, with everything in place, I set out on my walk along the selected route. I had a horrible tingling feeling in my back as I was expecting to receive a bullet between my shoulder blades at any minute. It was very difficult to walk in a relaxed manner knowing that someone unknown might be stalking me. I felt naked as I was used to having my aircraft around me when I was going into dangerous situations.

As I was getting close to the entrance steps to the underwater ballroom, I spotted a sudden movement. Instantly I worked out that any sudden movement must be danger, so I threw myself to my left. A gun went off, and I heard the bullet whistle by me and thud into a large flower pot. I heard a shot from a rifle behind me, and my attacker fell backwards down the steps to the ballroom.

A number of khaki clad figures raced past me and piled down the steps. They came back out dragging a man dressed in khaki that was wounded and moaning with pain. I went over to have a look at the person who had tried to kill me. It was the old Corporal who had picked Major Richards and I up at the train station, and brought us to Witley Park. He was the last person that I had expected to see.

When the house had returned to normal, and the extra guards had left the premises, the Colonel called us all together.

'I can now explain to you what happened today,' he said. 'Markus received a threatening note which had been pinned to his wardrobe with a knife. The note stated that if he went outside he would be killed. It also called him a rather unpleasant name. This afternoon we used Markus as bait, and we managed to lure the culprit into revealing himself. Luckily Markus wasn't hurt when he was attacked. The attacker was Corporal Kane who, as you all know, is the driver who takes you to and from the station. He was injured during the arrest.'

'Do we know why he wanted me out of the way,' I asked.

'Very sadly he learnt yesterday that his only son had been killed fighting off a German attack in the deserts of North Africa. I am afraid that the news pushed him over the edge.'

'Are you satisfied that the culprit has now been caught, and we can relax?' Vic asked.

'Yes, he was clearly acting on his own and nobody else was involved,' the Colonel answered.

'Let's all go and have a beer in the dining room. Markus has certainly earned one, and I feel that I need one,' Major Richards said, much to the delight of the assembled group.

Vic and Brian wanted to know all about my involvement in the afternoon's action, and we drank until dinner appeared. I was treated as a hero for my role in the whole affair.

Needless to say, a vacancy arose for a driver and Corporal Kane was removed from the estate. I sympathised with the Corporal and how he must have felt as a result of losing his son. The fact that he was quite old and had served in the last War had probably saved my life as he wasn't very nimble in his old age.

Chapter 23

I quickly settled back into my routine. The following Monday, six new trainees arrived at Witley Park, and the facilities went from being adequate to totally overcrowded. The winter weather wasn't good enough for us to spend much time outside, so we had to entertain ourselves indoors. We also had to stay within the confines of the estate, so tempers started to fray as we all got bored.

One very pleasant addition, on the entertainment side, was the showing of a movie on every Saturday evening. As well as the movie they used to show us a copy of Pathe News. It wasn't the latest copy with the news being a few weeks old, but I loved watching it as it reinforced what Major Richards had told me, Germany was losing the war. It obviously was bound to be biased as it was giving the allies progress in the war.

One of the new recruits was a twenty seven year old female, Francette Tranquet, who had lived a lot of her life in France prior to war breaking out. Her father was French, and her mother was English. I found her very attractive and good fun and we gravitated towards each other. For the Saturday night movie, we used to sit beside each other, and she used to help me out with some of the longer and more obtuse words.

One evening after dinner I went up to my room to find Vic Biddlecombe packing up his things.

'I'm leaving you this evening, Markus,' he said to me as I entered the room with a look of surprise on my face.

'Where are you off to Vic?'

'I am afraid that I can't tell you where I am going, but I think it is OK to tell you that I am flying out from Croydon this evening at around midnight.'

'That's extremely sudden isn't it,' I asked him.

'I have known for some time that I would have to leave at short notice, but I wasn't allowed to tell anyone. They told me at 5:00 pm that the weather was perfect, and I would be going tonight.'

'Well good luck Vic. I hope that it all works out for you wherever you are going.' I went across to him and shook his hand.

He picked his bag up and went downstairs. I shut off the light and opened the blackout shutters and shortly afterwards saw him walk out to the staff car with Major Richards. They both got in and left for the airfield in Croydon.

In the morning, I bumped into Major Richards after breakfast 'Did Vic get off alright last night, Sir?

'Yes, everything went well, and I saw him take off into the night sky over Croydon.'

'When will you know if he arrived safely? I asked.

'Hopefully he will be able to get a message through to us in the next few days.'

'I would be interested in hearing how he got on, Sir,'

'I'll let you know as soon as I hear anything. By the way, you will be getting a new roommate in the next day or so, his name is Lieutenant Matthew Osborne. He is around your age.'

Matthew Osborne arrived just before lunch the following day and was introduced to the others in the house just before we ate. I felt quite an old hand as there was only Brian Wilkinson and me from the original group. Matt, as he preferred to be addressed and I hit it off from the start. Dark haired, brown eyes, he was about six feet tall and had a build similar to mine. It turned out that he had gone to Monkton Combe School near Bath where he had been a member of the senior rowing eight. We had a lot in common, and he was a much more affable roommate than Vic had been. Vic had been remarkably quiet and had a worry frown all the time, and we had nothing in common to talk about. Matt was much more outgoing and full of energy.

The Friday afternoon of the week that Matt arrived I was called into the Colonel's office where Major Richards and Colonel Thorpe were already seated when I arrived.

"Good afternoon Markus how are you and Matt getting on?" The Colonel asked me.

'Oh fine. We are the same age and have a lot in common,'

'I have some particularly unwelcome news for you, Markus.' Major Richards leant towards me, tapping his unlit pipe on the desk and looking unusually serious. 'We have just heard that Vic Biddlecombe was killed at the landing site in northern France. There must have been a leak of information and the German SS were waiting for him when he landed by parachute.'

I was stunned. 'That's terrible news, Sir. Is there any chance that he might have survived?'

'No we have had confirmation from the French resistance movement that he was definitely killed,' the Major added.

'Anyway Markus that is not the main reason that we have asked to see us today.' the Colonel changed the direction of the conversation. 'We want to discuss with you the plans that we have for the rest of your training. Major Richards will now give you an outline of what we have in mind.'

'I have compiled this list setting out the areas that you will have to cover, so I think that it is best to use this as our discussion document.' He put the list on the table so as we all could see it.

The following was the list that he showed me:

Orienteering across country using maps and a compass - at least 50 to 100 miles -Devon/Cornwall

Survival in the open - Devon/Cornwall

Sailing - Derwent Reservoir, Co Durham

Knowledge of Jet engines - German and English - British Thomson-Houston factory in Lutterworth

Knowledge of the Me262 jet engined fighter

How to re-integrate into the Luftwaffe

Intended activation date April 1941

'I thought that I was going to do all my training at Witley Park, but you have me going all over England,' I commented.

'We wanted you here to start off with as we were taking an enormous risk in taking you on board and we needed to keep a particularly close eye on you,' the Colonel replied. 'You have done exceptionally well here, and we are satisfied that you won't go running back to Germany when our back is turned.'

'I am upset that you thought that I might abscond, especially when I have given my word,' I said, disconcerted that they hadn't trusted me.

'In the business we are in the only way to get our trust is to earn it. If you hopped back to German held territory, there a lot of people you have seen in this facility, whose lives would be at risk, in fact, we would have to train a whole new bunch of operatives,' the Major added.

'When do I start on this training programme?'

'You will be travelling to Cornwall on Monday to try your hand at orienteering. Your first week will be with Sergeant Paul Young who will be teaching you all you need to know about living rough. You had better learn well, because, in the second week, you will be on your own,' the Major said, smiling at me.

My first thoughts were:

I must be mad to consider setting out across a part of a country that was an enemy of mine up to very recently. I still spoke English with an exceptionally strong German accent, so if stopped by the locals for some reason, I would have a major problem.

'What happens if I am stopped and they discover that I am a German?' I decided to ask.

'I'll answer your question with one of my own. What would happen to you Markus if you are on the run in Germany and are stopped by the SS?' the Major responded.

'All hell would break loose.'

'So?' the Major added.

'I have to make sure that I don't get picked up,' I replied.

'That's 100% correct, and we will not be informing the local police or Home Guards that there is a friendly German on the loose in Cornwall.' The Colonel thought that this last remark was hilarious.

Chapter 24

Monday morning I was up before 6:00 and ready for my lift to Bodmin in Cornwall. Just after 7:00 am, a car pulled up outside, and a female driver got out and came towards the house to collect her passenger. The car was a big step up on anything that I had previously been in and my driver obviously looked after it extremely carefully.

'Good morning Sir, are you ready to go,' she asked me, taking my bag out of my hand as we met.

'Good morning, what a fabulous looking car and you obviously look after it exceptionally well,' I said, pouring charm into my words.

'Yes, it is a Wolseley 2.3 litre and I am very proud of it,' she said, giving it a friendly pat.

She loaded my bag in the boot and instructed me to sit in the back.

After the two check points, where they scrutinised my papers and my orders, we headed off for the main road to the West.

'Are you based locally,' I asked her.

'I have strict instructions not to talk to you Sir. I don't know what you do at Witley Park, but we are given strict orders that we mustn't talk to our passengers' she explained. 'You will have to find some other way of entertaining yourself until we get to Bodmin.'

'That's a shame, but I suppose that rules are rules,' I replied. It seemed very strange to be sitting so close to someone and not being able to talk to them.

It was a long time since I had been in the world that didn't belong to Witley Park, and I watched with interest as we passed through the English countryside. For some reason, I started to think about home. Would I ever see my mother and granddad again, and help out in the bakery. Memories of Chris invaded my thoughts and what might have been if this terrible war hadn't removed him from my life.

A loud horn blast woke me from my dreams. I had obviously fallen asleep. There were sheep on the road blocking our path, and my driver was endeavouring to clear a way for us to pass through.

'Sorry to wake you Sir, although it is probably time that you woke up as we will arrive in about ten minutes.'

'I must have nodded off, and I missed most of the wonderful views. I must apologise.'

'We have made quite good time, and we will be there just after 1:00 pm, so you can relax for another ten minutes'

As predicted by my driver, we pulled up in front of the Westberry Hotel in Bodmin after a further ten minutes.

She took my bag out of the boot of the car, saluted, and drove off leaving me in my new surroundings.

As I was standing there looking at the front of the hotel, a uniformed man came out of the front door and approached me. I noticed the three stripes on his sleeve.

'Good afternoon Sir, my name is Sergeant Young, and I will be conducting your training over the next two weeks.' He saluted me and grabbed hold of my bag. 'Let's go in and get some lunch, and I will tell you a bit more about myself.'

We approached the reception desk.

This is Lieutenant Becker who I told you about when I checked in earlier,' he said to the receptionist. 'Can I have his key please?'

He took the key and conducted me to my room.

Once in the room he dumped my bag on the bed and turned around to address me.

'Sir, my superiors have outlined to me what you are being trained for and your Nationality. I think it best if I do most of the talking, and that as few people as is possible, hear you speaking,' he explained. 'If we are out of earshot of others then there will be no problem in you talking to me. For obvious reasons, we must be extremely careful.'

'Thank you Sergeant, I obviously don't want to create a situation that will endanger you or I.' I was unaware at that stage what would transpire in the not too distant future.

Over lunch, he explained to me what he had been doing in the war so far. He had been part of the British army that had confronted the German invasion of Norway earlier in the year. He had managed to avoid injury and capture and been evacuated back to the United Kingdom. Once back in the UK he had been recruited into the new Commando unit and had undergone extensive special training. Finally he had been asked to get involved in teaching secret agents survival skills, so here he was, and I was his second pupil.

'Compared to you Sergeant I have had a remarkably easy war. I just sat in the seat of a fighter plane and was carried across the skies.'

'I like to feel the ground under my 'pins'. I wouldn't like the idea that there were thousands of feet of air below me if I happened to get shot down.

'We did have parachutes and, in fact, I was saved by one.'

'Well I will be teaching you how to create your own survival parachute on land. If you get into trouble you must be able to escape and remain under cover, wherever you happen to be.'

'I am sure that I will enjoy it, just be easy on me at the start.'

He smiled a cynical smile back at me. 'I think that enjoy may not be the right word Sir.' He got stuck into his lunch.

That started a week of intensive training in all aspects of surviving in open country without the support of the local populace. The weather was wet and cold, and we left the hotel early in the morning and spent the day in the local countryside. By the time the evening came, I was very glad to get back to the warmth of my room. A car came and picked us up at 7:00 am every morning and used to take us a distance of around twenty miles making sure that it was a different direction each day. I was blindfolded at the hotel before I entered the car, so I had no idea in which direction the car went after it left Bodmin. I then had to find the way back to the hotel. This week I had the assistance of Sergeant Young, but the following week, when I did my test, I would be on my own.

On the third night after we arrived in Bodmin, we were sitting having a beer in the bar when the landlord came over to us. He bent down to speak to me.

'We have a problem. I overheard some of the locals talking, and they were saying that there was a German staying in the hotel and that they were going to do something about it.'

'Did they say what action they were going to take?' the sergeant asked.

'No, but they were getting quite excited about it,' the landlord added. 'I must go now as I don't want to be seen talking to you.'

'We'll find somewhere else to stay and send over for our bags. Thanks for warning us,' the sergeant said.

We got up and slipped out of the door into the street, keeping a good look out to make sure that there was nobody waiting for us in the shadows.

'I saw another place at the entrance to the town when I arrived on Monday, so we'll try there,' the sergeant suggested.

'I am sorry for creating a problem Sergeant, I had no idea that they would react like that.'

'We will just have to keep a low profile, and they will think that we have left Bodmin. No more beers in the evening,' the sergeant said.

Luckily the boarding house that he had spotted was able to accommodate us, and the landlady sent across to the hotel for our bags once it was dark and the pub was closed.

After breakfast on Friday Sergeant Young came into my room.

'I have a surprise for you today. We are going to do a dummy run for your cross country trip next week. This time I will be with you, but I will allow you to do a lot of the decision making.'

'Will we come back here each night?' I enquired.

'No we will spend Friday and Saturday nights in the countryside, sleeping wherever we can find some shelter. We also won't be bringing anything with us to make it as close to a real situation as possible.'

'Doesn't sound like much fun?' I managed a forced smile. I wasn't looking forward to this adventure as the weather outside was looking decidedly wintery, and it was raining.

I was blindfolded as usual and then taken in the car about forty miles away from Bodmin where we were dropped off in the middle of nowhere.

I thought to myself:

I started this war as a pilot and had some comfort; look at me now, stuck out in the middle of nowhere, frozen stiff, in driving rain, with an English Sergeant as my mentor. I must be mad.

The next sixty hours were like a nightmare. We only had food and shelter wherever we could find it, and in the three days I hadn't been dry once. If we had been doing the task in the summer, it would probably have been tolerable, but climbing around the countryside in the dead of winter wasn't enjoyable.

By the time that we returned on the Sunday afternoon to our lodgings the relationship between the Sergeant and me was decidedly strained to put it mildly. I have never enjoyed a bed so much as I did on the Sunday night.

Chapter 25

I was given Monday off to recover. At dinner that evening he gave me the news that I was dreading.

'Well Sir, I hope that you have had a good day's rest and are fully recovered from the three days we spent in the countryside?' he said to me just after I had sat down at the dining table.

'Yes, I have recovered, but I am not looking forward to having to do it all on my own,' I replied.

'I am pleased to inform you that you won't have long to wait. You will be dropped off, on your own this time, tomorrow morning and will have to make your way back here. You will have three days to cover the fifty miles and you will not be allowed to organize any lifts with the local populace.'

I dreaded the task he was describing to me, but there was no other alternative offered to me. I would have to do it or die in the attempt.

Tuesday morning I was blindfolded in the usual way and then helped into the car. To confuse my sense of direction, they drove around the county of Cornwall in circles. Finally they stopped, and I left the sanctuary of the car with nothing but the clothes I was wearing. I had till Thursday to get back to Bodmin. In other words, I was expected to spend two nights in the great outdoors with zero luxuries other than a couple of bars of chocolate that were in my pockets.

The first day and a half went surprisingly well. To my immense relief the rain had eased off a bit, so at least I didn't have the water deluging down on top of me, running down my neck. The ground was still awash, and in some places I had to make long detours around areas that were completely water logged. On the first night, I managed to find farm buildings to sleep in and even managed to scrounge some food.

On the Wednesday, I started to have significant problems as the ground underfoot became wetter and wetter. I appeared to be travelling through an unusually large swamp, and it was extremely difficult to find areas that would take my weight without me sinking into the mud up to my knees. To make any progress, and avoid the worst of the clinging mud, I decided to move closer to the road where the ground seemed to be firmer. The problem I now had was that I was in danger of being spotted by someone travelling along the road, and they naturally would wonder what on earth I was up to and might report me. It was riskier walking close to the road, but at least I was making progress.

It wasn't long before I approached some buildings where I saw three farm girls putting out some fodder for a flock of sheep and some cattle. There was no way that I could risk staying close to the road as there was no cover to protect me from their view. I would have to go back into the swamp.

I ducked down out of sight and started to move away from the road. The mud got worse and worse, and I began to sink, but I still managed to keep moving and just hoped that the underfoot conditions would get better.

Then my greatest fear happened. I sank lower than my knees, and there seemed to be a suction pulling me down. Sergeant Young had informed me that there were areas of bog that were like quick sand and into which you could be sucked to your death. It looked as if I had stumbled upon one of them. He had told me that if I ever got sucked into one that I mustn't move my legs too much as that would speed up the suction process, but what other options were available to me. If I didn't break the silence and call for help, I was going to be sucked into the swamp, and never seen again. Rather naturally I started to panic.

I called out in the loudest voice that I could muster, hoping that the girls I had seen feeding the animals would hear me. By this stage, the mud was up to my stomach. I only had a few more minutes left to call out. I renewed my shouting.

I heard the squelch of people approaching and was tremendously relieved to see two girls looking in my direction.

'Hold on, we will get a rope,' one of them called out. She turned and ran back to the buildings.

A few minutes later she came back with the third girl, but also with a horse.

I had now sunk up to my chest, and time was running out.

'Catch this rope and we will use the horse to pull you out,' she said as she threw the rope towards me.

Unfortunately, throwing a rope was not one of her fortes and she eventually had to ask one of the others to try.

The rope came straight across my shoulders, and I was able to grab hold of it. I tied it around me under my armpits and hung on tight. They inched the horse forwards and gradually I was extracted from the swamp.

As I came out of the mud, hanging on for dear life to the rope, my trousers and underpants were sucked off me and left behind in the mud. I emerged naked from the waist down in front of the three girls. The clothes around the upper half of my body had been pulled upwards by the action of the rope, so I was left very exposed. My rescuers were highly amused by the outcome of their rescue mission.

'Thank you ladies for saving my life,' I said. Their grins turned to puzzlement as they realised that I had a pronounced German accent.

'Who are you and where have you come from? You sound German,' one of them asked.

'I am a German, but I am working with the British army,' I replied. 'All my papers are in my trousers, which are now in the swamp.

I had pulled my shirt and coat down as far as I was able, hiding my nakedness, but I was still exposing most of my lower half for them to see.

'Do you think that I could get something to cover me while we sort this out?' I asked.

'Well, I suppose that there is no chance of you being able to run away since you have no trousers or shoes, but we will still have to hand you in,' the girl who appeared to be the leader said.

Feeling really stupid I walked with them to the building where they had been working. They found a sack that had contained feed, and I managed to wrap that around me.

What looked like the oldest of the girls then got up on the horse and went off to get help.

About an hour later we saw a very old and dilapidated van approaching.

A policeman and two members of the Home Guard got out and came over to where I was sitting. To increase their official status the two Home Guard members were carrying First World War rifles.

'The girl here has told us that you are a German, is that correct?' the policeman asked.

'Yes, that is correct. I am on an exercise organized by the British army. I got stuck in the swamp, and these girls rescued me.'

'You will have to come with me to Bude police station. We will sort it all out there' the policeman continued. 'Have you got your orders and papers with you?'

'No, all my papers are in my trousers, which are still in the swamp.'

The policeman smiled. 'Well that's a first for me. I have never seen a grown man pulled out of a bog by a group of girls leaving his pants and boots behind.' He scratched his head as he took Markus to where the van was parked, still chortling away.

Back at the police station in Bude, I was locked up in a tiny cold cell with the promise that they would try and get a pair of trousers for me.

The key turned in the lock and the policeman who had arrested me came in with trousers and a cup of tea. The trousers were far too small, but at least they were better than the sack I had been using to cover my modesty. The tea was warm and was most welcome after what I had been through.

Shortly afterwards the door was unlocked again, and I was brought to an interview room where a police sergeant was waiting to talk to me.

'What is your name and rank?' he fired at me.

'My name is Markus BEKER, and I am a Lieutenant in the British Army.'

'Where are your papers proving who you are and why you were on the moors in the middle of winter?' He didn't seem to be convinced by my story.

'My papers were in my trousers, and I lost those when I was pulled out of the swamp.'

'That's a good one, and you also expect me to believe that you are a British officer with an exceptionally strong German accent'

'Might I suggest that you phone my superior officer, Major Richards, who is based at Witley Park in Surrey? He can verify my story. There is also Sergeant Young who has been training me in Cornwall for the past two weeks. He is in Bodmin at the moment,' I replied.

'This Sergeant Young could also be a German spy. I will phone Major Richards and ask him to come and identify you. In the meantime, we will have to hold you here.'

Twenty four hours later, after a night in a freezing cell, I heard the lock being turned, and a familiar face stuck his head around the door.

'Lieutenant BEKER, the police sergeant here doesn't believe that you are an Officer in the British army, so I have come to get you out.' I looked up to see the cheery face of Major Richards puffing away on his pipe. 'I went via Bodmin to let Sergeant Young know what you had been up to and to get your clothes. No doubt you would like to put on a pair of your own trousers for the trip back to Bodmin.'

'Thank you. The trousers that they rustled up for me here are far too small.'

'I am afraid that you failed to complete your test, so you are going to have to do three more days on your own in the great outdoors at another time to be arranged.'

'I know that I failed miserably in the task I was set; however, I felt that it was better giving myself away than drowning in a swamp,' I said contritely.

'This time we will take you to a different area of the country where you will have less of a challenge from the underfoot conditions.' The Major smiled sympathetically.

'I don't mind being out in the open, it was travelling through the swamp and the bog land that was pretty impossible,' I added

I was delighted to get away from my prison cell in Bude police station, although I didn't blame them for the inconvenience of being detained. For once I welcomed the Major's smoke.

We returned to Bodmin in the comfort of the car to find an amused Sergeant waiting for us.

My survival instructor was highly amused to hear the detail of what had happened.

'I would have given a week's pay to have seen you being pulled out of the swamp by three girls, without your trousers and boots. It must have been highly embarrassing for you but highly amusing for the girls.'

'To be perfectly honest, I was so happy to be rescued from a muddy death that I barely noticed the fact that I didn't have any trousers or underpants on. You're right, the girls did think it was highly amusing.'

'Well Markus I want you to give the Sergeant here a full account of how you got on,' the Major interjected. 'Give him every detail from the time you were dropped off until you were picked up by the police. We will leave for Witley Park as soon as you are finished.'

It took me about an hour to communicate all the details and then we left for Surrey. My orienteering training had been eventful, to say the least, and I still had the three day test to look forward to.

'Don't get too upset by failing your test. You did remarkably well up to the point where you were sucked into the swamp, and you certainly have gained a lot of experience from your ordeal. Those girls know you quite well too, don't they?' he smiled.

Ten minutes later we left the Sergeant in Bodmin and headed for home.

Chapter 26

Witley Park didn't seem to have changed much since I had left it ten days previously although the total blackout meant that there wasn't much visible by the time we got back. I was delighted when I found that Francette Tranquet had stayed up to greet me and that she was adamant that I give her all the sordid details of my adventure. We had been soul mates, who enjoyed each other's company before I had left for Cornwall, but I hadn't seen her as a special friend. I was touched by her concern for me. We drank and talked until my energy ran out and my eyes started to close. We then both went upstairs to our respective beds.

The following morning I was called into the Colonel's office. As usual, Colonel Thorpe and Major Richards were waiting for me when I entered.

'Good morning Markus, I hear that you had some interesting experiences in Cornwall on your orienteering course,' the Colonel said, with a smile on his face.

'Yes, I am afraid that I didn't cover myself in glory during my test and was rescued by some land girls.'

'I understand that they want you do redo the test, but I have another urgent job for you to do before you go off again,' the Colonel said, taking on a more serious tone. 'Major Richards will explain what we want you to do.'

'Is this new job connected with my training?'

'No, it is something totally unrelated. Perhaps I should give you the details now,' the Major explained. 'You are aware that the SS were waiting for Vic Biddlecombe when he landed in France and that they shot him.'

'Yes, I was extremely upset when that happened as we had shared a room together and had become quite good friends,' I said.

'When that happened we were convinced that there was a leak somewhere along the chain. The French Resistance were adamant that it wasn't at their end, so we had a look at our end. Much to our surprise we believe that we have found the source, and it appears to be extraordinarily close to home.'

'But the other agents in this house don't know about each other's projects. You insist on us not talking about our missions, and Vic never said a word about what he was up to.' I was starting to think that maybe they thought that I had leaked information.

'Don't jump to the wrong conclusion Markus. We are certainly not pointing the finger at you or any of the other trainee agents. You all have too much to lose, and we trust all of you,' the Major stated energetically. 'We have heard that there is a man with a German background who has been seen in the local pub "The Cat and Fiddle" and the Colonel's Secretary, Elizabeth Walters, has been seen talking to him. In fact, we believe that an intimate relationship has developed between them.'

'What do you want me to do?' I didn't like where this conversation was going, and the role they had in mind for me.

'We would like you to visit "The Cat and Fiddle" and try to get to know this man. We need a bit more information before we can be sure that Elizabeth is, in fact, the leak. Are you willing to do that for us?'

'If you think that I can help, I will give it a try. When do I need to go there?'

'We have taken the landlady of "The Cat and Fiddle" into our confidence, and she will phone us the next time that he comes in. He usually arrives at about 5:30 pm, has a drink with Elizabeth and then they leave at around 7:30 pm. We have also told the landlady that we will place our own man undercover in her Pub and that he has a strong German accent.'

'What happens if I bump into Elizabeth? She knows that I am based at Witley Park. Will she not be suspicious?'

'In fact it will be better if she is there as it will increase your credibility. You can tell them that you have become disillusioned by your training process and what you have been asked to do and that you are thinking of escaping back to Germany,' the Colonel suggested.

'I will help in any way that I can, and I will be prepared to go this evening. I just hope that this guy turns up.'

'I will organize a pass for you so as you can get in and out through the checkpoints. You should wear ordinary clothes and not your' uniform,' the Major suggested.

'I don't think that I need to remind you about being extremely careful and certainly don't lower your guard during the whole time that you are outside the confines of Witley Park. If your first meeting goes well we will give you false information relating to the other agents that you can pass on to them,' Colonel Thorpe added.

'I just hope that one of the locals doesn't report me to the police as happened in Cornwall,' I said.

'Well at least you will have your trousers on.' Major Richards smiled.

I left them in the office and returned to my room to prepare for my evening's task.

I was down in the lounge by 5:15 pm waiting for my notification to proceed from the Major. An hour later the Major still hadn't come to see me, and I was still patiently waiting when we were called in to dinner at 7:00 pm. A cloud of tobacco smoke came towards me.

'I think that you can stand down now for the evening Markus as it looks as if he isn't coming tonight,' the major said.

'Presumably I should be ready to go tomorrow night, Sir,' I replied.

'Yes, and you should get on with your normal training tomorrow. Just make certain that you are on your starting blocks by about 5:15 pm tomorrow evening.'

I grabbed hold of a plate and piled food onto it from the buffet, sitting down at the dining table. Shortly afterwards Francette came in to get her dinner. My heart gave a leap when I saw her enter the room, and I protected the chair beside me to make sure that she would be able to sit beside me.

After dinner, we both grabbed a drink and went to sit in a corner of the lounge where we wouldn't have to talk to the others. I enjoyed her company and her gentle voice with the strong French accent. The gentle scent of her French perfume wafted across to me. I had been so tied up in my own survival and future that I had forgotten how much I enjoyed female company. Since I left Susie in Kiel, at the start of the war, I had been starved of the opposite sex. Francette had rekindled a need in me.

'When do you have to go and be tested on your orienteering skills Markus?' she asked me.

'They still have to arrange a date. I am hoping that it will be in the New Year when the weather gets better. I would prefer not to have to go through what I endured last week until the weather improves.'

'I was due to leave this week, but they have delayed my mission for some reason,' Francette said.

'I am glad about that. It's nice to have your company. I really appreciated finding you waiting for me when I arrived back from Cornwall last night.'

'I enjoy your company too Markus.' She leant across and gave me a peck on my cheek and squeezed my arm.

Dark haired, petite and exceptionally attractive, Francette smiled at me seductively. She had my complete attention now and a piece of my heart.

'Do you know Markus that I have a room to myself, and it is close to yours,' Francette said retaining her seductive smile. 'Why don't we go upstairs and make use of my single room and finish our drinks there.'

That was the sort of invitation that I didn't have the will power to refuse. I smiled in agreement.

Amazingly enough she had managed to make her room look feminine unlike the masculine environment that my room portrayed. There was no chair in the room, so we had to sit on the side of the bed. She had scrounged a bedside lamp from somewhere so she switched off the main light and we sat there in the romantic glow of the smaller lamp.

She leant into me and put her arm around my waste. The scent of her perfume excited my senses.

'Are you ever afraid of what you have volunteered to do Markus,' Francette asked me.

'If I think about it, I do start to worry, but I find that if I put all my efforts into my training that the anxiousness leaves me.'

'I was OK until I was given my date to leave here. I can't tell you what I will be doing, but it is extremely dangerous with a lot of risk and I am particularly conscious of what happened to poor old Vic.'

'I still have a lot of training to do, so I haven't even thought about what will happen when I leave here. I'm glad I didn't return from Cornwall and find that you had gone, I would have been extremely upset.'

'Would you Markus? I need you to hold me to give me the strength I need to keep going. I am very afraid.'

I turned to face her, and we relaxed onto the bed until I was holding her close to me. I put my lips to hers, and we kissed, gently at first, but that soon graduated to highly passionate. All the anxiety and tension of the last two weeks went into my embrace, and she responded with equal passion.

I held her face in my hands and increased the energy of my kissing. We were lost in each other's embrace, and there was no way that we had the brakes or inclination to stop what we had started.

The embrace moved through the usual stages to love making. We slipped our naked bodies under the covers and lost ourselves in each other. By the time that we had satisfied our desires it was safe to say that our tensions had vanished, and we were both lost in our love for one another. I slipped into a deep sleep still in the arms of Francette.

I woke up to feel a tap on my shoulder.

'Markus, do you think that it is time for you to go back to your own room. Matt will be wondering where you are.'

'Do I have to leave you Francette? Matt is a man of the world and will understand.'

'Better not risk it though Markus. It is now 3:00 am and time that you were in your own bed'

'Oh you are a spoil sport Francette. Why don't we run away together and leave all this?'

'Because we both have a job to do and I want to complete my mission no matter how scary it is.'

'Can I slip back here tonight?'

'We'll have to see about that, won't we? I don't want to be branded as a loose woman'

'You can be my loose woman any time Francette, but you are banned from being anyone else's.'

'You can have one last hug, and then you must go.'

Our bodies touched again, and a hug was not going to satisfy the desire exploding in both of us. Half an hour later I finally managed to escape from her bed and make my way to my own room. Climbing into my own bed, I lay there thinking of how much better my life had suddenly become. I fell asleep grinning like a Cheshire cat.

Chapter 27

I woke the following morning with Matt shaking me.

'Get up sleepy head it's time to leave that bed of yours'

I pulled the covers up over my head intent on staying where I was.

'Where were you last night Markus? I heard you coming to bed at around 4:00 am and the last I saw of you downstairs was sitting with Francette. You haven't been a naughty boy have you?'

I pushed the covers back a bit and looked at him. He was grinning knowingly at me.

'I just went for a drink in her room, and we chatted for a very long time,' I suggested. She was very worried about her upcoming mission.

'Look at me and tell me with a straight face that you got up to nothing else.'

'We just talked,' I replied, avoiding his eyes.

'Then why are you grinning like a Cheshire cat?'

'I am just amused by your suggestion that's all.'

'If I see a similar smile on Francette's face this morning then that will confirm my suspicions. I am just jealous of you.'

Matt left the room to go and wash leaving me with my grinning face.

Matt and I were sitting together at breakfast when Francette came in. She gave me a big smile; Matt turned and gave me a knowing wink. 'What did I say Markus?'

In one night, my whole life had changed. Up to my romp with Francette I had been burdened down by the loss of my brother and felt that there was no real future to my life. I was firmly fixed in the past. A bit of love had changed all that, and I now wanted to succeed for a different reason.

Survival and having a future had moved up my list of priorities. It was also extremely important that I uncovered the person who had led to the death of Vic. Francette could be the next one to be killed as a result of an information leak.

I was ready and waiting downstairs by 5:15 pm. I wasn't disappointed this time as Major Richards came to get me at a quarter to six. He handed me a pass to allow me through the check points together with last minute instructions. The person who was the likely cause of Vic Biddlecombe's death was at the pub, "The Cat and Fiddle".

Although it wasn't even six o'clock it was pitch black outside, and, with the blackout, I had great difficulty finding my way. The major had given me a small flashlight to help me, but I didn't want to advertise the fact that I was leaving the estate and decided only to use it once I was through the gates.

I passed through the first guard house and then saw a glow in the distance which I presumed was the main checkpoint at the entrance to the property. Once through that I set off for the pub now using my torch.

The pub had a system of curtains at the entrance to allow customers to come and go without allowing light to beam out into the car park. I poked my way through the curtains and came out into the interior of the pub. The entrance opened into the main bar where there was a large fire burning. Off to the side there was a snug where women were allowed to drink, so I presumed Elizabeth would be there with her lover. There were only old men, too old to join the services in the pub that I could see.

I approached the bar where a lady I took to be the owner of the pub was in residence. She finished serving a customer and then turned to me. She raised her eyebrows at me in a questioning way.

'May I have a pint of beer please,' I asked in as confident a voice as I could manage.

'What brew do you want, will Watney's do you?' she asked.

I hadn't been in a pub since I had arrived in England, so I had to remember back to when I had been to a pub with my father and Chris in Harrogate before I had returned to Germany in 1937.

'Yes, Watney's is perfect thank you.'

She pulled my pint and brought to it to me. As she placed the pint on the bar, she leant across and spoke to me.

'He is in the snug.'

That's all she said to me. She took my money and left me to it. I picked up my pint and opened the door into the snug. Elizabeth and her friend were seated on the far side of the room. On my arrival, they both looked to see who was disturbing their privacy.

'Markus, what on earth are you doing here,' Elizabeth exclaimed.

'I was going mad locked up in that place, so I managed to get a pass out to get a decent drink in a better environment.'

'You sound German,' the man beside her said.

'Sorry Markus, I forgot to introduce Boris to you. He was also born in Germany but has spent most of his life living in London,' Elizabeth added.

'Hi Boris, it's nice to meet you. What brings you to Whitley?' I asked as innocently as I could muster.

'Oh, I live locally and commute into London to work in a bank. I met Elizabeth, and we have been going out together for the past year.'

'Why don't you join us at this table Markus, unless, of course, you are meeting someone else?' Elizabeth gave me a knowing smile.

'Thank you I would appreciate talking to somebody different. I have been cooped up in Witley Park for months now with nobody to talk to other than the other inmates.'

'Why are you there Markus?' Boris asked me.

'I'm sorry, but I am prohibited from telling you as it is all hush hush,' I replied.

'Judging by your earlier remarks you sound fed up with having to stay there, is that a correct assessment of your position?' Boris continued.

'I am becoming extremely disillusioned with what is going on and the role that they want me to play.' I wanted to appear to be disillusioned with my position to obtain his trust.

'You are welcome to come and talk to us any time that you want. We generally meet in this pub at least three times a week and always at the same time. Elizabeth can tell you which evenings we will be here as she usually knows by 3.00 pm at the latest.'

'That's very kind of you. It would help a lot to talk to somebody different. Give me an escape from my barracks.'

'What part of Germany are you from Markus?' Elizabeth asked me.

'I am from Kiel in the North of Germany. Do you know it Boris?' I replied. There was no way I was going to tell them that my home town was Lubeck as he might have some way of checking on me. I had to keep my Mother and Grandfather safe at all costs.

'No, I am from the South of Germany and have never been to the North even on vacation.'

'We have to go Markus. We will be back here on Saturday, and you are welcome to join us then,' Elizabeth suddenly interjected.

'That would be great. Will you be here at the same time?' I asked.

'Yes or a little earlier as it is a Saturday. Meet us here at five,' Boris said as he got up to leave. He shook my hand and left the snug with Elizabeth.

I remained in the snug a further thirty minutes before I felt it safe to leave the pub. When I got outside I didn't advertise my position by switching on the torch, but kept close to the walls, keeping my eyes open for trouble. I didn't think that I was at risk, but I had learnt that it was better to anticipate the worst, and be surprised when it didn't happen.

Although I arrived back in the house after dinner, I managed to scrounge some food from the kitchen staff. While I was eating, Major Richards came over and sat beside me.

'How did it go Markus? Did you actually talk to him?' he asked.

'It went better than I could have imagined. Elizabeth introduced me to him, and we had a pleasant chat.'

'Do you think that he was suspicious as to why you were there?'

'I explained that being cooped up in the house all the time was extremely boring, and I needed a break. I told them that I had been given an evening pass to go to the pub. They seemed convinced by my story.'

'If Elizabeth asks any questions, I will tell her that I authorised a pass for you. That should provide greater credibility to your story about being fed up in having to stay in the house all the time.'

'Thanks Major, she may check up on me.'

'Well done Markus. Have they suggested that you meet them again?'

'Yes, they will be there at 5:00 pm on Saturday and they have invited me to have a drink with them.'

'That's perfect, perhaps our little plan will work' The Major patted me on the shoulder leaving me to finish my meal

Saturday evening I joined them at 5:30 pm in the snug at "The Cat and Fiddle". We chatted for about an hour and then Boris leaned towards me.

'Markus, you sound remarkably negative about the way your training is going and what they have asked you to do. Are you willing to gather some information for me that might help Germany defeat England?'

'I don't have any information that would be of use to you,' I replied in an offhand manner.

'Elizabeth has told me that you are friendly with Francette Tranquet. Will you give me information about her mission?'

'I don't know anything about her mission. Trainees are not allowed to talk about what they are doing.'

'Let me say it in a different way. Are you willing to give me any information that you may come across? I will pay you very well.'

'If I do get some information that I feel that you might be interested in then I am willing to tell you.'

'Thank you Markus, you can rest assured that anything you tell us will be kept to ourselves and you won't be identified as the source.'

'When will I see you again Boris?' I asked.

'I will return on Tuesday of next week. You can come and meet me here at the usual time.'

'Thank you, I might just do that. I had better get back to the house as we will have our usual movie tonight and I don't want to miss that.'

This time I was the one to say my goodbyes, and I left them in the snug.

I got back in time to join Francette for dinner.

'Where were you Mr BEKER? Have you found a girlfriend in the local village and have abandoned me,' she said with mock anger.

'I was actually doing some of my training as an agent this evening.'

'In a pub?' She raised her voice, giving me a quizzical look.

'Yes in a pub. I can't tell you what I have been doing, but all will be revealed next week.' I smiled at her.

'Are we going to watch the movie this evening Markus or are you otherwise engaged?'

'I rushed back here so I would be able to take you to the Cinema.'

'Oh you are a liar; you don't even have to pay to take me to the movies.'

'I know, but it is the thought that counts. Can we take our drinks to your room afterwards for a private chat,' I asked, giving her a sexy look.

'That might be nice, provided you of course go back to your room afterwards'

'I promise, but it may be a few hours later.' I smiled.

I finally struggled back to my room at around three o'clock in the morning feeling rather pleased with myself. I must be falling in love which was a singularly dangerous thing to do in my profession in the middle of a war.

Chapter 28

Monday morning Major Richards approached me while I was eating my breakfast.

'Will you please join the Colonel and me in his office after you have finished your breakfast? Elizabeth will not be coming in today, so we don't have to conceal what we are up to.'

'Thank you Sir, I will be there at around 9:30 am.'

'The same scene as usual greeted me when I knocked and entered the Colonel's office. They were both seated on the other side of a round table waiting for me.

'I gather that you have seen Boris and Elizabeth on two occasions at the pub,' the Colonel commenced.

'That's right. I have had two conversations with them, and Boris asked me to supply him with information.'

'Have you agreed to his request,' the Colonel continued.

'I told them that I didn't have access to any information but that I would see what I could get.'

'Good. Did they ask you about any particular agent?' the Major asked.

'They asked me if I could get any information on Francette.'

'That's very good and activates the next stage in our plan,' the Major said looking extremely serious.

'We will give you the information you need on Francette. It will be entirely fabricated of course, but will be good enough to take Boris in,' the Colonel was taking charge.

'I am seeing them tomorrow evening. Will you have the information ready by then?'

'We have already worked out what we want to say so it won't take us long to have it written down. You can then transpose it in your hand and bring your piece of paper to the meeting,' the Colonel said.

'If you give it to me by lunchtime tomorrow I will have it transposed in time for the meeting.'

'OK Markus let us tell you what will happen then.' The Colonel was particularly forceful.

'It is essential that Boris is caught with the information on him,' the Colonel went on. 'As explained, you must re-write the information that we provide you with as it must be in your own hand. When you meet Boris it is essential that you give him the paper with the secret information. We will then arrest him as he leaves the pub, and we will also arrest Elizabeth as his accomplice.'

'Do you want me to follow him out,' I asked.

'Absolutely not; if he makes a run for it, we may have to open fire, and we don't want you caught in the cross fire.' The Major emphasised.

It all seemed extremely simple, and my involvement was minimal, once I had handed over the information.

The following day I set off for the pub, "The Cat and Fiddle", at 5:30 pm, feeling a lot more anxious than the previous times as this was the night they would be apprehended. Walking to the pub was the easy part, as I now knew the way and the hazards I had to avoid. When I went into the snug, to my immense relief, Boris and Elizabeth were sitting in their usual places.

'Let me get you a drink Markus,' Boris asked. 'What would you like?'

'A pint of Watney's would do me fine thanks Boris.'

Boris went up to the bar and attracted the attention of the landlady and purchased my beer.

Back at the table he placed the pint in front of me.

'How has it been for you Markus since we met last Saturday?' Boris asked me.

'Oh as busy as usual and as boring,' I replied.

'What movie did you see on Saturday night?' Elizabeth asked.

'An excellent one actually called "The Grapes of Wrath" with Henry Fonda staring. It was excellent.'

'They also show you the Pathe News don't they?' she asked.

'I don't believe all that it shows us. It seems to be made up of a lot of propaganda showing victories by the allies over Germany and Italy. I'm sure that it's a load of lies.' I wanted Boris to believe that I was still on the side of the Germans.

'That is the problem of living with the enemy. You are going to hear his side of the story,' Boris added.

'I have managed to get some information on Francette Tranquet for you. You seemed to be more interested in her situation than you were in the others, so I concentrated on her'

'You're a star Markus. Have you written it down for me?'

I took the piece of paper with the information on it out of my back pocket

'Here it is. Make sure that it doesn't fall into the wrong hands otherwise I will be in trouble.' I handed him the paper which he glanced at and then put into a pocket in the inside of his overcoat.

'If it checks out I will bring you the money the next time that I see you. I should be back here on Thursday as usual.'

'Boris we had better go, otherwise we are going to be late,' Elizabeth chipped in.

'Yes Beth, I know. I am finished here so we can go now.'

They both got up. Boris shook my hand, and they left the snug.

I remained, but I strained to hear any noise outside the pub. There was nothing beyond the crackle of the fire in the main bar and the murmur of the old men talking amongst themselves.

After ten minutes, my curiosity got the better of me, and I went out of the front door of the pub into the car park. The place was deserted, and there was no sign of Boris, Elizabeth, Major Richards or any police. What had happened? Had everything gone wrong at the last minute? At least the information that I had supplied was false, but there would be one seriously unhappy German out gunning for me.

I walked back to Witley Park feeling decidedly nervous and insecure. As I was finishing my dinner Major Richards came into the dining room with a big grin on his face. He came over to me and gave me a hefty slap on my back.

'Well done Markus. That couldn't have gone better. The two spies are locked up safely and can't do any more harm.'

The news banished my anxiousness, and I started to feel elated just like the Major.

'When I came out of the pub I saw nobody, so I assumed that they had got away. How did you do it so quietly and without any fuss?'

'We jumped on them as they left the car park and were fifty yards from the entrance. It was a bit of a risk, but we needn't have worried as they were taken totally by surprise.'

'Well I didn't hear a thing and assumed that it had all gone wrong. I assumed I was now a marked man.'

'You don't have to worry. Those two won't be out for another ten years.'

'I am so relieved and happy that it worked out so well'

'Come on I will buy you a drink to celebrate,' the Major suggested.

I had finished my meal, so we retired to the room that doubled as a bar and had our celebratory drink.

The following day the Colonel called all the trainee agents together and filled them in on what had been going on and how his secretary had been responsible for leaking information that had led to the death of Vic Biddlecome. He also spelt out what could have happened if it hadn't been discovered that his secretary was giving key information to the enemy. He praised me for my role in the exposure and capture.

After the meeting Francette sidled up to me.

'So that's why you went to the pub Markus. It wasn't another woman you were after.' She smiled and poked me in the shoulder.

'Well it was another woman, but not in the sense that you thought,' I replied.

'You are very brave to have volunteered as the bait.'

'The thought of you being in danger unless I did something was all the motivating force that I needed. You can now leave safely on your mission.'

'Oh, that's sweet Markus. As a bonus for looking after me you can come to my room this evening.'

'That's the best offer that I have had all day Francette and the only reward that I need.'

'You can supply the drink, and I will supply the room?' She smiled.

'Do you not think that we might spill it or do you plan on a quiet chat?'

'A quiet chat might be agreeable, but a little "amour" might be better.'

'I must get back to my work now. I'll see you at lunch.' I left and went to where I was studying some books on jet engines.

Chapter 29

Not much happened over Christmas 1940 as we were all confined to the house at Witley Park. We managed to get hold of some coloured paper and made Christmas decorations to take the bareness off the reception rooms. Francette was the creative one and her enthusiasm was infectious. I cut a branch off a fir tree that I found in the grounds of the estate and brought it in as our Christmas tree. Francette managed to make some trinkets to place on it; however, we didn't have any lights or candles, so it looked a bit drab.

Over the festive period I thought of home a lot and what we used to do in Lubeck at Christmas:

Where would I be next year and would I even be alive? How many of my friends in the Luftwaffe were still alive and were they experiencing the horrendous Russian winter. Although I was feeling blue, at least I had heat and friends around me and of course I had Francette.

Once the training stopped for the few days surrounding Christmas, Francette and I, spent almost all our time together. I started not to bother to go to my own room, but spent the whole night with her. It took too much courage to get out of a nice warm bed at two or three in the morning and walk in the cold back to my room. I wrongly assumed that nobody in authority would object to our relationship as they knew that we were an item.

At breakfast on the 29th December Major Richards came over to talk to me.

'The Colonel and I would like to see you in his office after breakfast Markus.'

My heart took an extra beat while I worked out in my mind why he wanted a special meeting. Perhaps he was going to give me instructions about the training I was going to receive at Power Jets. With some trepidation I knocked on the office door at 9:30 am.

On the instruction to 'come in', I entered the office to find the Colonel and the Major sitting in their usual chairs behind the round table. I sat down opposite them feeling like a guilty schoolboy.

'We have an extremely delicate matter that we would like to discuss with you Markus.' Colonel Thorpe started the conversation. 'It has come to our notice that a strong relationship has developed between Francette Tranquet and you. Is that the case?'

'Yes, we have become quite close over the past two months'

'I think that quite close is a bit of an understatement Markus. I do know that you have been spending a lot of nights recently in her room and presumably in her bed,' the Colonel continued.

'We have not tried to hide the fact that we are sleeping together although we have tried to be discrete,' I felt that I had to say something to defend myself.

'I am responsible for your training and for the welfare and safety of all the agents that pass through Witley Park,' the major said, looking extremely serious. 'I feel that the affair between you and Francette is compromising your security. All your attention must be on your training and on the thought processes required for you to have a successful mission.'

'This is a military training centre and the traditional disciplines expected at a military barracks are expected to operate,' the Colonel added. 'We are asking you to keep your relationship with Francette within certain boundaries that we can accept, and to sleep in your own room at night. Do you understand??'

'I'm sorry that I have overstepped the boundaries. I was unaware that there were rules governing where I was allowed to sleep.' I was genuinely apologetic for having broken the rules. Having been brought up in Germany I was well aware that one had to operate within strict rules

'I want you to understand why we are you giving these orders. To obtain the skills you will need to succeed behind enemy lines, you will have to focus on your training 110% of the time, and have no distractions. Your success and safety is my responsibility. I will not allow you to be compromised.' The Major tapped the table with his unlit pipe as he talked, emphasising his point.

'I understand fully what you are telling me, and you have my word that it will stop immediately'

'We will also be talking to Francette to let her know what we have said to you. We don't have a problem in you spending time together at meal times and in the evening; however, we are banning you from her room at all times. Do you understand?' The Colonel gave the final word.

I had gone into the meeting feeling like a naughty schoolboy and I left the meeting feeling even worse after my dressing down. At least they hadn't used the Headmaster's cane.

At lunch time Francette joined me at the dining table with her plate of food.

'Markus, did you have a difficult meeting with the Colonel and Major this morning?'

'Yes, and I gather from your question that you did too.'

'I am very disappointed in what they have asked me to do. You coming to my room made this whole training thing bearable.'

'I can understand why they have given us the order, but it is going to be extremely difficult knowing that you are sleeping just along the landing,' I replied.

'I don't see what harm we were doing. We did all their stupid training during the day and on top of that they expect me to live like a nun. It's not fair, and I told them that.' The look on Francette's face could have cut butter. She was obviously very upset.

'They must know what they are doing, and they emphasised to me that it was for my own good. Anyway I am due to go off for two months to Power Jets at Lutterworth near Derby so I won't be here anyway and you are due to leave in the near future on your mission'

'Oh Markus, you are a typical German, no emotion. I want romance in my life before I go off to get killed on some crazy mission.'

'Don't be so dramatic Francette. When we both come back after our missions I will sweep you off your feet, and we can spend all day every day together and even all night.' I smiled.

'Perhaps I will make a romantic man out of you eventually.' Francette punched me on the shoulder, and we both left the dining room to go to our rooms.

Matt was surprised to see me.

'Why are you looking so glum Markus and I didn't expect you back in our room as you normally go to Francette's'

'Let's just say that I am under orders which forbid me to go to her room.'

Matt gave a big guffaw. 'So lover boy has had his wings clipped by the top brass has he?'

'Something like that. I will have to make do with your company now.'

'I have missed your snoring and presence Markus. Welcome back.'

Chapter 30

Another year came to an end, and grimly the world moved into 1941. The war was still going on at many places around the world, and there was no indication that it would end in the foreseeable future. The winter weather enveloped Witley Park making all the occupants depressed and wanting to remain in 1940, a year that we knew and were safe in. The last thing any of us desired was to move into the New Year where so much danger awaited us in the missions that we were destined to carry out. I looked back to where I had been in January 1940 and the events that had overtaken me in the past year. I decided to take one month at a time in 1941 and do my best to survive.

I had hoped, when I agreed to work for the British that the war would be over before I would see active service as an agent. There was no sign of the war ending, and it probably would go on for another few years. Hitler had transferred his armies and air force to Russia after Germany had been defeated at the Battle of Britain, leaving the UK in splendid isolation. There appeared to be a stalemate as Germany occupied most of Europe, except for the unyielding British who were still resisting and were protected from attack by their air force and navy. With the French army defeated, the British didn't have the strength or resources to launch an offensive on their own and drive Germany out of Europe.

The next phase of my development as a secret agent was about to begin. I was being sent to a company called Power Jets where a brilliant engineer called Frank Whittle was developing a jet propulsion system. On my return to Europe in the spring, my mission would be to gather as much information as possible on the German jet engine programme, so to be effective, I would need to know all about jet engine propulsion. I had learnt a lot on the theory, but I now was being sent for two months, to work in the development process. I was hopeful that my three years studying engineering in Kiel would give me enough background knowledge for the task ahead.

On Monday 6th January I said my goodbyes at Witley Park and headed by train for London. Francette was not happy to see me go. With no date fixed for her to depart on her delayed mission, I was afraid that she would have left before I got back. We hugged hard and long before I left for the station.

My greatest fear in travelling on my own was being identified as a German if I had to speak for any reason. To avoid me having to buy tickets, they had issued me with a travel warrant.

Arriving in London I transferred by underground from Victoria station to Euston where I boarded a train to Rugby. I had been told that I would be met by an engineer from Power Jets.

On alighting from the train at Rugby, I spotted a man holding a sign with my name on it, "*Lieutenant Becker*". I noticed that my name had been spelt the English way to avoid any problems with people reacting to a German name. I appreciated their thoughtfulness.

I approached the man holding the name board.

'Are you Charles Johnson?' This was the name that I had been given.

'Yes, and you must be Lieutenant Becker?'

'Correct. Thank you for coming to meet me, but please call me Markus.'

Charles had a particularly friendly face and a wonderful warm smile. He must have been in his fifties with thinning grey hair and thick spectacles. He was much smaller than me, although his height was diminished further by a pronounced stoop. I surmised that he had been bending over, working on projects for most of his life. I took to him immediately and knew that I would enjoy working with him.

'I have a car and driver outside the station if you like to follow me.' He set off out of the station and turned left. We soon came to an old army car of some obscure make, and he put my bag in the trunk. The driver got out and opened the rear door for me, and I got in. Charles Johnson got in the back with me.

'It's not too far to the workshops in Lutterworth so we should be there in about forty minutes,' he said as he settled himself into the seat. 'Our funding is still not what we need for the development hence we have to make do with this rather old car, but it should get us there.'

'Is it a large factory?' I asked.

'It is a large factory complex owned by the British Thomson-Houston company. We only use one of the buildings at this stage, and it is just about adequate as we don't have a lot of people working with us.'

'Where will I be staying, is it close to the factory?'

'There is an old Coaching Inn in the centre of Lutterworth where we have booked you in. I am not too sure how good it is, but if it isn't to your liking we will try and find a better spot.'

'I am sure that it will be perfect. I am six feet three inches tall so the biggest problem I usually have is that the beds are too short, and I hang out over either end.'

'I'll drop you off there this evening and stick around while you check it all out'

'I appreciate you looking after me so well; you must be an exceedingly busy man'

'I am hopeful that you are going to ease my workload while you are with us. There is method in my madness.' He smiled at me in a knowing way. 'I believe you have done three years in a University Engineering School, so you should know your bolts from your screws.'

'Yes, I was mid-way through my last year when I was called up for the air force at the outbreak of war,' I replied.

'If you have a modicum of intelligence you will be fine and will be an asset to us during your stay here.'

When we arrived at the workshops, I was given a tour of the facility, and introduced to the rest of the staff. A strong smell of vapourized fuel was everywhere we went and hit the back of my throat. Frank Whittle wasn't there, so I didn't meet the genius who had been the originator of the new technology.

Charles explained to me that his boss had to spend far too much of his valuable time going around trying to convince the decision makers at the air ministry that the Jet Engine was the propulsion system of the future. Unfortunately, they had experienced a number of problems in the development and the engine hadn't been able to run at full power. After lunch, they did run the engine up to half power, and I was amazed at the noise and vibration that it generated. The smell of fuel increased considerably. Over the next two months, I was to get used to that massive noise. Even with ear muffs the noise was deafening

A few mornings later I was introduced to Frank Whittle. I had been warned that he had been on sick leave since the 10th December, but I was still horrified at how gaunt and tired he looked. It was a pleasant surprise when his energy and charisma came shining through as he spoke.

'Well Lieutenant Becker what do you think of my little operation here?'

'I am very impressed with what I see Sir. I had read up about the technology, but to see the engine running has convinced me that it is the future.'

'As a young engineer you can see the opportunities, but, I am afraid, the chiefs in the Air Ministry don't agree with you. I waste half my time talking to them when I should be working on the engine. Unfortunately, I have to indulge them as they provide most of the funds for the development, and they are not convinced. I am worn out chasing backwards and forwards to London.'

'I am sorry to hear that Sir. I think that what you have developed is incredible,' I said enthusiastically.

'Major Richards has told me that you have agreed to try and obtain information on the German jet engine Markus. We will do whatever we can to give you the knowledge you need for your job. You will work alongside Charles Johnson, who you have already met, and his team will use you to help them work on the engines. I can guarantee that you will learn a lot, but the hours will be long. The others do not know why you are here or about your upcoming mission, so be careful what you say.'

'I feel extremely privileged in being allowed to join your team for two months, and I will do everything in my power to contribute to the project during that time.'

'Any help will be greatly appreciated. You had better go and join Charles now and get stuck in. I'll talk to you every Friday to make sure that you are getting on OK.'

Very encouraged by my conversation with the brilliant engineer, I went off to find Charles.

Clearly the whole project was at a crisis point. The aircraft that had been developed to test the jet engine was ready, but the unit that the main engine supplier, Rover, was supposed to have built to Whittle's design still wasn't operational. The Power Jets team, based at the BTH factory, had cobbled together an engine from spare parts and other devious sources. This was the prototype that was now running successfully and was being refined to fit the air frame of the Gloster Meteor, the aircraft specially developed for the engine.

I have never worked so hard. I rolled out of bed at 6:00 am every morning, including weekends, and generally didn't get back to the Inn until ten o'clock each night. The whole team were involved in getting the engine ready to be fitted to the Meteor and the effort being made by the few of us had to be seen to be believed. The time flew by, February turned into March, and it soon was time for me to return to Witley Park. I was so involved in the atmosphere at Power Jets and the preparation of the engine for its first flight that I genuinely didn't want to leave.

On my last night, Charles, and a few of the technicians invited me to the local pub. They presented me with a little replica of the engine that an apprentice had turned on a lathe. I was very chuffed to receive such a gift and also to hear the nice words that they said about me.

'Markus, we want to thank you for being such an important member of our team for the past two months,' Charles said. 'You didn't have to work the long hours with us, but you did, and we greatly appreciated your efforts. When you see the Gloster Meteor flash by overhead, you will at least be able to say that you contributed to the engine flying that plane.'

'I also would like to thank you Charles for making the past two months so enjoyable and for teaching me so much about the jet engine. I will treasure this model for the rest of my life and remember very fondly my time with you in Power Jets.' As I made my little speech I held the model aloft in my right hand.

The following morning bright and early Charles picked me up in the same old car that had brought me to Lutterworth at the start of January, and I was driven to Rugby train station.

'Many thanks Charles for coming with me this morning. I am going to miss the team at Power Jets and just wish that I could stay with you until I see the Gloster Meteor fly,' I said, offering my right hand.

'We have enjoyed having you on the team for the last two months, and I just hope that the knowledge you have gained will prove useful to you.' Charles grabbed my hand and shook it vigorously.

'Thanks again Charles and I hope that I see you again sometime.'

'You never know Markus. This war brings a lot of surprises.'

I left him and headed into the station, to catch my train to London.

Chapter 31

Four hours later I was through the second checkpoint at Witley Park and was heading into the building. Having dumped my bag in my room, I went downstairs and knocked on the door of Major Richards' office. Even though it was after lunch on a Saturday, I anticipated that he would be in residence.

'Come in,' a voice answered.

I opened the door and stuck my head in to a cloud of tobacco smoke. Luckily the Major was all alone, so I had a chance of talking to him.

'I am back Major.'

'Did you have a successful time Markus?'

'It was really fantastic. They welcomed me as part of their team, and I was fully involved in all aspects of their work. After two months of immersion in their operation, I know all about jet engines and the unique problems encountered in their development.' My enthusiasm took over my tongue.

'I'm delighted to hear that you haven't wasted your time. You are going to be extremely busy between now and when you leave on your mission as we have planned in some activity for every day, starting with your exposure to small boats. You will be going to Derwent Water in County Durham to learn sailing for at least two weeks, and you will also do the orienteering test that you failed while you are there.'

'Has Francette Tranquet left on her mission yet Sir?'

'No, and you are back just in time to see her off. She is leaving this coming Tuesday. I have told you that piece of information in confidence Markus, so please don't say a word to anybody about it.'

'Thank you for your trust Sir. I am relieved that I am back before she left on her mission, I know how nervous she will be and how much support she will need.'

'Anyway Markus, welcome back to Witley Park. You can have a slightly easier weekend than normal, and I would appreciate it if you would give Francette the support she requires. That support doesn't include amorous activities in her bedroom.' He smiled.

'Thank you Sir. I will go and see if I can find her.' I got up and went to locate Francette.

I found her in one of the small rooms that we were allowed to use when we needed peace and quiet to study.

'Bonjour Francette,' I said as I went through the door.

She got up and gave me a loving hug.

'Bonjour Markus. How good it is to see you again. I have missed you.'

She held both my hands and looked up into my face.

'How did it go, Markus? I hope that you haven't found another girlfriend while you have been away in Rugby.'

'No, you can relax. I have been working every day from seven in the morning until ten o'clock at night.'

'Even weekends?' she asked.

'Yes, even weekends, but it was fantastic and I thoroughly enjoyed the work. How have you been? I hear that you are due to leave this coming Tuesday.'

'I am so glad that you have returned before I left Markus. I am terribly worried about what I have to do. I don't want to let anybody down and do something stupid when I get to the other end. I don't want people to be arrested or even killed because of me.'

'You will be fine Francette, and you can only do your best. I can guarantee that you won't do anything stupid you are far too intelligent.'

'I can't help thinking about what happened to Vic Biddlecome. He was shot dead just as soon as he landed, and he didn't stand a chance.'

'Don't forget Francette that the Germans were leaked the information about his arrival by Elizabeth. She is no longer able to provide details of the missions of the agents based here as she has been locked up for the remainder of the war.'

'One piece of very welcome news is that I won't have to use a parachute. They will be landing me by plane in a field controlled by the Resistance. I was so worried about using a parachute as I am not strong enough to control where it goes, and, in my practice jumps, I was landing quite a distance from the target.'

'It sounds as if they are looking after you and you will be safe.' I gave her a reassuring hug.

We spent the weekend together, walking and talking and generally getting to know each other again. I hadn't seen a Pathe News for over two months, so we went to watch the movie in the lounge that evening. The news reel was full of the bombing of London and also the bombing raids that the British were making against German positions in Europe. There was also a lot of hype about the victories that the British and their allies had achieved in North Africa against the Italians. Having been brought up in a country that thrived on propaganda, I didn't know whether what I was looking at was the truth or just fabricated stories to keep the British peoples morale up. Yes, I was suspicious.

On the Tuesday evening, I was having dinner with Francette, just before she was due to leave on her mission, when Major Richards came in, accompanied by his cloud of smoke, and sat down beside us.

'Are you all set to go Francette?' he asked.

'Yes I have checked everything a hundred times to make sure that I have no tell-tale labels or anything else to give me away.'

'We will be leaving at 8:30 pm sharp, so you must be dressed and ready by then,' the Major continued. 'Would you like to come along to see her off Markus?'

'I certainly would if that is possible.'

'We will have room for you and the car that is taking us to Weston-Super-Mare is bringing me back here later, so there is no inconvenience in taking you.'

'I'll be ready and waiting at 8:30 then.'

'That makes me feel a lot better Markus,' Francette said to me after the Major had left us.

'Under all that efficiency and bluster he is a thoughtful man,' I said, genuinely appreciative of his offer.

We were waiting outside the front door admiring the beautiful, still, moonlit night, by twenty past eight. It couldn't have been a better night for flying. As we stood there holding hands, we heard the drone of the German bombers flying overhead towards London where they would give the populace another torrid night. It brought the war closer to us at that moment.

A car pulled up, and, just afterwards, Major Richards came from the house to join us.

'What perfect weather Francette, you will unquestionably be leaving tonight. Let's go.'

The Major got into the front of the car with the driver, and Francette and I snuggled into the back seat still holding hands.

Far too soon we were pulling into the airfield at Weston-super-Mare, driving up close to a lone sinister looking Westland Lysander painted entirely in black. It seemed to be an exceptionally small plane to be taking Francette so far. The Pilot was already on board doing his final checks and seemed to be impatient to take off.

I got out with Francette, and the Major gave her his last words of wisdom. Finally it was my turn to say good-bye, and I took her into my arms. I would have liked to have held there for hours as I didn't like the idea of her going off on a highly dangerous mission.

'I have to get on board Markus, can you please let me go.' She smiled up at me.

'I'll only let you go if you promise to be extremely careful and not take any unnecessary risks,' I replied.

'I am going to be alright, and have this strong feeling that we are going to meet up again, get married and have loads of kids.'

'I will be thinking of you all the time, and we will meet up again later in the year. Please look after yourself.'

We let go of each other, and the Major helped her climb on board the plane. The Pilot started the engine and the plane taxied out to the start of the runway. There was a surge in the noise as the pilot hit the throttle, and the plane trundled down the runway and lifted off into the moonlit night sky. It was soon lost from sight, and we climbed back into the car and returned to Witley Park.

'She is a remarkably brave girl Markus and has bags of talent to match her determination. I am confident that she will come back'

'She is a remarkable girl, and I will miss her. I just hope that someone she trusts doesn't let her down and give her away.'

'Unfortunately, that always is a risk in our game. I am fairly confident that the group she is going to is a highly committed one and she will be well looked after.'

'I hope so.' I sat back in the seat, closed my eyes, and thought of Francette. I knew that she was going to France, but she hadn't told me what part of that large country she was being sent to.

I thought to myself: *Wouldn't it be extraordinary if I ended up in the same part of France as she had gone to and we bumped into one another. It might create problems, but it would be nice.*

We arrived back at Witley Park at just after 2:00 am, but it was a Witley Park without the love of my life Francette. It was a very sad Markus that climbed into bed and eventually went asleep.

Chapter 32

The following morning I was called in to the Colonel's office for my briefing on the next phase of my training. As usual, Colonel Thorpe and Major Richards were sitting at the round table when I entered.

'Good morning Sirs,' I said as I sat down in the spare chair facing them.

'First things first Markus, you will be glad to hear that Francette arrived safely in France and also that the plane landed back in Somerset safe and sound,' the Major said, giving me a big smile. He looked just as relieved as I felt.

'We need to begin firming up a plan with you about your own mission and your proposed transfer to France,' the Colonel went on. 'As already discussed with you we believe that the best landing place for you is Cherbourg or on the Cherbourg peninsula somewhere and that you should approach the coast in a small sailing boat.'

'Is that not dangerous as I have never sailed before, even though I lived right on the sea in Lubeck,' I protested. 'I only know how to row.'

'Your story relies on convincing the Germans that you have escaped from a prison camp, have stolen a boat on the south coast and have sailed across the Channel for about eighteen hours,' the Colonel added. 'In fact you will be taken across the Channel in a fishing boat, which will tow your sailing boat. They will deliver you close to Cherbourg. We expect that one of their patrol boats based in Cherbourg will pick you up, so you won't have to sail terribly far.'

'I believe that sailing a small boat is quite a skill and also dangerous. I have rowed but never sailed, and I probably would capsize within a few meters of being released from the fishing boat.'

'That's why we have called you in here today Markus,' the Major now spoke. 'You are being sent to the North of England for an intensive sailing course where you will become a proficient sailor. You will also do your orienteering test in safer terrain than you experienced in Cornwall.'

'Is it not still a bit wintry for sailing?' I enquired.

'We can't do anything about the weather, but we are sending you to Derwent reservoir in Co. Durham which is a very large lake. You will get strong winds and waves without getting swamped,' the Major replied.

'Sounds good. When do I leave?'

'You will depart on Saturday. You will take a train from London to Chester le Street with your friendly instructor Sergeant Paul Young, who will meet you in London. He is an excellent sailor as well as being an orienteering expert.'

'When are you planning to send me to Cherbourg?' I asked.

'We want to try and get you organized by the 10th. April, but it will all depend on the weather. The winds mustn't be too strong, and the waves too high for your sail in the Channel,' the Colonel replied. 'After you are finished in Durham you will go to Taunton where you will spend a few days in a Prisoner of War camp. At your de-briefing by the Germans you will need to give accurate details of where you were held as a prisoner and how you escaped.'

'I hadn't thought of all that side of it. Will I have it all completed by the beginning of April?'

'It will be tight, but you should make it,' the Major replied. 'We will not send you on your assignment until you are one hundred and ten percent ready.'

'Is there anything in particular that you want me to do for the rest of this week before I leave for Durham?'

'Yes, we will work together compiling *'your story'* from the time that you were shot down until you escaped from the South of England in a small boat,' the Major answered. 'You will then have to learn it until it over-rides the truth.'

'Now that it is getting closer to the time I have to leave I am getting nervous. I can appreciate how Francette felt just before she left for France.'

'Just relax and put your whole heart into your preparation and everything will go smoothly,' the Colonel suggested. 'You are dismissed, and the Major will start with you this afternoon.'

'I'll come to your office after lunch Major Richards will that suit?' The thought of an afternoon in a tobacco smoke filled room didn't appeal to me.

'Yes, I will see you then.'

I left the two of them and went to search in the library for any books on sailing and the handling of yachts in general.

The rest of the week flew by, and it was no time before I was waiting for my lift to the station on Saturday morning. I met up with my old tormentor Sergeant Paul Young at Kings Cross Station as arranged and we both boarded the train for Newcastle. It was great to meet him again even though the end of our time together in Cornwall had been so embarrassing for me.

'Nice to see you wearing your trousers Sir,' he said when I approached him.

'And I don't plan on losing them again this trip Sergeant,' I replied.

We had a compartment to ourselves for a lot of the journey, so we were able to catch up on what each of us had been up to since we had last met.

At Chester le Street, we left the train and were joined on the platform by five other service personnel, who, after some discussion, we found were going to the same place as we were. An army driver came over to us and announced that he would be bringing us to Derwent Manor where we all were staying. He explained to us that the army had requisitioned the Manor as accommodation for military personnel training on Derwent Water. We all piled into his truck and set off.

After about ten miles, he turned off the main road onto a narrow laneway which brought us to an impressive very large and well preserved old house. When we entered the reception area we were welcomed by a huge open fire which threw its heat to all corners of the room. We were all logged in and allotted our rooms. I was delighted that I was billeted on my own and didn't have to share a room with any of the other service personnel.

After a late lunch, the same old truck brought a large group of about fifteen people, including the Sergeant and I, to the sailing club where my training began. I was introduced to what was going to be my torture for the next week, a Firefly sailing dinghy. It was twelve feet long and close to five feet wide and weighed around seventy five kilograms, without me on board. The big advantage was that it comfortably could accommodate a crew of two, but could also be sailed single handed.

The first two hours were spent in understanding the rigging of the boat and in putting on the sails. Just when I thought that we were never actually going to take to the water I was told to put on a life jacket, and we launched the boat with the Sergeant at the helm. The wind was strong, and we accelerated away from the shore. It was exhilarating, but I felt very insecure as any slight movement in the boat was transferred into violent action.

Just as I was getting used to it and starting to enjoy myself the Sergeant told me that he was going about which he told me meant that we were going to go back in the direction we had just come from.

He shouted, *'Going about, Now.'* He pushed the tiller suddenly away from him.

I let the jib go from the side it had been on and pulled it on the other side, and we quickly built up speed again. Just as I got settled, he shouted again, *'Going About, Now.'* We went around one hundred and eighty degrees again.

'You have to be quicker changing the jib Markus. We mustn't lose too much speed.' He barked out at me.

'I am scared of falling in. The boat lunges from one side to the other and I am the ballast keeping it upright.'

'Tomorrow I will get rid of that fear as we will deliberately capsize the Firefly and then get it back with the right side up.

If you sail a small boat, you quickly learn to get wet and then recover from your ducking.'

'I don't like the sound of that even if I am a strong swimmer and don't mind the water.'

'You have nothing to worry about and you will pick it up very quickly. We will go in now and call it a day.'

The following day we were out on the water early and after a few manoeuvres he announced that he was about to capsize the dinghy. As it turned over, he instructed me to climb over the side so as I was in the water alongside the centreboard. He turned the boat so as the sail, which was now flat on the water, was facing the wind. He stood on the centreboard, and the yacht started to come up. The wind caught under the sails, and the boat popped up rapidly. We both slipped over the side into the boat, and we were sailing again.

'That wasn't too bad Markus was it?' he asked me.

'I was amazed how fast it came up and with so little effort. Allowing the wind to do the work is brilliant,' I replied. 'But it is bloody cold, and my hands are freezing.'

'We will do a few more this morning and then you can sail solo this afternoon.'

'I am almost as worried about this as I was for my first solo flight.' I smiled nervously.

'At least if you fall in the water you won't have far to fall, and your boat will stay with you. Never leave your boat as it won't sink and all you have to do is hang on until you are rescued.'

I'll try to remember that.

That afternoon I took the boat out myself under just the mainsail. I didn't have the jib to worry about which made it a lot simpler. I got on remarkably well and didn't capsize once. At the end of the session, the Sergeant instructed me to turn the boat over. He came out with the rescue boat, just in case I got into trouble.

I had no difficulty in capsizing the boat, my problems started when I was in the water. What had seemed to be a straightforward operation yesterday, turned out to be extremely difficult. I couldn't manoeuvre the boat to face in the right direction, and, without the wind lifting the sail, I couldn't get the boat upright.

He came close and shouted instructions at me. Finally I managed to get the boat pointing into the wind, and I stepped on the centreboard. As if by magic the yacht righted itself, and I was able to climb aboard. Very wet and cold, but triumphant, I gave the thumbs up to the Sergeant.

'Well done Markus, that's the first one; I want you to do four more before you can call yourself a sailor.'

I muttered under my breath as I was already exhausted, soaked through and freezing. I started to wonder when hypothermia would set in.

By the fifth time, I was quite an expert and was able to get the yacht upright in about four minutes. I received a round of applause from the rescue boat.

I sailed the boat back to the shore and gratefully climbed out onto dry land. The Sergeant arrived shortly after me and gave me a hand putting the Firefly onto its trailer. We then pulled it into the dinghy park.

'Well done Markus, you did remarkably well today. It will all be downhill from here on in, and you should start enjoying yourself. Tomorrow, weather permitting you can sail with the jib, and if you are successful with that you will have cracked it.'

'I am looking forward to getting some dry clothes on and getting warm again. I presume I can change before we head back to the Manor.' My teeth were chattering and my body shaking.

'I think that they have some hot water in the sailing club so you can have a shower before you put on your dry clothes. I might do that myself.'

It was two extremely tired individuals that were welcomed back by the huge fire in the reception area at the Manor and went to their respective rooms.

Chapter 33

We had a drink before dinner to celebrate my solo performance and the fact that I had survived another day on and in the water. Prior to being requisitioned by the army Derwent Manor had been a hotel, so all the facilities such as a bar and a dining room were in place and able to cater for the needs of about thirty trainees plus their instructors. There were open fires in all the reception rooms and the bar, supplied with logs from the surrounding grounds of the Manor. That evening there was a group of six army NCO's who were obviously celebrating some achievement as they were getting quite drunk and making an unwelcome noise.

Paul and I took our drinks with us into the dining room to escape the loud voices as it was the last thing that we wanted after a day on the water. About half an hour later two of the rowdy bunch came into the dining room and unfortunately, plonked themselves down in the two spare seats at our table. They insisted on talking to us.

After a while, one of them looked straight at me.

'Are you German?' he said very aggressively. 'You certainly sound German.'

'I originally came from Germany some years ago,' I replied, trying to act calmly.

'You're the cause of this whole f..king war,' he shouted back at me.

I noticed that my companion had moved his chair slightly away from the table.

'I am a member of the British army and am on your side,' I said firmly

'We don't want your likes on our side. I have lost good friends because of you and your fellow f..king countrymen,' he shouted. His mate was trying to calm him down, but he was pushing him away.

'I'm sorry that you lost your friends, but it had nothing to do with me,' I countered.

He stood up and moved towards me, obviously intent on taking a swing at me. Sergeant Paul moved into action and grabbed him in a vice like grip. He frog marched him out of the dining room and into the hall.

Ten minutes later, my protective Sergeant returned to the dining room.

'What did you do with him Sergeant?' I asked him.

'They have an old pantry that has no windows but has a particularly solid door that I was able to lock, so I put him in there to cool down and sober up. He will be better in the morning.'

'I didn't like to flatten him, although that is what I wanted to do.'

'Better that you weren't the one to subdue him as he would have seen it as proof of his view of Germans. He should come to his senses in the morning. He also served in Norway and lost a lot of his platoon there.'

'I can understand how he is so bitter against all Germans, but it has shaken me up a bit.'

'Yes, it has rather ruined our evening, so I am going to go to my room, and I will see you bright and early in the morning.'

I also decided that I would leave the rest of my dinner and go to bed.

The following morning the truck took us to the reservoir after breakfast. A strong wind was blowing and there was driving rain whipping across the water, making it particularly unpleasant. I wouldn't have to fall in the water to get wet today; the rain would soak me through in ten minutes.

'Well Markus, you will be going out with the jib up today. The wind is quite strong, but you should be able to manage. The main thing to remember is to let everything go if you feel that you are going to capsize. The boat will turn head to wind, and you can then start again.'

'There are more waves today than yesterday,' I said, looking at the surface of the reservoir.

'If we were in the Channel I wouldn't think of letting you sail, but the waves on the lake aren't too bad so you should be able to manage. Let's just see how you get on.'

We launched the Firefly, and I climbed aboard while he held the dinghy. He pushed me off, and I was sailing with the wind directly behind me. I didn't have much control over what was happening as the boat started to plane on the top of the waves. If I didn't do something, I would end up at the other side of the reservoir and would have considerable difficulty getting back. I pulled in the main sail and the jib and slowly turned towards the wind. The boat lent over alarmingly; however, I used my considerable weight to keep it upright.

I gradually came to terms with the strong wind and felt more comfortable, although there was no opportunity to relax. Spray was coming up from where the bow was cutting through the waves, and it was intensely cold. I was still struggling to get the jib under control every time that I went about, but I didn't capsize the boat. So I was managing, but only just and all my attention was going into staying upright and surviving.

An event then took place that changed the whole pattern of my morning's sailing.

I was travelling parallel with the land, about sixty meters from the shore. The wind was coming from the direction of the shore, so I was leaning far out with my back to the land. Just as I moved to throw the tiller over to go about I heard what sounded like the shot of a rifle. At the same time, a jagged hole appeared in my main sail. I was being shot at.

I capsized the dinghy with the sail facing the shore, and I hid behind the hull, keeping as low as possible and hanging onto the centreboard. A hole appeared in the bottom of the boat as a second bullet found its mark. That was the motivation I needed to sink even lower in the water. Who on earth was shooting at me, and then I remembered the man who had sat down at our table at dinner the night before. It must be him. I just hoped that the Sergeant had been watching me and quickly realise what was going on.

I heard the report of another rifle, but no more holes appeared in my boat. I stayed put keeping the hull between me and the shore. After what seemed to me like hours I heard the support boat coming towards me. I was immensely relieved when it came around the hull, and I saw the familiar face of the Sergeant looking down at me in the water.

'You can get your Firefly upright again now. I have dealt with the problem. Our friend from last night decided that he wanted to get rid of you. He has a lot more to worry about now as I wounded him quite badly.'

I was too shocked to talk, but I just focused on getting the boat upright. Thankfully it popped up, but the holes made by the bullets meant that water was pouring in.

'You had better hop into the safety boat with me Markus and we will tow the Firefly to the launching area. If you try to sail back, it will sink with your weight in it. Are you alright?'

'Yes I am fine. Thankfully I wasn't hit. What a crazy man?'

I was so weighed down with my sodden clothes that he had to drag me into the support boat. There was a welcome party waiting for us as we pulled up to the slipway. I saw an army ambulance pulling into the car park obviously coming to pick up my wounded assailant.

The crowd came over to give us a hand getting the boats ashore and they inspected the bullet holes in the floor of the dinghy. Where the bullets had gone through the hull, the wood had splintered on either side, and there were gaping holes at least six centimetres long. There was also a sizeable rip in the mainsail from the first shot.

'You're an extremely lucky man,' Sergeant Paul Young said to me as he assessed the damage. 'I must congratulate you on your prompt action in capsizing the boat. That saved your life as you were then hidden behind the twelve foot long hull and he didn't know where you were.'

'Did you see him firing at me?' I asked.

'I heard the shot, and saw you going over. I assumed that he had hit you.'

'Where did you get a gun from to shoot at my attacker?'

'There was a soldier on guard duty near the gate, so I ran over to him and borrowed his gun. Luckily it was a Lee Enfield which I am familiar with, and I am also a marksman'

'Thanks for protecting me. I was getting worried as I was afraid that he would get in a lucky shot sooner or later.'

There was a commotion close to the ambulance as they brought a still swearing wounded soldier to the ambulance. Two military policemen had come with the ambulance, and they left in the back with their charge.

'I think that you have done enough for today, and the weather is getting worse. We will return to the Manor as soon as I can arrange a lift,' the Sergeant said sympathetically for once. I didn't know that he had a softer side.

Shortly afterwards the Major in charge of the training facility arrived to find out for himself what had happened. After he had gathered all the details, and was happy that everything was under control, he took us to the Manor in his car. An eventful morning had ended.

After what had happened that morning my training on Derwent Water went relatively smoothly and I became quite proficient. The biggest challenge I faced was moving about in the dinghy. I was too tall and too heavy. The Sergeant assured me that the boat that they would use to bring me close to Cherbourg would be a lot bigger than the Firefly, and I would have a lot more room.

Having passed my sailing challenge the next step was to do my three day orienteering test.

'Well Markus, I am happy that you won't drown yourself in the English Channel when you try to get to France by boat. It is now time for your orienteering test,' the Sergeant said to me on the evening after my sailing test. 'You will be set down close to Carlisle tomorrow morning, and you will have three days to get back to Derwent Manor. You should find it easier here than in Cornwall, and you shouldn't meet any swamps.'

'The weather isn't great, and it is extremely wet, but I feel confident that I will make it. Have you any idea what the weather forecast is like for the next three days?'

'There is rain predicted, but the cloud cover should prevent the temperature from dropping to too low a temperature.'

'I'll go to bed now to ensure I get a decent night's sleep before I set off. I imagine that I won't sleep too well for the next few nights.'

Three days later an exhausted, wet and cold Markus arrived safely back at Derwent Manor, to be greeted by a mightily relieved Sergeant Young. Compared to Cornwall the countryside had been a lot friendlier and also there hadn't been too much rain. I was delighted to have successfully completed my orienteering test as it had been hanging over me since I had failed so miserably before Christmas. The successful completion of my trek had given me a new confidence for the mission I had to embark on in April.

The following day I packed up all my belongings and said goodbye to Derwent Manor. It had been quite a challenging experience and I felt immense satisfaction at having come through it successfully.

The Sergeant accompanied me as far as London where he had to head back down to the West Country, I returned to Witley Park from where I was due to go and experience a Prisoner of War camp. I was sorry to have to say goodbye to Paul Young at Kings Cross Station. We had become good friends in our few weeks together, and he had taught me a lot that I hoped would benefit me in the future. He was a born survivor, and I needed his skills for my task ahead.

Chapter 34

Major Richards, in welcoming me back, was delighted to hear that I had passed both my sailing and orienteering tests.

'Well done Markus. You have now completed all aspects of your official training so we can now get on to perfecting your story. You must know every aspect of it so well that it will stand up to whatever pressure they put you under to try and get the truth.'

'By pressure, you mean torture Sir.'

'Yes by pressure I do mean torture, although, if we get the process right, then they will have no need to torture you.'

'When do I have to go to the POW camp in Taunton?'

'You can take tomorrow off to recover from your trip to Derwent Water. We will then take you there the following day. A week of total immersion in the camp should be enough for you to fully absorb what life is like in a POW camp.'

'Do you think that I will be in danger from the other inmates Major?'

'No, we can make it look like you have just been transferred to the Taunton camp from Yorkshire. Your story is that you were held in an interrogation centre near Harrogate, and then spent four months in a POW camp close to Catterick.' The Major leant back in his chair and related my story matter-of-factly. It all sounded terribly convincing.

'How will I be able to describe the camp at Catterick as I haven't been there?'

'I have obtained a collection of photographs of the camp and the everyday life in the Catterick camp will closely match the one you will experience in Taunton. I don't need to tell you that your story will have to be perfect before you are allowed to set off for France.'

'We'll talk again after you get back here from Taunton. I am sorry, but you will be taken to Taunton under guard, and you will also have to wear your old Luftwaffe uniform which, with a bit of luck, will still fit you.'

'It will be a strange experience wearing my old uniform again and going back to live as a German prisoner. I hope that I don't give the game away.'

'Good luck Markus. I will see you when they come to pick you up shortly after breakfast on Thursday. In the meantime relax and learn your story so as it is word perfect. I have had an envelope left on your bed, which contains all the relevant information you will need. Memorise every little detail.'

I left the Major's office and went up to my room. I now would have to prepare mentally for what lay ahead which would be the hardest part of the whole exercise. I found the envelope on my bed and inside were pictures of the POW camp in Catterick. There was also a plan of the camp showing where all the facilities were, so, with these two prompts, I familiarised myself with the layout.

As well as the photographs and the plan there was a list of the prisoners being held in the camp. The list included their ranks and the units that they had served in. In addition, there were some personal details of some of the men, mainly individuals that were the same age as me and who I would have naturally palled up with. I was extremely impressed, the Major had thought of everything, and I spent the next day and a half absorbing the information in the envelope. A nervous energy drove me on.

Suitably dressed and prepared I was ready and waiting in the reception area of Witley Manor on Thursday morning. Major Richards approached me.

'Are you ready for your next adventure Markus?'

'I think that I have covered everything, but I am feeling decidedly nervous,' I replied.

'Just remember that you don't have to offer much information. Only provide information to a superior officer and only if you are asked. I suggest that you demonstrate a grumpy disposition and snap at people who ask you questions. They will then leave you alone.'

'That sounds like a good plan. I will give the impression of being totally pissed off with life and disgruntled at being a POW.'

'Here comes your guard with their truck.'

The truck pulled up in front of the entrance and we went out to greet it. A corporal climbed out of the front seat and came over to us.

'Corporal this is the prisoner that you will be taking to Taunton. See to it that he doesn't escape,' the Major ordered.

'Yes Sir,' the corporal replied.

'He has been held here for interrogation and has been very helpful so don't be too hard on him.'

'Yes Sir.'

'Here are the papers to travel with him. You must personally make sure that these papers are given to the senior officer at the camp and I am holding you responsible for delivering them.'

'Yes Sir, you can rely on me to deliver him safely; Sir.'

The corporal took the papers from Major Richards and brought me over to the rear of the truck.

'Climb in,' he instructed me.

I climbed up into the back where there were two privates armed with rifles sitting on either side of the opening. I was pushed by one of the soldiers towards the front, and made to sit down.

'Sit there and don't budge. If you try to make a run for it we will shoot,' one of the privates said with great menace.

It was going to be hard to get used to life as a prisoner; however, it was only for a week so I would survive.

The truck was the most uncomfortable means of transportation I had ever had to use. The wooden bench seats along the side of the truck where really hard and the truck bounced at any slight bump in the road. I was bruised and tender by the time that we arrived at the gates to the camp. We passed through two entrance gates and stopped in front of a large black hut where I was pulled roughly from the back. I was marched into the building with one soldier at each elbow.

'Name?' An officious sergeant barked out at me.

'Oberleutnant Markus BEKER,' I replied in a confident voice.

'Age?'

'Twenty-four.'

'Your Luftwaffe Squadron?'

'I don't have to give you that information under the Geneva Convention,' I replied.

'Don't be a smart ass with me young fellow. I need to know your squadron.'

'Well I am not going to give it to you as I am not obliged to give it.'

The Sergeant turned to a Corporal who was standing close by with two privates.

'Take this block head to the cell in the guard house and lock him away until he is willing to give us the information we need.'

With that my arms were grabbed, and I was frog marched out of the presence of the Sergeant and towards a particularly drab looking building close by. As I was being marched I looked around me. About twenty meters away there was the main area of the camp surrounded by two high fences containing masses of barbed wire. Beyond that, I could see a lot of long low huts and the prisoners wandering around.

They didn't bring me into the compound but marched me to the isolated building. Inside there were a number of cells. They opened one and threw me inside.

There was no heating in the building and the place was freezing. I didn't have many clothes on, so I rapidly reached an uncomfortable temperature. There was a horrible smell of disinfectant.

'Hello, can you hear me?' a voice called out.

I was so tied up in my own misfortune that I didn't hear clearly at first.

'Hello, can you hear me?' the voice called out again.

I moved towards the door. 'Yes, I can hear you. How long have you been in here?'

'I was thrown in here yesterday, and I spent the whole night here. I am absolutely frozen. Who are you?'

'My name is Markus BEKER, and I have just arrived at the camp.'

'Hi, my name is Lothar Meier, and I have been in this camp for seven months.'

'How did you get captured,' I asked

'I was co-pilot of a bomber, and we got shot down on a night bombing raid to the midlands of England. I managed to parachute down, but most of the rest of my crew perished. How about you?'

'I was a Me109 pilot and got shot down over Kent. I was lucky enough not to be injured, and I parachuted down.'

'When did you get shot down?'

'It was last July during the Battle of Britain.'

'Why are you only getting to this camp now?'

'I was interrogated in a large house near Harrogate for at least two months, and then moved to a camp in Catterick, in the North of England. Have you been here all the time?'

'I broke my leg when I landed, so they brought me to a hospital first and then when I was able to walk they transferred me here.'

'Why have they locked you up in this guard house Lothar?'

'I got involved in a fight with a cocky 109 pilot.' I heard him laugh. 'Why are you in here Markus?'

'I refused to give the Sergeant my Luftwaffe squadron number when he was taking down my details'

'It sounds as if you encountered our stupid prick Sergeant 'Mad-dog'. Keep away from him as he is always looking for an excuse to throw you in here and he is always barking at you.'

'I'll keep that in mind for the future. I'll talk to you later Lothar.'

'Keep warm Markus.' I heard him chuckle again.

I thought to myself - *That was particularly useful. Getting thrown in the brig would help authenticate my story. I hadn't planned it, but I was getting credibility and a reason that I had been moved from Yorkshire. I was a troublemaker.*

Chapter 35

A few hours later I heard the main door to the guard house open and my door was unlocked. The Corporal stuck his head into the cell.

'Up you get. The Colonel wants to see you.'

I decided to keep my mouth shut and just go along with them.

'Goodbye Lothar,' I called out as I left my cell

'Good luck Markus, I hope that I don't see you back here.'

This time I was allowed to walk on my own and the two guards didn't grab my arms. My small group marched over to what looked like an administrative building. The complex was also outside the main confines of the camp.

We entered the building and approached a door.

'Wait here,' the Corporal instructed.

He knocked on the door and immediately opened it. I didn't catch what he said.

'You can go in. When you enter, salute the Colonel'

I entered the room and saluted the Colonel who was standing behind his desk. I expected to see a young man, but the Colonel was in his late fifties or perhaps even early sixties. He had an impressive head of silvery grey hair and a large handle bar moustache. His twinkling eyes were on the move assessing me.

'Sit down Oberleutnant BEKER,' he said with a surprisingly strong voice, obviously used to taking charge.

'Thank you Sir.'

'You haven't made my job easy have you, getting disciplined so early in your stay with us.'

'The Sergeant annoyed me with his attitude, but, on reflection, I think that it might help my credibility.'

'That is as maybe, but you have still given me a problem. I am going to have you sent to the main camp which isn't going to impress my Sergeant as he would like you incarcerated until at least tomorrow in the guard house'

'Thank you Sir and I am sorry for causing you a problem.'

'I'll get over it and anyway he was a bit hasty in having you locked up. You are within your rights under the Geneva Convention not to give your squadron number, and I do try to stay within the rules'

'I will try and stay out of trouble for the rest of my time here, and I appreciate you letting me out.'

'Let's hope that the rest of the week goes smoothly' He got up and opened the door.

'Corporal, take this prisoner through to the camp and see that he meets Major Horst Winkel or one of the other senior German officers.'

This time we marched towards the entrance in the barbed wire fence. Once through there I was taken to a hut in the middle of the block. The Corporal went inside and came back with an extremely serious but elegant looking Major from the Wehrmacht. He and his two guards left me in the presence of the Major.

'Oberleutnant, my name is Major Winkel, and I am the most senior German officer in this camp. You will take your orders from me and not from the British.'

I stood to attention and clicked my heels, 'Sir, my name is Oberleutnant Markus BEKER of the Luftwaffe, and I have been moved here from a camp in Yorkshire.'

'You are welcome Oberleutnant. Come inside and we will talk together for a few minutes before I assign you a bed in one of the huts. I need to know something about you before I put you in with a group.'

We went down the length of the hut until we came to a separate room at the end which I gathered was the private room of the Major.

'Tell me what has happened to you since you were taken prisoner until you arrived here today. You don't have to go into too much detail; I will ask you specific questions if I need more information.'

I then related the story to him that I had prepared with the assistance of Major Richards. Major Winkel sat there in front of me nodding his head as I gave him all the details.

'What happened when you arrived this morning?' Major Winkel asked as I neared the end of my story.

'They asked me for my squadron number, and I refused to give it to them. I was then locked up in an isolation cell.'

'I suppose it was that twit Sergeant 'Mad-dog' up to his usual tricks.'

'Yes, it was the Sergeant.'

'How come that they have let you out so quickly?'

'They took me to the camp commander, and he told me that I was being released and sent into the main camp. He told the guards to bring me to see you. He said that he was releasing me as he wanted the camp to operate under the normal rules outlined in the Geneva Convention.'

'The Colonel is from the old school; he served in the First World War and was brought back out of retirement to run this camp. He's not too bad.'

'I didn't expect to be treated so civilly having been locked up for a while. He struck me as being a gentleman.'

'Did you happen to talk to Lothar Meier when you were in the cell? Is he reasonably comfortable?'

'Yes, I had a long chat with him and he appears to be surviving. He did complain that he is extremely cold.'

'Oh, he'll come through it alright. He is always ending up in there due to his terrible temper. He is always getting involved in fights. When the guards come in to break up the fight they always grab him and throw him in there for a few days.'

'Which hut will you be putting me in Sir?'

'I'll put you in hut H with a lot of other Luftwaffe officers. You may even know some of them.'

'Are we finished Sir? Can you possibly get someone to show me to hut H?'

'Yes, I have heard enough from you. You are dismissed, and I will get Curt to show you to your hut.'

'Thank you Sir.'

I had survived my first inquisition. I was thankful that Major Richards had prepared me so well. He would have been proud of the way I had given all the details of my imprisonment. I reckoned that I had done a good job. I now would be able to relax and learn more about being a POW. Fortunately none of the Luftwaffe officers in Hut H knew me, and I had never met any of them.

After two days, the monotony was starting to get to me. How on earth did they put up with this lack of activity, week after week? There was nothing to do. First thing every morning there was a bit of activity as we all had to go on parade. They checked the numbers to make sure that nobody was missing. During the day, some of the men played football; others did exercises to keep fit and others read the few books that had been sent from home. There was also a drama group who were rehearsing a play. I was amused to see that all the female roles had to be played by male prisoners, but there was still a problem in getting people to play the female parts. It wasn't considered manly, and there were a lot of comments which weren't flattering. I was darned glad that I was only programmed to stay a week in this hell hole.

The following Wednesday I was slipped a piece of paper by one of the guards. I went in search of a quiet place where I wouldn't have company and opened it.

Thursday, at around eleven o'clock, you are to pick a fight with a prisoner and create a significant disturbance. You will be arrested and locked up. That night you will be removed from the camp and taken away. This is your ticket out. Destroy this note after reading it.

I had been wondering how they were going to get me out without causing suspicion. This was quite an ingenious plan as they then could tell the remaining prisoners that I was a trouble maker and, for the second time, I was being moved.

After the parade the following morning, I decided to join the football game. I reckoned that it would be easier to pick a fight in a game when emotions would be running high, than just walking around the compound.

I was quite aggressive in my play and feathers were getting ruffled on the other team. Finally, I made a nasty tackle and the player that I had fouled squared up to me. This was just what I wanted, so I hit him. One of his team members came to his rescue and started throwing punches. My team members gathered around to support me. There was a monumental brawl.

The guards were standing by waiting for the fight to start, so they quickly moved in.

'Who started this?' Sergeant 'Mad-dog' shouted.

'He did,' the man that I had first hit replied, pointing at me.

'Yes, it was him,' his other team members shouted, now all pointing at me.

The guards frog marched me out of the fenced off area to the cell where I had been locked up on my arrival. Lothar had been long since released back into the camp, and it was empty, so I had nobody to talk to.'

Safely locked up, I stayed there for the remainder of the day. A few hours after sunset they came to get me. I was loaded into the back of a truck and driven out of the camp. A few miles from the camp, the truck stopped, and I was transferred to a car which took me back to Witley Park. My time in a Prisoner of War camp had come to a successful end.

As I went in through the entrance door of Witley Park, I smelt the odour of tobacco smoke. Major Richards duly greeted me.

'Welcome back again Markus. Did you have an enjoyable time in Taunton?'

'Let's put it this way, I survived and am alive to tell the tale.'

'Get changed out of those clothes and meet me in the bar. You can then tell me how you got on as a prisoner. You are too late for dinner.'

Chapter 36

I went to my room and changed into casual clothes and joined the Major in the bar, relieved to be back in civilisation. What a contrast to the POW camp in Taunton. Here, I was treated as an individual and had a lot of perks such as proper food and a drink when I wanted it. So far my decision to work with the British was paying off.

'Will you have your usual beer Markus?' the Major asked me as I joined him at the bar. 'I think that you have earned it.'

'That would be very welcome thank you. My life at the camp was basic to put it mildly, and I felt under pressure the whole time that I was there.'

'Well you can relax now until you set off for France.'

The first beer went down extremely smoothly and the second and the third. I hadn't had any dinner, and the meal that I had eaten at the camp was meagre, to say the least, and a long time ago. I was getting drunk, and by midnight I was more than drunk. In fact, I hadn't been as drunk since my student days in Kiel.

The next thing that I knew I was being shaken awake and dragged out of bed. I learnt later that the Major had ordered a few of the trainees to take me to my room, remove my outer clothes, and put me into bed in my underclothes. I don't remember any of what happened, I was too drunk

Rudely pulled from my bed, my head was still spinning from the drink. It was dark so I couldn't see who was pulling me out of bed. They didn't stop there. They dragged me unceremonially out of the room, down the stairs and brought me to a room at the back of the building. I was tied to a chair and they left the room, leaving me totally on my own.

I hadn't been in this particular room before even though I had been living in the house, off and on for at least four months. It was about four meters wide and five meters from front to back. The door was facing me. A single glaring light bulb lit the room. The walls were painted a hideous pale hospital green. The same disinfectant smell that had been in the guard house at the POW camp pervaded the air. What was going on? There hadn't been one word uttered during the process of dragging from my bed into this barren room. Roped into the chair, wearing nothing but my underclothes, I was feeling extremely vulnerable. The worst part of it all was that I had nothing on my feet, and the floor was made out of flagstones. The cold was intense as there was no heating in the room.

My senses started to come to life as the effects of the alcohol wore off. I now had another problem. Having had so much beer to drink the night before my bladder was full. It was most uncomfortable as I fought the desire to get rid of the liquid. I held back as long as possible, but in the end I had no choice, my bladder won over my desire not to wet myself, and I let it go. The release was immense, but I and the room was now stinking of urine and I was saturated from the waist down.

There was no window in the room, so I had no idea what time it was or how long I had been incarcerated. What seemed like hours later I heard the door being unlocked, and I expected a person I was familiar with to come through the door and tell me that it had all been a terrible mistake.

A totally unknown officer came through the door. He was dressed in a Captain's uniform, had thin angular features and had the appearance of an undertaker. He looked down at me and wrinkled his nose.

'Oh you filthy creature you have pee'd all over yourself and the floor. I will have to get this cleaned up before we can start.'

He stormed out, slamming the door behind him.

That certainly didn't make me feel any better. I had expected a friendly face and all I got was a scowl and a strong rebuke. I was still none the wiser as to what was going on.

The door opened, and a Private entered with a bucket of water and a mop. He threw the bucket of cold water over me and then mopped up the mess on the floor. I now had water dripping off me, and I felt even more uncomfortable. If I had felt vulnerable before, I was now starting to get genuinely worried. He sprinkled disinfectant around the room and left.

The door opened again, and the unpleasant officer re-entered. He sat down opposite me. The Private who had cleaned up my mess took up guard duty just inside the door. He also didn't look too happy.

'Name?' he barked at me.

'Lieutenant Markus BEKER.'

'Why are you lying to me Oberleutnant?'

'What do you mean, lying to you?'

'Don't answer back. You are an officer in the German Luftwaffe.'

'Yes, I was an officer in the Luftwaffe, but I am now in the British army as Major Richards can verify.'

'Don't be stupid, how could you transfer from one army to the other? You are lying.'

'But it is the truth. I have agreed to work for British Intelligence.'

'That is absolute rubbish. Don't you think I would have been told if you had changed sides and were now working for the British?'

I just sat there in total disbelief. Was this man a raving lunatic, or had I done something to undermine the trust that Major Richards had placed in me?

'I am going to leave you here, to think over your situation. I will come back later, and you had better decide to tell me the truth.' He got up and left the room together with the Private. I heard the key turn in the lock, locking me in.

I was still tied to the chair. I was soaked from the waist down, I was sitting in a pool of water, and, with my bare feet on the cold floor, I felt totally exposed and naked. My mind was totally confused, and I didn't know what to do or say. I had never known despair in my life, but in the space of a few hours my whole life had come tumbling down around me. What did this horrible man want me to say and how could I get him off my back?

They left me sitting there for what seemed to me like hours. I had no way of knowing what time of the day or night it was as the room had no windows. Eventually I heard the lock being turned, and my persecutor came back in plus his trusty Private.

'What year were you born in Lubeck?' He started asking me totally different questions.

'I was born on the 5th February 1917.'

'Do you have a twin brother?'

'Yes.'

'Where is he now?'

'He was killed in the Battle of Britain in July of last year.'

'Did you kill him?'

'No, in fact, he was the one that shot me down.' Where were these questions leading? I didn't like the fact that they had brought my brother into it.

'I know that he shot you down, but you then killed him when he landed. Isn't that correct?'

'No, that is not correct. He was killed when he hit power lines and was thrown out of his cockpit.'

'That's not the truth, is it? You killed him and stole his uniform, hoping to get away.'

'I did take his tunic to help me escape. He was dead, so he didn't need it.'

'You are a thoroughly nasty piece of work to kill your own brother just to save your own skin. I'll leave you now. I will come back later to hear the truth.' He stormed out of the room with the guard. I heard the door being locked.

How could he possibly believe that I would kill my brother? Tears came to my eyes as I thought back to that fateful day last July when my brother had been killed. I, unfortunately, wasn't able to prove that I hadn't killed him, and I had switched my tunic for his to enable me to escape the scene and go to my father.

I was trapped and now feared what the outcome of this interrogation would be. Was I actually being accused of murder? All I could do was tell the truth.

I hated the waiting and the games my mind was playing. Why had I been pulled out of bed in the middle of the night and subjected to such humiliation? I had been doing so well, and Colonel Thorpe and Major Richards had been so pleased with the way that my training was going. I had been turned from being a hero into a criminal overnight.

Physically I was starting to wilt. I was shivering with the cold and feeling weak from hunger. I hadn't eaten for about a day now, and my large frame needed its sustenance. I was also becoming dehydrated from the after-effects of the alcohol I had consumed last night.

The door opened, and the interrogation continued.

'Are you going to tell me what you did to your brother?' he asked me.

'I didn't kill him. He was already dead when I removed his tunic.'

My interrogator suddenly smashed a stick down on the table, startling the life out of me, and he stood up.

'I am tempted to use this stick on you. What do I have to do to make you to tell the truth?' he shouted at me glaring into my eyes.

'I loved my twin brother, and there is no way that I would have killed him. It is exactly as I have told you.'

'I don't believe you, but continue with your story up until you got back from the POW camp in Taunton.' He sat down again and leant back in his chair, scowling but listening.

I related all that happened to me including details of my training and the events that took place in Cornwall. He didn't interrupt me, but just listened.

When I had finished, he leant forwards in his chair, putting his arms on the table that stood between us and steepled his fingers.

'What is your name?'

"Lieutenant Markus BEKER assigned to British Intelligence.'
'Are you sure? Do you not want to convince me that you are Oberleutnant Markus BEKER of the Luftwaffe?'
'No, I am now a member of British Intelligence.'
He got up from his chair and leant towards me across the table. I thought he was going to hit me. Instead, he smiled.
'Well done Lieutenant you came through that test remarkably well.' He came around the table to untie the ropes binding me to the chair.
My mouth dropped open, and I was speechless for a few moments.
'What do mean it was a test,' I finally gasped, highly annoyed at what they had done to me.
'I am sorry for what you have been through, but we needed to see how you would bear up under interrogation and out of your comfort zone. I was asked to come and put you through a few hoops. Let me go and get Major Richards as he has been a bit concerned for your welfare and state of mind.'
The guard followed him out and came back a few minutes later with a cup of tea for me.
My interrogator and Major Richards came back into the room.
'How are you feeling Markus after what we have put you through for the last twelve hours? The only way of demonstrating what an extended period of interrogation does to you was by letting you experience it,' the Major said genuinely apologetic.
'I suppose getting me drunk last night was part of the process?' I enquired.
'Yes, we wanted you to be as inconvenienced and as uncomfortable as we could make you'
'Well all I can say is that you did an extremely good job of it. I have never felt so humiliated and uncomfortable in my life. At no time did I get any indication that it was a test. I was convinced that it was for real, especially when he started accusing me of murdering my brother.'

'I think that we have kept you long enough in this room. You probably would like a hot bath, some warm clothes and some food?'

'Can you please tell me what time it is?'

'It is 6:00 pm, so you have time to have a bath before dinner. I am sure that you are hungry.'

'I can safely say that I have never been hungrier, and my body is crying out for food.'

'I'll see you in an hour then.' I grabbed a blanket that had appeared from somewhere and wrapped it around me as I left my place of torture.

Chapter 37

I have never enjoyed a bath more. After the events of the worst day of my life which had started around 4:00 am the previous night, soaking in a hot tub restored my self-esteem and confidence.

As I lay there, I thought back to the hell I had endured. At one point, I had thought that my freedom was at an end and that I would be incarcerated for the remainder of the war. If they had pinned the murder of my brother on me, I might even have been imprisoned in a gaol, rather than in a POW camp.

When they finally had told me that it was just a test, a weight had been lifted off my shoulders, and I had been brought back into the real world. How could they have done such a thing to me without giving me any prior warning?

Eventually, I managed to work up the courage to leave the sanctuary of the now quite cold water, and dry off. After dressing in warm clothes, I went down to eat dinner.

Major Richards asked me to join him at the table where he was sitting with my interrogator.

'You can join us here Markus, and we promise not to talk about the events of today. I will go over the experience with you in the morning after breakfast. The Colonel will be with me'

'I appreciate that Sir. I need to unwind for a bit now, and I don't think that I want another beer for quite a while.' I smiled.

'I won't be here in the morning and would like to give you one comment before we drop the subject,' my interrogator said. 'You stood up to me remarkably well and didn't let me bully you. Don't let the person doing the interrogation get the satisfaction of feeling that they are intimidating you.'

'Thank you Sir. I'll remember that if I ever should be captured and interrogated.'

After dinner, they went to the bar; however, I declined and retired to my bed to get some well-earned sleep.

In the morning, I spent a good two hours relating my experiences to Colonel Thorpe and Major Richards. They spent more time analysing the feelings and state of mind I had experienced during the process than they did on what I had actually said.

'What we tried to show you yesterday is how your body affects your mind when it is out of its comfort zone,' the Colonel observed.

'We got you drunk so that you would start off at a considerable disadvantage. You were placed in a hostile environment and were only wearing your underclothes. You also had no socks or shoes on. To make it even worse you had no option but to pee all over yourself and then you were doused with cold water.'

'I felt intensely uncomfortable and at a great disadvantage. It was also a highly embarrassing experience when I peed all over myself and the floor.'

'Was it made worse by not having anything on your feet?' the Major asked.

'Definitely, I felt vulnerable and exposed. I might as well have had no clothes on. I couldn't have felt more naked, even if they had taken my underclothes off. It was a strange feeling and made me feel extremely threatened.'

'It is all part of the process of breaking down your defences. If you ever get caught Markus, remember that they will try to humiliate you in whatever way they can. It is extremely difficult to be strong sitting there with no clothes on.'

'It's a darned good reason for making sure that I don't get caught.' I gave a wry smile.

By the time I was finished, the debriefing I had a totally different understanding of what I had been through. I had to agree with them that the only way that I could have gotten the experience was to be subjected to the mock interrogation. I was extremely grateful that I wouldn't have to go through the process again.

For the next eight days, I worked hard perfecting my story. I now knew how word perfect I would have to be if I was going to survive an interrogation by an expert. My experience in the pale green room had sharpened my desire to learn.

On Saturday the 5th April, I was called into the Major's office. 'Do you think that you are ready to be sent back to Europe Markus,' the Major asked me.

'I am probably as ready as I will ever be.'

'The Colonel and I have discussed your status in considerable detail, and we believe that you are as ready as you ever will be. We also have a favourable weather forecast for Thursday 10th April, which is the date that we have tentatively selected for you to leave. How do think that sounds?'

'To be perfectly honest it will be a relief to be at the point when I can leave. I am ready to go.'

'That's what I hoped you would say. We have arranged for you to transfer to Poole in Dorset tomorrow. You will meet up with your old friend Sergeant Young, who is already there. He has found a boat for you, so that is why you are going to Poole. You need to get familiar with it. He will then be in charge of getting the boat and you to Yarmouth on the Isle of Wight. You will set out from there for France on the evening of the 10th April.'

'That sounds really good. Will he do something with my personal things that I will have to leave behind me?'

'Yes, he will bring all the items that you can't bring with you back to us here and we will keep them for you.'

'Will he be with me on the fishing boat that takes me across the Channel to Cherbourg?'

'Yes, he will stay with you until you leave the trawler which will be close to Cherbourg.'

'That takes a load off my mind. I trust him and know that he will make sure everything is under control, and he will do his best to make sure that I reach land safely.'

'I will have a final meeting with you this afternoon to cover any remaining details, such as the process of getting information back to us here in Witley Park.'

'Thank you Sir. I am very relieved to be under starter's orders at last.'

I left his office and went for a walk in the grounds to get my thoughts straight:

Was everything going to go to plan or would I end up being shot as a spy? Did I have the knowledge and courage required to succeed as a spy? Was I doing the right thing in turning against my former country or should I just go back to my squadron and fly for Germany? Would my mother and grandfather in Lubeck brand me as a traitor or would they understand why I had changed sides?

My thoughts strayed to Francette who was now somewhere in France acting as an agent. *I couldn't let her down. She believed in me, and we had arranged to meet again when we were both back in England.*

Then there was my twin brother Chris who had been killed last July. *I had promised my father that I would work for the British because of my involvement in Chris's death. For all their sakes, I had a duty to go through with it.*

I returned to my room to pack, having convinced myself that I had made the correct decision.

Chapter 38

Needless to say, I didn't sleep much that night as my brain was covering all eventualities, only slipping into a deep sleep around 4:00 am. I was shaken awake at 7:00 and had to rush to be ready to catch the train in time to get my connection to Poole. I had to take a train from the local Witley station to Woking where I changed for the Poole train. I just made it and arrived at Poole as arranged at midday where Sergeant Paul Young was waiting for me.

'Good morning Sir,' he said as he gave me a salute. I saluted back.

'Good morning Sergeant. We meet again on the last leg of my long journey.'

'I have booked us into a small hotel, close to where the boat I have purchased for you is moored. I have organized some lunch for us there and will take you on board afterwards.'

'That sounds like an excellent plan. How do we get to the hotel?'

'It's within easy walking distance so we will walk if that is alright with you.'

As we walked through the town, I looked around me, lost in my thoughts. Poole was very different to any other places that I had previously seen in England. There was no bomb damage that I could see and all the old buildings, which oozed character, were remarkably well preserved. We emerged onto the quays where there were a lot of small boats moored. Poole appeared to be situated at the head of a large inland lagoon, and there was water as far as I could see. In the distance, at the far end of the lagoon, I spotted a narrow inlet which presumably was the outlet to the sea.

As we walked along the quayside, the Sergeant pointed to a yacht moored parallel to the quay alongside two other boats.

'There's the boat that you are going to use. It's called *Olympus* and is twenty one feet long. It was made in 1928, so it is still quite seaworthy. I reckoned that it was perfect for the task in hand.'

'It's a lot bigger than the Firefly that I sailed on the Derwent Reservoir, and it even has a small cabin,' I commented.

'We'll take it for a spin after lunch and see how you like it. After your experience of sailing the dinghy, you will find it remarkably easy to handle this one. Let's hope that there is a decent wind later as it is a bit gentle at the moment.'

'I would prefer to have a gentle breeze for my first sail.'

We passed a ferry terminal, and I noticed from the signs that the ferries went from the quay to Brownsea Island, which I was told was the large island I could see in the middle of the lagoon.

I dumped my bag in my room and joined the Sergeant in the restaurant of the hotel. Fortified by a particularly good lunch consisting of extremely fresh fish, I then changed, and we set off for my first sail in *Olympus*.

The first lesson that I learnt was, you don't put up the sails in a larger yacht until you have left the mooring. I was shown every aspect of the boat including how to prepare the engine for starting and what each rope was for. I was given the proper names for everything, but promptly forgot them. There was far too much to take in all at one session. After a while, I was just about able to come to terms with the fact that the left was '*Port*' and the right was '*Starboard*'.

I also experienced the effects of a much larger current than I had met before. When we released the boat from its mooring, we were swept by a strong current away from the quay and towards the open water. There was a real danger that we would collide with other moored boats, and I was posted on the bow, to push off from any boat we got too close to.

Eventually we reached open water, and the speed of the current slackened off. I then learnt that you had to point the bow of the yacht into the wind before you raised the sails. The motor was switched off, and silence greeted us as we hissed through the water solely under sail.

'Here you are Markus; you can take the tiller and sail the yacht. Head down the lagoon towards the exit keeping quite close to the shore as it is bit too shallow close to Brownsea Island.'

How much nicer this was than sailing the Firefly. I could stand up and look around me without the risk of falling over or capsizing. This yacht with its deep keel was in no danger of going over, and I felt a lot safer. Perhaps it would have been a bit different if the wind had been stronger.

We spent the afternoon sailing around Poole lagoon and by evening I was able to do everything on my own. We even dropped anchor to give me that experience.

Monday and Tuesday we set out early, returning to our mooring beside the quay late in the evening. The hotel supplied us with sandwiches, so we didn't have to return for food and we were able to go out through the entrance of the lagoon into the open sea. Luckily the weather behaved, and we didn't have any high winds to deal with. My stomach did react a bit to the movement, and I felt decidedly queasy on occasions; however, much to my relief, I didn't have to deposit my food over the side. My enthusiasm for lunch wasn't great, but I made up for it at dinner in the hotel.

On Tuesday evening, we took *Olympus* to a slipway, where the Sergeant had arranged for the boat to be placed on a trailer ready for transfer to the Isle of Wight on the Wednesday.

As the day approached for the start of my mission, I was getting more anxious. I had anticipated that I would find it difficult to get to sleep at night as I was mentally covering all the eventualities I was likely to encounter. To my surprise and immense relief the hours spent in the salt air cured my insomnia, and I slept the sleep of the dead. The few beers that I had each evening also might have helped.

On the Wednesday morning, an army lorry arrived, to take the yacht, and the two of us, to Yarmouth on the Isle of Wight. I was getting much closer to the hour of my departure for France, and now there were only just over twenty four hours to go. The lorry brought us to a slipway at Lymington, opposite the Isle of Wight, where we put the boat back in the water and from there we sailed to Yarmouth. For my last night in England, we stayed in a pub close to the harbour.

As we were eating dinner, at around half past seven, I got a very pleasant surprise. I smelt the scent of tobacco smoke approaching.

'Good evening Lieutenant BEKER, do you mind if I join the two of you?' It was Major Richards.

'Of course you can. You are the last person that I expected to see out here on the island.' I am sure that my face showed my surprise.

'I like to see all my charges off on their missions after all the hard work I have put in getting them trained. You can take me for a sail tomorrow and show me how proficient you are at the helm of a yacht.'

'You should be safe enough, he has been quite a good student and does remarkably well considering how tall he is,' the Sergeant chipped in.

'Can I buy you both a beer?' the Major asked us.

We sat there in the pub for a few more hours talking about anything other than the War. I made sure that I kept my intake to a minimum, mindful of my recent experience of drinking with the Major.

In the morning, I was up at 7:00 and sitting having my breakfast when the other two joined me.

'How are you feeling today Markus?' the Major asked me.

'I am slightly apprehensive about tonight, but other than that, I am in good form.'

'Everything is going to go well. The weather is set fair so the only problem may be that you won't have enough wind to sail the yacht to Cherbourg; however, you do have an engine and we will make sure that you have plenty of fuel.'

'What is making me anxious are the unknown factors. What happens if they start shooting at my boat before they realise it is an escaping German pilot on board?'

'I don't see why they would shoot as they won't see you as a threat,' the Major replied.

'Yes, but they will be surprised to see a yacht coming across the Channel from the English side.'

'Once you tell them your story, their suspicions will be answered, and they will welcome you. You do speak good German!' The Major smiled and slapped me on the arm. 'What have you got planned for us today, Sergeant?'

'We'll give *Olympus* one last thorough inspection and then go for a sail up the Solent towards the river Hamble. We can have lunch in a pub that I know at Bursledon which is up the river.'

'Sounds good to me Sergeant. I envy you guys and the so called work that you have to do swanning around in boats on the Solent.'

The Sergeant checked everything meticulously from bow to stern. The only problem he found was one halyard that was quite worn and which he reckoned needed replacing.

He called me over to show me the problem.

'I will replace this rope for you as it could break if the winds get a bit strong. I will pick one up in a chandlers on the Hamble when we go there for lunch. I need to get you a rope that has a bit of age, so nobody recognizes it has been replaced. An escaping POW wouldn't have been able to go and buy a new halyard.'

Seeing the check was over the Major asked, 'Are we able to leave the harbour now Sergeant?'

'Yes. I have finished the checks and everything, other than one rope that needs replacing, is looking one hundred per cent.'

He switched the electrics on and pressed the button for the engine. The starter engaged, and the engine turned, but it didn't start. There wasn't a single indication that it wanted to start. It didn't take long for the battery to go flat giving us another problem.

The only alternative was to get the starting handle out and try to start the engine using that. Each one of us had a go, but no matter how hard we swung the handle the engine wouldn't start. I was now in a position where my mission, starting that evening, was in danger of not having a boat to travel in.

'Have you any bright ideas Sergeant as the situation is critical,' the Major said, sucking on his pipe and looking forlornly at the engine.

'Well, the engine was working perfectly up to last night when we moored here, so there can't be much wrong with it.'

I climbed up onto the harbour wall and looked around to see if there was anybody who might be able to help us. On the other side of the river, I spotted a boatyard with the name Hales painted on the side of the building.

'Major I have located a boatyard which is within walking distance, maybe they can help us?'

'I'll go and have a talk to them. Most of these places have been stripped of their expertise by the war, but maybe they have someone who was too old to be called up,' the Sergeant said.

About half an hour later he came back towards the boat with an old man, who I hoped was a mechanic or someone who could get the engine going. The Sergeant was wheeling a trolley on which there were two batteries.

As they arrived on the quayside beside the boat, the Sergeant introduced the old man to us.

'Major, Lieutenant, this is Sam. He is a mechanic and has offered to help us start the engine. We have brought two fully charged batteries to help in the process.'

'I have also brought some new spark plugs and will fit those first before we try anything else.' Sam said as he climbed down into *Olympus*. 'The chances are that you simply flooded the engine, and the spark plugs are old and gave up the ghost.'

'Let's hope that is all it is,' the Major added.

Sam connected one of the batteries, changed the spark plugs and pressed the starter button. After one cough, the engine came alive and blew a cloud of black smoke into the harbour. We were back in business.

Sam shook all our hands and left us to it, taking our flat battery to be recharged. The Major told him that as soon as they got back he would come and settle up with the owner for what we owed him. I was extremely thankful that the problem had arisen in Yarmouth and not when I was far from land and in need of starting the engine to get to France.

The rest of the day on the Solent went a lot smoother, and there were no further problems. We picked up and fitted a new halyard while we were moored for lunch on the Hamble, and we arrived back in Yarmouth by 5:00 pm.

As I came into Yarmouth, I noticed an old fishing trawler tied up to the Quay. I suspected that my means of transport to France had arrived. The Major left us and went over to talk to the skipper of the trawler.

There was a lot of nodding and smiles and then the Major came back over to us.

'That is the boat that is going to bring you close to Cherbourg tonight. I have briefed him on what is expected of him and told him to leave at 10:00 pm this evening. That should take you close enough to Cherbourg to be released by 4:00 am which in turn will give him enough darkness to return to England by morning,' the Major explained.

'So, we are all set to go Major,' I added.

'Yes and the weather is still perfect for your mission. I am going to leave you now as I want to get back to Witley Park tonight and there is no need for me to stay here any longer. Just remember all that you have been taught, and you will come home safely.'

He went across the bridge to Hales to pay them for repairing the engine, and forty minutes later I walked over to the ferry with him and shook his hand as he left me to go on board.

With his departure, I now felt that my mission had started. The umbilical cord had been cut.

Chapter 39

The Sergeant and I had a meal together in the pub where we were staying before we returned to *Olympus* to prepare the boat for its trip across the Channel. It was an impenetrable darkness that enveloped us when we left the pub, and it took us time for our eyes to adjust to the night. The blackout meant that there were no lights showing, even at the ferry terminal. The main thought going through my mind was - *how was the skipper going to find his way out to the Needles Lighthouse in this dark.*

In discussions with Sergeant Young, it was decided that I should leave everything I didn't need for the final trip to Cherbourg, in a bag with the Landlady of the pub we had been staying in. If a German patrol vessel did happen to come close to the trawler then the *Olympus* would be pushed off with me in it, and they wanted nothing connecting me with the trawler to be left on board.

All hatches on the yacht were sealed shut, and it was tied up to the trawler and towed astern. We crept our way out of the harbour, turned to port, and headed for the Needles. I was amazed at how the skipper found his way as I couldn't see the lighthouse. When we had chugged past the cliffs at the western end of the Isle of Wight which were just visible on the port side of the trawler, we turned again and headed for France. Even though it was a fairly calm night, there was a swell that made the trawler roll slightly. I started to wish that I hadn't eaten so well. I felt decidedly queasy.

'You don't look too good?' the Sergeant commented.

'The rolling of the trawler is making me seasick,' I replied.

'That will make your story even better when you are eventually picked up. It is reasonable to assume that a Me 109 pilot stuck in a boat for several hours is going to get seasick and be totally miserable.'

'It won't be terribly clever if I am unable to sail the yacht,' I said, slightly annoyed at his comment.

'I am only being realistic. If you had sailed your yacht *Olympus* all the way from the English coast, which you are supposed to have done, then you would be in poor shape and suffering, so it is better if you suffer now.'

'Thanks; that makes me feel a lot better,' I added. I clearly wasn't going to get any sympathy from the Sergeant.

We heard the noise of a fast launch. The loud engine noise died.

'Whoever it is has cut their engines because they think that they have heard another boat. We can expect visitors,' the Sergeant whispered in my ear.

As suddenly as the engines had gone silent, they roared into action again, and a dark shape approached us. The beam of a spotlight suddenly cut the night air and illuminated the trawler. If this is a German vessel, then we were in trouble as we hadn't had time to release the yacht.

'Stop and cut your engines, we are coming over to inspect you,' a voice called out in English. Relief flooded me as I realised that it was an English patrol boat.

A rubber inflatable approached and came alongside. Two men, an officer and a rating climbed aboard while their colleagues in the inflatable covered us with their guns.

'Can I see your papers please,' the officer asked.

The sergeant handed over the papers authorising our mission.

'That seems all in order. We will just inspect the boat to make sure that there is nobody else on board, and you aren't carrying anything illegal,' the officer added.

They gave the boat a quick once over and then got back into the inflatable.

'You can proceed and good luck on your mission.' The officer saluted and went back to the patrol boat. We all breathed a massive sigh of relief.

'We had all better have a swig of whiskey after that,' the skipper said as he handed us a flask. 'I keep this on board for medicinal purposes.'

At 3:30 am, Sergeant Young informed me that it was time that I got ready as I would be released in about twenty minutes. He explained that the distance to Cherbourg was approximately five miles and that they were releasing me in a position to allow for the strong current that flows in Channel.

'So all I have to do is head due south, and I will get close to Cherbourg.'

'Yes, but I imagine that as soon as it gets light you will be spotted and picked up.'

'I have no idea how to navigate a boat, so I hope that you are right.'

'Watch your compass and you can't miss. There is nothing but France in the direction that you are going.' He smiled.

Shortly afterwards the trawler cut its engines, and the forward motion stopped. My yacht *Olympus* was pulled alongside, and I got in. The Sergeant came aboard with me to help me haul up the sails and to get the engine running. The skipper of the trawler kept us head to wind while we got the boat ready.

'Keep the engine running in case you need it, other than that I think that you are ready to go.'

He shook my hand and stepped back on board the trawler taking the tow rope with him. I cast off and was under way towards France, leaving my mother hen, the trawler, behind me. The engines engaged, and the trawler turned one hundred and eighty degrees and motored back to England with a last wave in my direction. I was now totally on my own. A German pilot shot down and captured by the British in July 1940 and now returning to fly for the Luftwaffe in an ingenious escape. Would they believe me?

Compared with my experience of sailing the Firefly on Derwent Water this was a doddle and quite uninspiring. Sunset would be at 6:30 am and by then I should be extremely close to the French coast. I started to enjoy the experience although I was still suffering from sea sickness.

I had plenty of time to think of what faced me in the morning. One of my main thoughts was - *what if there is fog and I can't*

see the French coast and also if the visibility is poor, the
patrol boats won't be able to see me?

I needn't have worried as dawn brought a beautiful sunny morning with exceptionally good visibility, and I could see the port of Cherbourg in the distance.

So far so good.

Chapter 40

I heard the sound of a fast boat before I saw it. Focussing on where the noise was coming from, I eventually saw a heavily camouflaged vessel emerge from the background of the coast. In fact, I spotted the large bow wave before I made out the shape of the boat.

I steeled myself for the encounter with my fellow countrymen that was about to take place. The bow wave headed straight towards me until the patrol boat stopped about forty meters away. An officer shouted to me through a loud-hailer.

'Turn around and get away from this area, it is protected and no civilian boats are allowed to enter Cherbourg.'

I stood up in the boat and shouted back to him, 'I am a German pilot who was shot down and captured. I have escaped from custody in England. Can you take me on board?'

He obviously didn't hear me and continued to shout, 'Turn around and go away, or we will have to sink your boat with you on it.'

I took off my jacket and pointed to my Luftwaffe trousers and my shirt. 'I am a German Officer, please take me on board.' I put my two hands together in a mock prayer.

He obviously still couldn't hear me, so he ordered his vessel to move closer to try and find out what I was saying. The sinister grey patrol boat with its powerful throbbing engine moved to about ten meters away from where I was standing in the cockpit of *Olympus*. It towered over me.

The officer came down to the guard rail and leant towards me. 'What was it that you were trying to tell me?'

'My name is Oberleutnant Markus BEKER, and I am a Luftwaffe officer who has escaped from England and I have just sailed across the Channel in this stolen boat.'

He quickly realised that I was speaking flawless German. We will come alongside and decide what we are going to do with you.

I had been so absorbed in my rescue that I hadn't heard the aircraft. In the same way, the crew of the patrol boat had been focusing so much on me that they had also missed it. Too late we realised that we were about to be strafed. A Spitfire came in a dive out of the sun towards us with its guns blazing. Panicking as I had no cover, I jumped over the side and swam as hard as I could away from the yacht. The patrol boat took off with its engines flat out.

Olympus took a direct hit and bits of timber flew in every direction. If I had stayed on board, I would now be history. By jumping in the water and swimming away from the boat, I had survived.

The Spitfire climbed and then swooped back down to attack the patrol boat. I watched the action from the water where I was bobbing in my life jacket. *Was I going to drown so close to the land, or would the patrol boat escape and come back for me?*

The Spitfire eventually gave up its sport of chasing the patrol vessel, and it, in turn, came back for me. They used a boat hook to unceremoniously drag me from the water soaked through and unusually heavy from the wet clothes. I looked around the patrol boat, checking what the damage to the patrol boat was like. I was informed that none of the crew had been injured, and the patrol boat would be able to make the port of Cherbourg, under its own power.

The officer took me down below and found some dry clothes which miraculously fitted my large frame. He then organized some coffee for us.

'That was too close for comfort,' he said to me as we sat down at the table in the cabin that they used as a mess. 'Luckily none of my men was injured in the attack, but we did receive some hits.'

'I am sorry for putting you and your crew in danger,' I said in an apologetic tone.

'We should have been more vigilant. Unfortunately, we were all focusing on you as it is most unusual to find a pilot sailing a yacht first thing in the morning.' He smiled.

'I escaped from a POW camp in the South of England, stole a boat and sailed across the Channel. I managed to find France more by luck than good navigation, so I was extremely glad to see you heading towards me this morning.'

'I had better go up on deck while we enter the harbour. There will be a lot of explaining to do when we tie up. If you want to join me on the bridge, you may. You will get a good view of the port as we go through the booms.' We both finished our coffee and headed up to the bridge.

It was evident that Cherbourg was quite a significant port as there was a lot of naval activity. The harbour was protected from the sea by two booms, positioned to prevent attacks by submarines and other enemy vessels. There was a portion of the boom which was opened for us so as we could enter the port. We motored over to a part of the harbour where there were a quantity of other patrol boats moored.

As we tied up, there were a lot of comments from other sailors gathered around the other vessels. They were all eager to find out what had happened and how we had suffered the damage.

'If you come with me, I will introduce you to the officer in charge of the port, and he can decide what he does with you. I will have to fill out a report of the attack by the Spitfire and complete a lot of paperwork.'

During the walk from the harbour into the town, I noticed that there was quite a lot of bomb damage.

'I see that there is evidence of bombing in the harbour area. Do you get many raids?' I asked the skipper who had rescued me.

'We get a few days of bombing from the British, and then they seem to forget about us for a while. It is almost as if we are at the bottom of their list of priorities and they only come if they have nothing else on.'

'You would think that Cherbourg would be bombed every day as it is very close to the South Coast of England.'

'There isn't a lot to interest them here, and I suppose that they have a lot of higher priority targets elsewhere. Believe me, when you have to live through a raid you know all about it. We don't want any more.'

We eventually arrived at a building festooned with German Swastika flags. On entering, my guardian brought me over to a desk where he told a man in uniform to arrange an appointment for me to see the Kommandant. I was shown an area where there were some benches and was told to wait.

Clearly I was wasn't considered high priority as I had to wait at least two hours before I was told to go up the stairs and knock on the Kommandant's door. A lady in uniform came to the door and brought me into an outer office. After two hours, I still hadn't reached the Kommandant, but at least I was getting closer.

This time my wait was a lot shorter, and, after about ten minutes, I was ushered into the presence of the Kommandant.

Totally bald and with wire frame glasses, he looked to be in his fifties. He had a round bald head, a round body and would have been a funny person if he hadn't been the Kommandant.

'You want to see me,' he barked at me. 'I am a busy man so make it quick.'

I gave him a summary of my story. How I was a German pilot, shot down in the Battle of Britain, interrogated for two months, and then held as a POW. I explained that I had managed to escape, steal a boat and sail as far as Cherbourg.

'That sounds quite a story and I congratulate you on escaping. What do you want from me?'

'Well, I have no papers so can't travel, and I want to return to my squadron as soon as possible. Are you able to issue me with papers, Sir?'

'The easy answer to that is No. You will have to go to the SS to get papers. I will ask my secretary to type out a letter to the

SS branch in charge of issuing papers, and there shouldn't be any problem.'

'Thank you Sir, I am extremely appreciative of your help.'

'You can wait outside while she gets the letter ready. Please tell her to come and see me when you leave my office.'

I stood up, saluted and left the room.

Shortly afterwards I was given the signed letter, and I left to try and find the offices where the SS were based. I expected that a precursor to my receiving my papers would be an interrogation, so I had that to look forward to.

Chapter 41

The SS were based in the old police station which was a dark dirty grey building set back on a side street about one hundred meters from the harbour. There wasn't even a Nazi flag flying over the building, but there were two sentries outside the door which gave away its location.

I approached the building intending to walk through the front door. One of the sentries put his rifle across the entrance barring me from entering. He didn't say anything.

'I have been told I have to report to the SS to obtain my travel documents,' I said, hoping that he would let me enter.

'Name?' he asked.

'Oberleutnant BEKER of the Luftwaffe.'

'Why have you no papers?'

'I was shot down and have been a prisoner for nine months.'

'Why aren't you with your squadron?'

'I was shot down in England and have just got back to France.'

This was getting ridiculous. I had anticipated an interrogation, but not with a sentry!'

'We have been told not to let anybody into the building today. You can try again tomorrow morning.'

And that seemed to be that. There was no way that I was going to be able to get my papers today, and even tomorrow seemed doubtful. What would I do in the meantime?

I decided that the best approach would be to return to the Kommandant's office and see if I could see him again. The soldier on duty on the reception desk was remarkably helpful and got in touch with the Kommandant's secretary. She came down the stairs to see me, and to find out what the problem was.

She worked her magic, and the outcome was far better than I could have expected. A member of the Kommandant's team was allocated to take me personally over to the offices where the SS operated, and he was to make sure that I saw the appropriate person.

Two hours later I had the necessary papers and felt a free man again. I also had been able to obtain my papers without having to endure the ordeal of an interrogation. The fact that there was someone from the Kommandant's office with me seemed to oil the wheels. I smiled at the sentry on my way out. He didn't smile back.

I went back to the building occupied by the Kommandant. I wanted to try and locate my squadron, so as I could get back to them. I saw a Major of the Luftwaffe sitting waiting in the reception area, so I went over to him. He appeared to be not much older than me.

'Excuse me Sir; my name is Oberleutnant Markus BEKER.' I saluted. I have just arrived in Cherbourg, and I am trying to find out where my squadron is so as I can re-join them.'

'Are you a pilot Oberleutnant?'

'Yes Sir, I flew 109's and was shot down in the Battle of Britain.'

'Well, don't worry about finding your own squadron, you can join mine. We are based not too far away at Caen. In fact, the reason I came to meet with the Kommandant today is to try and get a few more pilots, so it looks as if you are the first one.'

'Does your squadron fly 109's?'

'Yes, so it is absolutely perfect for you. My name is Konrad Bahm, and I am the person in charge at Caen. Welcome to my group.'

'Thank you Sir. I am delighted to find a squadron so quickly.'

'If you like to come back here at 5:00 pm, I have a car coming to pick me up and you can travel back to the airfield with me. Here is some money to buy yourself some food and a coffee while you are waiting for me.' He handed me some notes.

'That's very kind of you, I am absolutely starving. I will see you again at 5:00.' I was delighted to escape from the building and return to normality. I found a little restaurant that had some other service personnel in attendance, so appeared to be safe, and bought myself some food and a beer. It was all going exceedingly well so far, my imagination had painted a very different picture.

I returned to the Kommandant's office and couldn't see any sign of my benefactor, so I sat down and waited. After about twenty minutes, when my anxiety was starting to mount, Major Konrad Bahm descended the stairs and walked over to where I was sitting.

'Are you ready to go Oberleutnant?' he asked me.

'Yes. There is nothing to keep me here, in fact, I will be glad to get away from all this bureaucracy,' I replied.

We walked towards the harbour and eventually found his driver who was patiently waiting for him. As we approached the car the wail of sirens commenced.

'Let's get out of here; there is a raid on the way.' He started to run the last few meters to the car.

We jumped into the car, and he told the driver to get out of the port area sharpish. As we sped up the hill out of the town, we heard the 'thrump' of bombs exploding in the port area. I was back in the war where death was not far away. Eventually, we were out on the open road with the bombs left behind us.

I noticed the Major pick up a sub-machine gun which he cocked and held on his lap. Seeing the alarm on my face he explained.

'We have to travel down the whole length of the Cherbourg peninsula, and the hedges are exceptionally high. The French Resistance is active in the area, so I want to be prepared in case we are attacked.'

I thought to myself: *We don't actually stand a chance if the French Resistance fighters are hiding behind the hedges they will ambush us, and we won't see them before a hail of bullets hits the car and wipes us out.*

I was now more scared than I had ever been in my life and wished that he had not mentioned the possibility of attack to me.

Fortunately we weren't attacked, and we reached the airfield at Caen safely at around eight o'clock. The Major had his orderly show me my accommodation, and I joined him for dinner in the mess. He introduced me to the other pilots who were sitting around having a drink after their dinner.

One of the first facts that I was told was that the squadron was spending very few hours in the air as there was a severe shortage of fuel. Any fuel that was available was being stock piled in case the area was attacked. Flying was limited to just keeping the pilots' skills at an acceptable level.

As an experienced 109 pilot I was put in charge of training the recent recruits, so I got more flying in than most. The greatest advantage was that we didn't fly combat missions, so the threat to me personally was minimised. The nearest we came to danger was when we flew sorties to attack enemy shipping in the Channel, but these occasions were few and far between as they used a lot of our precious fuel. The biggest problem that we had as officers was maintaining a high level of morale. The pilots had joined the Luftwaffe because they liked to fly and they wanted to help the cause of the Fatherland. They were now based at an airfield in France, where it was too dangerous to go out into the town and where they were grounded because of a lack of fuel. Boredom set in, and morale plummeted. The only alternative to their present predicament was to volunteer to go to the Eastern front and fly against the Russians. There wasn't a long list of applicants wanting to transfer.

The Major wasn't too hard a taskmaster, so I found it the perfect place to contemplate what steps I needed to take to fulfil the main part of my mission. I somehow had to get into the squadron who would be flying the new jet engined fighter. While I was settling in to my new squadron, I was unaware that I had been seen in Cherbourg on the day that I had arrived from England. I had been spotted going between the various offices trying to get my papers.

Chapter 42

Francette Tranquet:

Francette's heart missed a beat when she rounded the corner and saw the German checkpoint fifty meters ahead. She was cycling to Cherbourg to gather information on the numbers and types of vessels that the Germans had stationed there. It was too late to turn around as it would look highly suspicious and the motor cyclist she saw parked beside the checkpoint would easily catch them. She would have to brazen it out and hope that her forged papers would get her through.

She cycled up to the barrier and offered her papers to the soldier at the checkpoint.

'Where are you going?' the soldier asked.

'I am going with my brother to Cherbourg, to see my uncle who is dying.' she replied.

'Where do you live?'

'We live in Carentan where my brother is a fisherman.'

The soldier carefully inspected her papers to ensure that they were not false. She had used them at other checkpoints before, and they had been accepted, so she was confident that they would pass inspection here.

'You know that Cherbourg is a prohibited area so I really shouldn't let you through.'

'I was aware of that, but I thought that you would allow me through as my uncle is so seriously ill,' Francette replied.

He went over to his superior officer who was sitting in a staff car parked nearby and she saw them talking for a few minutes. They looked over at Michel and her, a number of times, as they worked out what to do. Finally, the soldier came back to them.

'The Oberleutnant says that I can let you through, but I must give you a special twelve hour pass which will expire at ten o'clock this evening. You must be out of the area by then.'

'Thank you, I am extremely grateful. I will make sure that I will be out of Cherbourg by 20:00 hours this evening.' Francette added in a contrite manner.

They drew up a pass to cover the two of them, stamped it, and gave it to them. They then hopped on their bicycles and cycled away from the checkpoint towards Cherbourg, an immensely relieved pair of Resistance fighters.

It was just over a month since Francette had landed in France. She had felt extremely frightened when she had left Markus and Major Richards at the airfield in Weston-super-Mare, but had put on a brave face for Markus's benefit. Getting on board that tiny plane made her realise how dangerous her mission was.

It was an hour and a half later that the pilot indicated to her that they were in the area where he was expected to land. As they flew low over the area, there was the flash of a light from the ground. The pilot flashed a light on the underside of the aircraft to indicate to the reception committee that this was the plane that they were expecting. The next thing that Francette saw was a row of lanterns being lit on the ground, and suddenly there was a landing strip. The pilot made his approach and expertly landed the aircraft. It was extremely bumpy, but they were safe, and the Lysander was undamaged and would be able to take off.

She was helped from the plane with her small suitcase and the wooden box containing her radio. She was led from the area by two men, the plane then took off, and the lights were extinguished. The whole operation hadn't taken much more than ten minutes.

She learnt from the two men who had met her and who were now taking her back to Carentan that the field where they had landed was close to a little village called Sainteny. They came to the gate that led from the field onto a road where there were three bicycles. One of the men took Francette's suitcase with her personal belongings while she strapped the box with the radio to the carrier of her bicycle. She just hoped that they wouldn't come across any Germans on their way to Carentan. She was told that there was a curfew in operation, and nobody was supposed to be out after nine o'clock at night.

Luckily they didn't encounter any of the enemy on the way, and they reached a fisherman's cottage on the other side of Carentan without any problems just before dawn. Francette had settled in remarkably quickly in the month that followed her arrival. She spent most of her days confined to the cottage and anybody that she needed to talk to came to see her rather than vice versa. It turned out that Michel owned the cottage and that he wasn't married, so there was only the two of them living there. She sent radio messages back to England once a week. She had been told to keep her radio contacts to a minimum unless there was a serious emergency as the Germans were capable of tracking down transmitting points.

The only alarm happened one night when Michel drank rather too much brandy and became very passionate. Francette had to bring her combat training into play which greatly surprised Michel as he ended up flat on his back on the floor with a heavily bruised rib cage. He didn't try it again and, in fact, warned his Resistance friends: 'Don't try it on with Francette.'

With their twelve hour pass safely in their possession, they successfully negotiated two more checkpoints before arriving at the port area of Cherbourg. They found a Boulangerie on one of the quays where they were able to buy some croissants and coffee. Francette assessed the portion of the harbour that she could see from the Boulangerie, drawing up a list, in her mind, where the best viewing points would be. She would have to be extremely careful not to arouse the suspicion of the many German service personnel she saw wandering around.

As she was sitting there having her coffee, she suddenly froze. She spotted her Markus walking along the quay with a young naval officer. He had his Luftwaffe trousers on but he was wearing some type of tunic that she had never seen before. His head was bare, and he was looking weathered, like a fisherman. She ducked down behind a screen so as he wouldn't see her.

What on earth was he doing in Cherbourg? He must have started his mission and have somehow arrived here. She could have bumped into him on the street and what a disaster that would have been. How good it was to see him again. He vanished up into the town leaving her heart fluttering.

Later on that day, she was on her way back from the area of the harbour where the fast patrol boats were moored, when she saw him again. He was walking this time with a senior officer; they got into a car and headed off out of the town. He heart beat faster again. What a pity that she couldn't wave to him or let him know that she was here. It was painful just to ignore him.

She met Michel at the Boulangerie they had drunk coffee at earlier in the day as arranged. They jumped on their bicycles and started to ride up the hill out of Cherbourg. Just then the air raid sirens went off and they heard the whistle of bombs descending. Should they continue cycling or should they take shelter? They decided to keep going as their safest option. Their decision turned out to be correct as it was the port area that was being bombed.

Two hours later they arrived back in Carentan. Francette was in a great mood having seen her beloved Markus even if she hadn't been able to talk to him. That glimpse of Markus had shown her that she had much deeper feelings for him than she had thought. There was now another reason why she must make sure that she survived this mission and got back to England to see him.

Chapter 43

Back to Markus:

I was talking to the Major in his office one day at the beginning of May when he was interrupted by a telephone call. I listened as he talked to the person on the other end of the line. From the side of the conversation that I could hear, it sounded as if someone was asking him to choose pilots for a new squadron.

When he put the phone down I asked him as casually as I could, 'are they looking for pilots for something special?'

'Yes, that was the Kommandant at Cherbourg asking me if I could let him have one or two experienced pilots for a special project in Germany. He said that he would give me six pilots who have just finished their training in return.'

'What is the new project?' I cheekily asked.

'They are forming a new squadron at Leipheim to fly the new Me262 jet engine fighter.'

This was the moment that I had been waiting for, and it had just landed in my lap.

'Do you think that I could be considered as a prospective pilot?'

'I don't want to lose you from my team, especially as I am receiving six raw pilots who will need to be made combat ready and you are the best person to train them.'

'I would really love to apply for this new squadron if I could be spared,' I pleaded.

'I'll think about it and let you know tomorrow morning.'

When I left the Major, he was looking a bit disconsolate. I, in turn, was feeling extremely excited as I was convinced I could persuade him to let me apply for the new squadron.

The following morning, he informed me that he had given my name to the Kommandant, and he was confident that my application would be considered.

Two days later I received orders to travel to Leipheim, in Germany, where I would undergo extensive tests, medical, physical and flying, to see if I was suitable.

The first problem that they had was with my height, however, when I explained that the way I had got around this problem in the past was to have a special seat made they relented on that one. Physically I passed all the tests with flying colours, and I was also medically in perfect working order with 20:20 vision.

The aircraft that I had to use for the flying tests had to be one that I was not familiar with. The fighter that they selected for me was the Messerschmitt Bf 110 E version. I had never flown one before, but after the problems I had to overcome when flying the 109, this was a lot easier. The biggest difference was that it was a twin engine fighter and was not as nimble as the 109. If I was to pass all the tests and be selected as a pilot for the Me262, I would have to fly the 110 like a pro.

The officer putting me through my paces flew with me as it was a three seater airplane. He gave me all sorts of tasks to complete while we were in the air. I never knew what he was going to ask me to do next as he gave me no warning. This included on one occasion stalling the engines, diving and then getting them, going again. He must have had complete faith in my ability as if we had plunged into the ground, he would have been killed with me, and the heavy fighter did not have dual controls. A pleasant thought!

I had three long days where my flying skills were tested to their limits. I noticed that the number of pilots being tested gradually got fewer as the week progressed, so presumably there was a high fall out rate and those no longer around had been sent back to their squadrons. On the Friday afternoon, I landed the Messerschmitt Bf 110 after a particularly tough session and was told through my headphones:

'Well done Oberleutnant BEKER you have successfully passed and you are now a member of the squadron that will test fly the Me262. You have proved to me that you are an exceptional pilot. Congratulations.'

Out of the twenty pilots who had collected at Leipheim on the Tuesday evening, there were only four who celebrated with a drink that Friday evening. I had been focusing so much on what I was doing that I hadn't noticed the high attrition rate. One pilot had crashed a 109 on landing and obviously he had failed, but I wasn't aware why the others had been kicked out.

A thought crossed my mind: *If I had not been skilful enough to pass the tests, what would have happened to my spying mission? It would have been over before it had begun.*

I received a pleasant surprise for having been accepted as a test pilot. I was allowed to go home to Lubeck for a few days before returning to my squadron in France. I would have to report to my new role as a test pilot at the end of May. I hadn't seen my mother and granddad for a long time so it would be nice to catch up with them.

Leipheim was in the southern part of Germany, so it was a long train journey through Nuremberg, where we had been for the Hitler Youth rally's so many years ago, through Hanover and Hamburg and then finally on to Lubeck. I was mentally and physically exhausted after the few days of qualification, so I dozed a lot of the journey. There was very tight security on all the trains that I took and my papers were checked frequently even though I was in uniform. I arrived at 9:00 in the evening and by the time that I knocked on my mother's front door it was almost 10:00 and she was in bed. What a surprise she got when she opened the door and saw me standing there.

'Markus, oh how good to see you. I didn't think that I would see you again.' She hugged me and broke down in tears.

'I escaped from England and joined up with a squadron in France, and now I am going to be based at Leipheim in southern Germany. Sorry, but I had no way of letting you know.'

'Come in, come in, Markus, you must be worn out after your journey.'

We went into the kitchen where my mother started to poke the fire.

'Mum, don't bother with the stove I am exhausted and will just eat some bread before I go to bed. Sleep is more valuable than food at this time.'

'How is granddad, I am looking forward to seeing him in the morning?'

'I have some unpleasant news for you Markus. I am afraid that he passed away about four months ago. We had a very severe winter, and he caught a bad cold which went to his chest. I went in one morning to the bakery and found him dead on the floor of the bakery. Thankfully, he went quickly and didn't suffer at all.'

'It must be terribly lonely for you here Mum without any of the family around. What has happened to the bakery?'

'I am running it myself, with the help of Horst Bielenberg. He is a thirty year old man who was invalided out of the army after he had his leg blown off.'

'I wish that I was in a position to help you, but I have to return to France next Wednesday. I will help while I am here.'

'Oh, don't worry about me Markus. We have very little flour these days so we can't bake much, and Horst is well able to cope.'

'I take it that you heard about what happened to Chris?'

'Yes, a letter from your father got through, and he explained everything, but maybe you can tell me more of the details when we have a chance to talk tomorrow.'

My mother got me out some bread although there wasn't much to put on it. She gave me another hug and had another weep before we both headed upstairs to bed.

In the morning, I never heard her leave the house, and I only woke up at 10:30 am. I dressed and went over to the bakery to get what I could for my breakfast. The familiar smells of the freshly baked bread warmed my heart.

I saw for myself what my mother meant by saying that they didn't have much flour. It was no longer possible to give each customer a loaf of bread and, in addition, the loaves were now much smaller. To make the bread go around she had to cut each loaf in half. They also were now only making two basic types of bread, all the fancy stuff was now a thing of the past. I thought to myself:

This is the brave new Germany that Hitler has promised us; this is what we are fighting for. There wasn't fuel for the planes at the front, and there wasn't food for the citizens. How could Germany possibly win a war with such shortages?

It was depressing watching my mother serve the customers and seeing the sadness in their faces. Her new helpmate Horst Bielenberg was also a sad sight as he struggled around the bakery on his crutches. He told me he had been injured in the Netherlands in the first few days of the war, and had been fortunate in only losing his leg. The rest of his tank crew had been killed in the same attack.

I walked around my beautiful city of Lubeck and was relieved to see that the main part of the old town had not suffered bomb damage. Some isolated bombs had been dropped around the docks area, but the rest of the city had not been touched. As I walked, I looked at the faces of the people. There were remarkably few smiles, and there were no young people. The children were probably at school, and, anybody between the ages of eighteen and fifty years of age was off fighting on some remote battlefield. There was a look of despair on people's faces.

I would have to talk to my mother about Chris when she got home from work that evening which I certainly wasn't looking forward to. I had decided that I wouldn't tell her anything about my mission and just to give her the story of my escape and my new squadron. If anything went wrong and I was captured, they probably would come and check out my story with her. I didn't like to lie, but what she didn't know wouldn't hurt her, and it was far too dangerous to give her any information.

We spent that entire evening talking about the family and what I had been up to in England when I had been held as a prisoner. It was a very good test of my story as I reckoned if my mother didn't suspect anything then my story was good and hopefully watertight.

Wednesday came around far too quickly, and it was time to leave for Caen. I had received a message during my few days in Lubeck that I was to go to Warnemünde which was 100km up the coast from Lubeck and pick up a brand new Me Bf109 which had just come off the assembly line. I was to fly this aircraft to Caen. The big benefit of this arrangement was that it would save me a long train journey across Germany and France to Caen.

I said good bye to my mother not knowing that this was the last time that I would see her alive.

The journey by train to Warnemünde from Lubeck was painstakingly slow as I had to change trains at Bad Kleinen and Rostock and the connecting trains didn't arrive when they were supposed to. It was an overcast day with heavy showers and was dark and dreary just like my mood. If this weather was the same in Warnemünde then I wouldn't be able to fly, and I would need to stay overnight. It was, and I was delayed; however, it gave them time to adjust the seat for my height so as I could fit into the cockpit. While I waited, they showed me the assembly line where they were making the 109's.

When I woke up the following morning, I was extremely encouraged to see it was a beautiful sunny morning. I was airborne by 10:00 am heading for Cologne where I would refuel. I finally reached the airfield at Caen at 5:00 pm that evening. If I had gone by train I would only be arriving at the same time, so my extra night's delay hadn't been too inconvenient and I had enjoyed being back in the air rather than stuck in a railway carriage for over a day.

Chapter 44

For the remaining two weeks in Caen, I was kept fully occupied training the new pilots. Fuel was still extremely scarce, so flying time was kept to a minimum. I had to teach them in a class room environment which wasn't ideal as there was no substitute for putting what I taught them into practice in the air. Luckily it was quiet, and there were no attacks planned in our theatre of the War. The enemy was quite content to focus on other areas and left our area of Normandy alone.

On Friday 30th May I said goodbye to Major Bahm and left Caen to take up my new role as a test pilot at Leipheim. As the train chugged its way towards Paris, I had plenty of time to contemplate the next stage of my mission. My task was to find out all about the new Jet Engine that would power the Me262 and pass it on to my bosses back in Witley Park. As soon as I had done that I could leave Germany and head back to England via Sweden or Spain. The ideal would be steal a jet engined fighter and fly it back to England, but that probably would be a highly dangerous and unrealistic exercise.

Before I left Witley Park, Major Richards had gone into considerable detail as to how I was to get the information back to him. There was an agent with a radio who lived near Leipheim, and he would be keeping an eye out for notes from me. I had been given precise details of a large flat stone in a park beside an old castle called Stadt Leipheim Gussenhalle. I was told to put two pebbles on top of the stone whenever I left a letter under it. The agent would walk by and periodically check on the stone and if he saw pebbles on the top he would pick up the note. He then would radio the information back to Witley Park. It shouldn't be too difficult for me to arrange a reason to go into Leipheim, to make a drop. Unlike Caen, where there was danger in going into the town, Leipheim was in Germany, and I would be able to visit the bars and shops whenever we were off duty.

I envisaged that I only would need to carry out my role as a test pilot for about two months, at the maximum, and it might even be less if I got the information that I needed.

That evening we were called together by the head of the Me262 project and told what our programme would be for the next few months.

'Welcome to Leipheim,' he said. 'We are at the start of something tremendously exciting and the Luftwaffe is about to be the first air force in the world to fly jet engined fighters.'

He then went on to tell us about the enormous advantage that the new engine would give the Luftwaffe, in the battle against Germany's various enemies.

'You four gentlemen will be remembered for your outstanding achievement in being the first pilots to fly a jet propelled aircraft. Congratulations on being selected for this exciting challenge.'

'When will we get a chance to fly the plane?' one of my colleagues asked.

'There is a slight problem in the development of the engine, and they don't have a working model ready yet; however, the air frame is ready and has been fitted with a conventional engine and propeller in the nose. You will be able take the new plane into the air and become familiar with it. We need to check the air frame out before the new engines are fitted. Next month, the jet engines are expected to arrive.'

'Have the new engines been tested in the air?' I asked.

'No, you will be the first ones to test the engines in flight mode, but I do have a good piece of news for you. The first planes will also be fitted with a conventional engine as a back-up. If both the jet engines pack up for any reason, you will simply start your old engine and use it to land.'

'How many planes will there be at the start?' one of the others asked.

'There will be one to start off with and then, when more engines are available, we will have one for each of you. After your tests, which qualified you for your new job as a test pilot, you have been ranked 1 to 4 depending on your competency. The person at number 1 will do the first jet engined flight and at the moment that is Oberleutnant Fritz Wendel. We will continually review the list based on your day to day flying.'

The following morning we were introduced to the Me262. Sitting on the airstrip outside the hanger it looked a beautiful looking beast. Painted the dark Luftwaffe grey it was extremely streamlined and sleek. It was a really well designed aircraft even if it did look slightly odd with a conventional propeller engine fitted in the nose and blanks where the jet engines should have been. I was very impressed with the new plane. This was the only jet engined aircraft that the people looking at the fighter had seen so they couldn't make any comparisons. I was in the privileged position of having seen the Gloster Meteor, the British equivalent. The Me262 definitely looked the better plane, but it obviously would depend on the efficiency of the engine, the speed it could go at and its manoeuvrability.

In the ranking of pilots I was number three, so would be third to fly the new plane. In fact, they moved me down to number four as I had the usual seat problems and they had to adjust the seat before I took my turn. The following day they let me fly first which saved them having to adjust the seat again, and that was the pattern for the following days.

Finally, the noise of jet engines assaulted my ears. A Me 262, fitted with jet engines, had arrived, and I was able to write my first note to be placed under the stone at the castle in Leipheim. I used the code that I had been trained in, so, to an untrained eye, it looked gibberish

Me262, twin engined fighter, first aircraft delivered, 2 jet engines and one conventional engine per plane, No specs yet.

I took a trip into the town in the evening and placed the note under the stone, leaving two pebbles on the top as arranged. It was easy, and there was nobody else around.

When I went back two days later the pebbles had gone from the top of the stone, and the note was gone. The system was working.

I was watching when Fritz Wendel, still ranked top pilot in our small group, attempted to take off for the first time on the 18th July. In fact, when the plane was roaring down the runway, he had to pile on all his brakes and come to a screaming halt as there was no lift. The air from the engines was blasting over the aileron on the tail which in turn forced the plane back onto the ground. After a discussion with the designers, he tried again. This time he touched the brakes at take-off speed, and this overcame the problem. He took off with a roar into the skies over Leipheim. I was witnessing a whole new era in flying.

Shortly afterwards he landed safely, and we all ran over to where he had parked the aircraft to congratulate him. There was a sudden deathly stillness when the engines were switched off, giving our ears a rest.

I wrote in code: *First test flight of Me262 with jet engine today; Successful; More test planes arriving in next few weeks; Impressed with the design.*

I went down the town that evening and dropped the note off in my 'letter-box'.

It was all going too well. Near the end of August, a serious incident occurred that caused a significant upset to my plans.

The third test plane arrived and was allocated to me to test. The first two Me262's had been giving a lot of problems and both the pilots had needed the propeller engine to get them home on a few occasions. The jet engines were simply not reliable enough and kept cutting out. One engine failing was not a serious problem as the plane could land on just the one, but if two cut out then the pilot had to start the conventional engine, and this took a little while as the plane descended towards the ground.

As luck would have it, on my first trip, both engines failed. I had taken off without any problems, and, as it was my first flight, I had decided only to make one circuit of the airfield before landing. It was totally different to any other flying that I had done as everything happened so much faster.

As I was on my way in to land, both engines failed. I was in the final stages of my approach, and there was no time to start the conventional engine. The plane lost speed rapidly and started to nose dive into the ground. I used all my strength and height to pull the nose up, and the plane belly flopped into the ground. That is all I remember until I came around in an ambulance heading for the hospital.

I looked up and saw an orderly looking down at me. I tried to move.

'Don't try to move Sir. You've had an accident and have a broken ankle and goodness knows what other damage.'

I tried to talk, but I was still too dazed and couldn't form my words. I lay back in considerable pain feeling the blood congealing on my face.

At the hospital, I was brought directly into the operating theatre where I was greeted by an elderly surgeon.

'We are going to knock you out and re-set that ankle of yours and we will also check whether anything else is broken or out of place,' he said, poking at my right leg at the same time.

The next thing that I remember is waking up in a hospital bed with my right leg up in the air. As usual when bad things happened to me the smell of disinfectant assaulted my nostrils. As I regained consciousness I started to feel pain in other areas of my body, but I was alive.

They gave me pain killers to try and neutralize the pain, but as well as getting rid of the pain they made me sleep. That evening I was agreeably surprised when the other three test pilots came into my ward and approached the bed.

'Hi Markus, how are you?' one of them asked me.

'Not too good I am afraid, but I am glad to be alive. When the engines failed on my approach, I thought that I was a goner.'

'We were all watching, and we also thought it was the end of you. Those bloody engines will be the death of all of us, they are so unreliable.' Fritz Wendel added.

'The boss has grounded the other three aircraft until they can sort out the stalling problem,' one of the others said.

They stayed with me for a few more minutes, but I couldn't keep my eyes open, and I started to drop off to sleep again. Seeing that I was exhausted they left. They came to see me in relays after that and I enjoyed their company.

Three weeks later I was released and spent the next month hopping around the airfield on crutches. I obviously wasn't able to travel into the town, to put any more notes under the stone, during that time. I was given the task of writing up all the reports that had to be compiled after each test flight and of reporting back to the designers. I was based in an office, and the pilots used to have to come and see me after each flight and give me a full report. From an information gathering point of view it couldn't have been better as I was getting all the data I needed to report back to Major Richards, the only problem was that I couldn't get into town to the drop-off point.

Finally, I did make a report.

I wrote in the code: *Sorry crashed and was in hospital; New engine very unreliable; Major engineering problems; Uses a lot of fuel; Top speed 500 km; Not very manoeuvrable; Climbs well; Engines overheating; Major re-development required; Long delays; Shortage of spare parts.*

I got one of the support staff to drive me into the town around 5:00 pm and hobbled from the centre to the drop-off point. Bending down to place the note under the stone was a considerable problem. Having fallen over once I finally managed to do the job, I then went back to the centre of the town to get my lift back to the airfield.

Chapter 45

By the middle of October, my ankle had improved to the stage where I was able to hobble around without the use of crutches. I still was not fully mobile, and certainly wasn't strong enough to make a long trek to either Sweden or Spain. Because of my bad ankle I was starting to formulate a plan as to how I might be able to 'borrow' a plane and fly to freedom. I reckoned that I could take off without arousing suspicion, but obviously landing would be a problem.

From an information gathering point of view, I had more than enough at this stage. My role as the report writer for all the test pilots had given me a massive database of information on the performance of the jet engine and the Me262, and this was now stored inside my head.

After an additional three weeks of rehabilitation, during which time I received physiotherapy and did extensive strengthening exercises, I was now fit enough to undertake the walking required. I would make one final drop at my 'letter-box' and would start on my escape route one week later. Just in case I disappeared on my back to England, I would make my last report as detailed as possible. I wanted to make sure that all the essential information would get back to Major Richards in England.

I selected my escape route having decided that the safest option would be to fly to the unoccupied part of France and then walk over the Pyrenees into Spain. I had been given the name and address of a contact that lived in Lourdes, and he would organize for me to be taken across the mountains on a secure track.

I spent a considerable amount of time compiling and coding my last note, and I made my way in to Leipheim to drop it off at the 'letter-box'. As normal, I picked up two pebbles to place on top of the stone, to indicate that a new envelope was under the stone, and I approached the location. I noticed a man and a woman sitting on a bench about twenty meters beyond the stone. They had arms around each other, and I discounted them as a threat as they looked like two locals having a quiet cuddle. I thought about aborting my task, but, on reflection, didn't see any need to change my plans.

I had another good look around as I usually did, and then, seeing nothing untoward, I approached the stone, leant down and placed the note in the hiding place. Finally, I put the two pebbles on the top. I glanced at the couple sitting on the bench, they hadn't moved, so I walked back towards the entrance and the road back into the centre of Leipheim. As I turned the corner onto the main road, two men jumped out and grabbed my arms. They were two members of the SS.

I tried to fight them off.

'If you escape from us we will shoot you,' one of the men barked at me.

'We have been waiting for you,' the other said in a menacing voice.

'I was just walking in the park,' I said as confidently as I could muster.

Just then the couple who had been on the bench joined us. The man was carrying the envelope that I had just placed under the stone.

I was in big trouble now as, although it was in code, all the details of the Me262 and its engine were set out in my note. Even if they couldn't decipher the note, I would be shot as a spy.

I was frog marched along the pavement towards a car. The left hand side rear door was opened, and I was forced into the back.

Both SS men got into the back of the car, one on my left and one on my right. The male member of the twosome from the park got into the front still clutching the unopened envelope. There was no sign of the lady.

The car brought us to the local police station which was doubling as the local SS offices. I was pulled roughly from the car and then thrown into a cell. I heard a loud click as the lock was turned. The worst had happened, and I now was a prisoner of the SS.

I had always feared being captured by the dreaded Gestapo. I had heard so many stories of the methods that they used to obtain information and how people taken by them just disappeared. I was about to find out first-hand what it would be like, and I wasn't looking forward to it.

I had been caught red handed delivering the note. It would be impossible for me to plead innocence as they had the hand written note and it wouldn't take terribly long to prove that it was my writing.

There was a rough wooden bed without a mattress against one of the walls of the room on which I lay down. I closed my eyes and mentally prepared for the ordeal that lay ahead of me. The dank smell of a prison cell surrounded me.

My thought process went along the following lines:

I was clearly guilty so they wouldn't waste their time trying to prove that I was a spy. They must have captured my contact and extracted details of the drop-off point. What else were they aware of?

I anticipated that the Gestapo would want to know where the information was going and who my contacts were in whatever country I was spying for. They would also want to know why I had changed sides and had agreed to work for the enemy. Top of their list would be to find out the code I was using, so as they could find out what information was in the note that they had in their possession. Obviously they would want to know what other information I had sent back to my contacts.

My basic analysis in some way made me a feel a lot more confident. I now reckoned that I knew what I had to defend. I made a decision there and then that I would die rather than give them the information that they wanted from me. I owed that to my father and Chris. If I was fortunate, the end would come quickly.

They left me, with my thoughts, in that cell all day. The room was about two meters by three meters. It had been painted a dark green many years ago. There was a single bare bulb glaring from the ceiling. I recalled my experience at Witley Park when I had been pulled from my bed in the middle of the night and stuck in a room such as the one I was now in. Being November the temperature outside was getting near to freezing point so this room, bereft of any heating, was intensely cold. The pee pot in the corner gave off the strong smell of urine.

I glanced at my wrist watch when I heard the key turn in the lock. It was 8:00 pm.

They took me to another small room where there was a table and a chair. I was told to sit down and wait for the officer to arrive.

After another hour had passed, the door opened, and an SS officer came in accompanied by a Private who stood guard at the door.

'Oberleutnant BEKER you are a disgrace to the Luftwaffe. I want you to take off your uniform now.' He leant towards me and ripped off my shoulder flashings which indicated my rank.

I stood up and took off my uniform, which left me dressed in my shirt, underpants and socks.

'You are a traitor and a spy and will be shot. You have betrayed your fellow test pilots, and I have a good mind to get them to make up the firing squad.'

I sat there and said nothing.

'If you decide to co-operate and tell me everything that I need to know then I will spare your life and you will be sent to a normal prison. If you don't co-operate, then you will be shot. Will you co-operate.'

I continued to sit there saying nothing.

'You are a silly man. We know that your mother lives in Lubeck, and if you don't tell us what we want to know she will suffer. Surely you don't want her to suffer?'

What bastards they were. I had never envisaged that they would go after my mother. Would she understand? I still couldn't give them the information that they wanted.

'My mother knows nothing about this. She thinks that I am still an officer in the Luftwaffe, and she knows that I escaped from a POW camp in England and came back to Germany. She is also aware that I am a test pilot based at Leipheim.'

'We shall have to tell her what a scum you actually are then won't we?'

'Please leave my mother alone.'

'She will be brought to the same place as you are going. Tomorrow, you will be transferred to a castle in Munich, which is our main interrogation centre. I can tell you for certain that you will not get out of there alive unless you decide to cooperate. I will give you till tomorrow morning to make your decision. If you tell me everything, then I will not send you there, and your mother will be able to remain in Lubeck.'

He got up and left the room. I was taken back to my cell where some bread and water had been left for me.

In the morning, after a night in which I barely slept, the same SS officer asked me if I had decided to give him the information he required. I told him that I would never tell him anything.

Shortly afterwards they tied my hands and feet together and loaded me in to a car with two guards and I was driven to Munich.

I wasn't taken into the castle itself, but was taken around the back to some outbuildings which had been the stables and carriage houses for the castle at some stage. They had been converted into very basic cells. The remainder of my belongings were taken away from me, and I was issued with a loose fitting brown prison suit.

The SS Officer in Leipheim had told me that nobody got out of this place alive, so this was where I would be tortured and end my days. He had also said that they were bringing my mother here.

In the early morning, they came for me.

Two burly guards entered my cell and grabbed hold of me. I was brought to one end of the building, to a large room that looked as if it was the interrogation centre. There were all sorts of pieces of strange apparatus around the room which I reckoned I would find out all about in time. I was strapped into a chair.

The largest man that I had ever seen entered the room; he was twice the size of the guards who were large men. Wearing black trousers, leather boots and a tight fitting leather jacket he looked very intimidating. His face was large and round, topped off by an unusually tight haircut and he had muscles bulging out from everywhere. He had a very mean look. If I hadn't been scared, I was now.

He came towards me and grabbed my hair, lifting me and the chair off the ground. I winced with the intense pain.

'Do you want to start telling us something before I get going on you more seriously?' he asked me.

I was afraid that if I tried to speak I would groan or indicate in some way that he was hurting me, so I remained silent.

He put me down and then quickly picked me up again. The pain I felt doubled in intensity. He held me in one hand and slapped me hard across the face with the other.

He had plenty of ways of inflicting pain, and he kept going until finally I passed out.

I regained consciousness, naked and soaked through. A bucket of cold water had been thrown over me, to bring me round. I looked up to see an SS Officer staring down at me.

'Are you ready to talk yet?' he asked me.

I shook my head. I was in so much of a daze that I couldn't speak.

'Take him back to his cell,' he ordered the two guards. 'Your mother should arrive later, and we will see if you are man enough to talk to protect her.'

They shoved my sodden prison suit into my hands, which were tied behind my back, and dragged me back to my cell. I was thrown onto the wooden planks of my bed. They hadn't untied my arms and my legs, so I had no alternative than just to lie there, still naked.

As I lay prone on the bed staring up at the ceiling, I noticed that the light coming through a window close to the roof, way above my head, vanished to be replaced by darkness. It must be night again. They came to get me shortly afterwards.

I was firmly tied to the chair, and waited, in trepidation, for my torturer to begin his process again. Instead of the 'hulk' the SS officer came into the room and stood in front of me.

'Your decision not to give us information has now caused the death of your mother. Are you proud of that?'

'What are you talking about? I haven't even seen my mother.'

'If you had told us all you know she would be alive today.' He put his face really close to mine as he made that statement. I smelt the smell of his stale sweat.

Was he trying to scare me and was this some trick he had decided to use to break me down.

'She was being flown from Lubeck to Munich today, and the plane was shot down by your RAF friends shortly after it took off. All on board were killed,' he said triumphantly.

'I don't believe you. It is a ploy to get me to talk.'

'It is no trick and your mother is dead.' He spat this last statement out at me, turned around and stormed out of the room.

I was stunned. My mother had been killed. It hardened my resolve, there now was no way that I was going to tell them anything. This war had killed my brother and now my mother. I would be next.

I was left strapped into the chair with my thoughts for a further two hours. The SS Officer came back into the room, accompanied by the 'torturer'.

'Do I have to give Heinrich the order to interrogate you further or are you going to see sense and give us the information that we need?' he asked me.

'I am not going to tell you anything.'

The Officer left the room and my body and mind had to endure further suffering. I passed out again at some stage. He would throw water over me to bring me around and then start the process again. I was proud of myself as I was holding out and was still determined to hold out as long as I could remain in charge of my body and mind.

Chapter 46

I woke up on the bed in my cell, but didn't remember being taken there. I had no idea how long I had been tortured for. I was still just about alive, so that was a positive, but how much longer would I be able to withstand the pain. They had untied my hands, so now I was able to pull on my prison suit to cover my nakedness.

My battered and tortured body just wanted to rest, and, at this stage, I would welcome the release of death. My body and mind had suffered enough and couldn't take much more of their treatment. If I had bed clothes or something else that I could make into a rope I would hang myself; however, they had anticipated my thought process and I had nothing that I could use to kill myself.

There was no heat inside the outbuildings, and moisture glistened on the inside of the walls over the moss that had grown there. I was frozen stiff, and what clothes I had were wet through after my soakings in the torture room.

In the morning, they came to collect me and bring me back to the torture room. They retied my hands behind my back before we left the cell. I was surprised to see the SS Officer waiting for me when we entered the interrogation room.

'Good morning Oberleutnant BEKER, I want to apologise for the rough treatment that you have been receiving from the hands of Heinrich here. We should be treating you a lot better, and we haven't even given you any food to eat for a few days.'

I stood there in amazement. It was the last thing that I had expected. I actually relaxed a bit.

'We are going to bring some hot water to your cell so as you can wash and shave like a true German Officer and we will also bring you some food. We cannot expect you to behave as a Luftwaffe Officer if we do not treat you as one.'

'Thank you, I would appreciate that,' I said, very surprised by the new approach.

The ropes tying my hands and my legs were removed, and I was returned to my cell. The door of the cell wasn't locked when they left me, so I was free to go.

Should I make a run for it?

I washed in the hot water that they brought and pondered my changed circumstances.

I wasn't convinced by the change of attitude. They did bring me some food for breakfast, and they brought me a tunic to wear, but why did they leave the door unlocked. It must be a trick, and they wanted me to try to escape. They would shoot me as I was making a break for it. I would stay put and not give them that opportunity.

In the evening, I was brought back into the torture room to meet the SS Officer.

'We have treated you as an officer today, so are you going to behave like a German Officer and finally tell us what you have been up to and who your contacts are?' The friendly attitude had disappeared.

'I think that you know the answer.' I smiled.

'You will be taken back to your cell now. I want you to think very carefully about your situation. Tomorrow you will be shot if you have not agreed to give us the information and the code.' He spoke unusually slowly, making sure that I knew exactly what fate lay ahead for me.

I was taken back to my cell for the last time. I would never give them the code and the other information, so I was as good as dead. They would take me out and shoot me the following morning. I had already worked out that even if I told them everything they would still shoot me. I was dead one way or the other.

I lay down on the bed, listened to the familiar noises of the prison and shivered. Whether I was shivering from the cold or from fear I don't know, probably a bit of both.

The dominating thought in my head was:

I had let down a lot of people who depended on me; Major Richards, Chris, my father and Sergeant Paul Young, to name

four. Was there anything that I could have done? I was
probably stupid to proceed when I saw those two people
sitting on that bench close to my drop-off point. If, If, If...
Then my thoughts went to Francette. I would never see her
again. I hoped that she was safe. At least I had experienced
love in my life and had very fond memories of making love in
her bed at Witley Park.

As I lay in my bed, lost in my thoughts, I heard a noise in the
passageway outside that sounded like rats scratching at the
door. The outbuildings had plenty of openings where the rats
would be able to enter the building. I hoped that one wouldn't
come into my cell as I had fear of the horrible creatures.

The noise of the rat was replaced by the sound of a key being
inserted in the lock, so it obviously wasn't a rat. They must be
coming to get me again; perhaps this was the start of my final
moments. The guards who came to get me usually made a lot
more noise. I was curious as to what was going on.

The door slowly opened, and a person came through into my
cell.

'Markus, its Walter,' a voice whispered.

'Walter who?' I asked, anticipating another trick.

'Walter Peters, your old friend from University in Kiel,' he
replied in a whisper. 'Keep quiet, I am here to help you.'

Walter was dressed as an SS Officer.

'Here, put this on.' He handed me another SS uniform that he
was carrying.

I did what I was told and quickly pulled on the trousers, a shirt
and a tunic.

'I remember that you are a size 48, so I brought you boots to
fit.' He smiled.

The boots fitted perfectly, and I topped it all off with a peaked
SS Officers cap.

'Let's go Markus. Follow me.'

He carefully looked out the door and seeing that it was all
clear, led the way to a door at the rear of the building, which
he opened with a key. We came out on the side of the

outbuildings farthest from the main castle. He led me along paths through the wooded land that surrounded the castle until we came to a road which he told me led into the centre of Munich.

Walter stopped in a dark gateway where we couldn't be seen, and he took out a small torch.

'Markus, here are your papers. I managed to get these put together for you together with a rail pass to Frankfurt. There is a train that leaves at 5:30 am and I suggest that you are on that. You need to get out of Munich as soon as you can before they discover that you have escaped.'

'Walter, how can I thank you enough for what you have done. Will you be safe? What happens if they find out that you helped me?'

'You are the only brother that I have ever known Markus. I had to help you. It was an act of fate that I happen to be based at the castle and that I heard you were being held in the outbuildings. They won't suspect that an SS Officer with my record would do anything like this.'

'Walter, thank you so much for risking your life for me. They were going to shoot me today, and that would have been the end.'

'I know Markus. You had better get going away from this place.'

I gave him a hug and left him. About thirty minutes later I arrived at the station.

My plan was to take a train as far as Frankfurt and then find an airfield where I could steal a plane. I then would fly to the South of France.

Chapter 47

As I expected my papers were checked at the station before I was allowed to proceed to the platforms, but Walter had done a good job, and I wasn't stopped. I was a bit worried that the black eye and split lip that I had as a result of the activities of Heinrich would give me away, but there being a war on meant that there were others in uniform looking worse than me.

The train was due to leave at 5:30 am; no train arrived. This was all I needed. If they went in to my cell to bring me out to be shot, they would find that I was no longer there. The first place that they would look for me would be the train station.

I watched the hands of the station clock crawl around. Six, Six thirty, Seven...... Just as I was deciding that it was too dangerous to wait any longer the train pulled in. I climbed on board the train and found a seat in a carriage filled with other officers. Walter had fixed me up with a pass for first class as he had quite rightly assumed that an SS Officer would not travel with the 'plebs'. I reckoned that if they were looking for Markus BEKER they would not look in a carriage full of officers. In fact, when they came around checking tickets and papers they didn't even enter the carriage that I was in. I started to relax.

I closed my eyes and reflected on the events of the night.

While we had been walking together through the woods, Walter had explained to me how he had found out that I was imprisoned at the castle. He had overheard the SS Officer, who had been in charge of my interrogation, telling a colleague that he was interrogating an exceedingly stubborn Luftwaffe pilot named Oberleutnant BEKER. Later Walter had asked him what Oberleutnant BEKER was supposed to have done, and he had been told that he was a spy leaking secrets about the new jet engined aircraft to Britain.

He told me that he had only joined the SS to avoid being sent to the Russian front. He didn't approve of their methods but had to appear to go along with them in order to avoid suspicions. Walter had been praised for having cracked a terrorist cell, so he was considered a trusted Nazi. When he had heard that I was been held captive, he had decided that he had to help me escape and so he had come up with the plan that had resulted in me now being on board this train headed for Frankfurt.

If I was to survive, now was the time that I needed to put all the skills that Sergeant Paul Young had taught me, into action. My route to freedom would not be easy. This was exactly the type of situation he had trained me for.

I chanced talking to one of the other officers in my carriage and found out from him that the best airport for me to go to in Frankfurt was at Egelsbach, about twelve kilometres from the centre of the town. He said that a car was meeting him and as he was going close to the airport, so he would give me a lift.

I left the train in Frankfurt, together with my new friend, and he dropped me at the gates of Egelsbach airfield. I now had to make a plan as to how I was going steal an airplane, preferably one that I had flown before. One thing worrying me was that I always had to adjust the seat to fit my large frame, and I obviously wouldn't be able to do that in this case. I just hoped that I would fit in. My preference would be to try and steal a Messerschmitt Bf 110 which had more room in the cockpit than the 109 and also had a longer range. I had a minimum of one thousand kilometres to fly.

I had one significant advantage; I was wearing an SS Officer's uniform. All service personnel, not in the SS, were terrified of people wearing that dreaded uniform. I decided to try and get the maximum benefit from that fear.

I spotted a group of eight 110's on the far side of the airfield, well away from the terminal buildings. They had dispersed the aircraft around the airfield as we had done at Caen in case of attack. I decided to try my luck there first. I walked across to where four mechanics were working on the planes. A fuel bowser was in attendance, so obviously they were getting the planes ready for a sortie. A full fuel tank would take me over two thousand kilometres, so there was plenty of fuel to get me to Toulouse even if I got lost.

'Good morning, do you look after this aircraft all the time?' I asked the technician working on the first aircraft I came to.

He looked down at me, a suspicious look on his face.

'Yes Sir. Why do you want to know?'

'If something goes wrong we need to know who was working on the plane.' I replied, trying to make him feel uncomfortable.

'I can assure you that this plane is as good as I can make it with the parts that I am able to get.'

'Why, are there shortages?'

'Yes, we can't get a lot of the spare parts and we have to repair the old ones even when they are not serviceable. We also take bits from planes that are beyond repair.' He was now looking decidedly uncomfortable and wondering if he had said too much.

'I am sure that your officers wouldn't want you talking like that, but don't worry I won't say anything.' I now had him on my side.

'Thank you sir.'

They finished filling the last aircraft with fuel and the bowser headed across the airfield towards the buildings on the other side.

'I flew these before I joined the SS, do you mind if I sit in the cockpit just to get the thrill of it again,' I asked the mechanic.

'No Sir, go ahead.'

I climbed up into the cockpit and moved the seat back as far as it would go. I squeezed myself in and managed to sit down. Once in the seat I pushed again and obtained a little more space. I now would have enough leg room to be able to fly.

A few minutes later I was in luck. A truck came to pick up the four mechanics and they all headed back towards the other side of the airfield to the hangers leaving me on my own.

Things had gone better than I could have expected. I now had plenty of time to start the engines and take off. What's more, it was a fabulous sunny day for November, perfect for flying.

I engaged the engines one at a time, and they both started without any problems. I didn't notice any unusual activity around the terminal buildings, so there was no need for panic. I taxied out at a leisurely pace fighting the instinct to speed up. I didn't want it to look different to any other take-off that the people on the ground were used to. Having flown the 110 for my tests at Leipheim, prior to my becoming a test pilot, I was well used to its eccentricities and I had no trouble getting it into the air. Once up I headed west for France.

How easy was that? Yesterday I was a prisoner in a castle awaiting execution and today I was flying free, heading for France. Perhaps everything was going to work out after all.

I would have to fly over occupied France; however, a Messerschmitt in Luftwaffe livery wasn't a strange sight in the skies over France. The problem would be when I started to fly over Vichy France as it was a no-fly zone. It was obviously my lucky day, and I had a trouble free flight and touched down in Toulouse just over five hours later as the light was starting to fail. By the time that I was down it was quite dark. I parked my aircraft on the opposite side of the airport to the terminal and vanished into the countryside. If I had planned it, I couldn't have timed it better. If there is a God, he must be looking after me.

My biggest problem now was that I was dressed in a German uniform, in unoccupied France. If I was spotted, I would be arrested and returned to the occupied sector. What would Paul Young do now? He definitely would get hold of a change of clothes. My biggest problem in getting clothes was that Frenchmen, in general, were not as tall as I was. I decided to find somewhere to sleep and try and find some clothes in the morning.

I awoke in a barn the following morning to another sunny day and was relieved to see that French women do their washing early and hang their clothes out to dry. I had a large selection to choose from although the finished product looked a bit strange.

I made my way to the train station, successfully purchasing a ticket and I boarded the train for Lourdes dressed as a local. It was amazing to think that there was a war going on in the rest of Europe as people here were going about their daily business and there was no visible presence of police or military at the station. I had the feeling that I was getting closer to freedom.

Two and a half hours later I arrived in Lourdes and went looking for the house of my contact. His name was Bernard Guillot, and he lived at 6, rue Ramond. I had been instructed to locate the Hospital, which was right beside the station, and then follow Avenue Alexandre Marqui until I came to rue Ramond. It was not far from the station.

It was with some trepidation that I knocked on the door of number 6. The curtain moved on the window of the room that was to the right of the door. A minute later the door opened, and an old man appeared.

'Oui?' he grunted.

'The birds are flying over the Pyrenees today,' I said in English. This was the phrase that I had been told to use when I met him.

He smiled a toothless smile back at me.

'Enter mon ami,' he said as he held the door open for me.

'Thank you. I am extremely relieved to have found you.'

He brought me down a narrow passageway to a room at the back of the house.

'Meet Tom who has also arrived today. You will be leaving this evening, so you can support one another.'

Tom looked up at me suspiciously having heard English spoken with a decidedly German accent.

'Hi Tom. I speak with a German accent, but I am on your side and am escaping from Germany. My name is Markus.' We shook hands.

'Glad to meet you Markus. I was shot down over France and the Resistance brought me here to Bernard.'

'What were you flying Tom?'

'I was number two in a Lancaster, and we got hit by flak. As far as I know I am the only one of the crew who escaped,'

'I used to fly Me109's and, in fact, flew in a Messerschmitt Bf 110 from Frankfurt to Toulouse yesterday when I escaped.'

'I will bring you some food,' Bernard said, heading for the kitchen.

Just after six that evening Bernard came in with a young lad of about sixteen to tell us that we were leaving.

'This is my nephew Thibaut, and he will show you the way to the border. He will make sure that you get across before returning here. He will take you as far as he can with cart, but then you will have to walk.

We shook hands with Bernard and then went outside. There was an old horse and cart, with straw spread out on the floor, drawn up outside. We climbed on board, Thibaut took the reins, and we set off up the mountain. I was glad that we had the ride in the cart as it was forty kilometres, and it was all uphill.

After two hours, Thibaut pulled the cart into a laneway, and he tied the horse to the trunk of a small tree. He got a nosebag for the horse out of the cart put it on and then we left on foot up a narrow winding path.

'We walk now. Ten kilometres to border,' Thibaut said in faltering English. It was exceptionally steep, and it was hard to get our footing on a terribly slippery track.

The ankle I had broken quickly let me know that it didn't like this climb. It was very painful, but I was determined to keep going. Tom helped me up the steeper bits where there were just rocks.

Three hours later we came out on the top of a hill and saw the road disappear below us into the dark. Thibaut stopped.

'Is Spain Sirs,' Thibaut said, pointing downwards. 'I leave here.'

267

'Is border,' I said so as he could understand.

'Yes, back there.' He pointed behind us. 'In Spain now.'

I shook his hand and thanked him as did Tom. We were now on our own and had to make it to Gibraltar which was one thousand kilometres away at the foot of Spain.

Without Tom, I don't think that I would have made it. When I was at the end of my tether he would keep me going and when he was down I lifted him. He also spoke some schoolboy Spanish which helped us a number of times.

By various means, we made it. Using the train whenever we could and lifts from farmers at other times, we inched our way towards Gibraltar. The last leg as far as the border we did in a fishing boat which we picked up in Malaga. The whole journey took us two weeks.

Gibraltar was a hive of activity and the most active military base that I had ever seen. Fortunately there were plenty of flights returning to England and Tom, and I managed to get seats for the two of us on one leaving in two days' time. In the meantime, we slept and ate alternately recovering from our trip down the length of Spain. The impossible had happened; I had escaped from my death cell in Munich and was now a free man again.

I managed to send a coded message to Major Richards in Witley Park telling him that I was alive and was on my way back to England. I wasn't allowed to tell him where I was or when I would be flying back to England as that was all classified.

Chapter 48

It was still dark when we touched down at Kenley airfield
close to Croydon in the South of England on the 5th of
December 1941 after a long and uncomfortable flight from
Gibraltar. I said a fond goodbye to Tom, my constant
companion since leaving Lourdes two weeks ago. We
exchanged addresses and vowed to keep in touch. He was
returning to his squadron, and I didn't have a clue what I
would be up to. Perhaps they would give me some time off
over Christmas, and I could go and see my father.

I scrounged the use of a telephone, so as I could call Major
Richards.

'Hi Major, it is Markus BEKER. I have arrived.'

'Welcome back Markus. I will send a car for you, so just wait
there. Croydon is not far away from us here, so the driver
should be with you in approximately two hours.'

'Is there any news of Francette Sir?' I am extremely anxious to
hear if she is safe.

'I can't talk over the phone. I will tell you when you get here.'

I managed to scrounge a cup of tea and a sandwich as there
was no food available on the eight hour flight from Gibraltar
and I was starving. Having eaten I found a quiet corner where
I would try and get some sleep.

The next thing that I knew, somebody was shaking my
shoulder to waken me.

'Are you Lieutenant BEKER?' I looked up to see a slightly
flustered female corporal standing over me.

'Yes; are you from Witley Park?' I asked her, trying to get my
thoughts together after my deep sleep. They had obviously
changed the driver since I had left Witley Park in April as I
had never seen her before.

'If you like to follow me Sir I will take you to the car.'

They hadn't changed the rules since my previous experiences
of being driven, and the journey back to Witley Park was
silent. As I approached the house where I had been trained,

and had spent so many weeks, I got quite excited. I had completed my mission if a little fortuitously and was returning safely against all the odds.

The Major must have been waiting for me as he came out to greet me in the hallway as soon as I went through the front door. I had never thought that I would welcome the smell of tobacco, but, as he approached so did a cloud of smoke from his pipe.

He shook my hand. 'It is so good to see you back all in one piece Markus, although you do look a bit bruised around the face and you still have evidence of a black eye.'

'Do you have my bag here Sir as I could do with a bath and a change of clothes?'

'I have put you in your old room, and you will find your bag there. I suggest that you bath, change and then come down for lunch. We will start your debriefing after lunch.'

'That sounds like an excellent plan. It's fantastic to be back.' I shook his hand again and went up to my room.

Suitably refreshed and with a good meal inside me I sat down with the Major and the Colonel at 2:00 pm to start the debriefing process.

I was told that Charles Johnson, the Engineer I had worked with when I was at Power Jets, was coming to Witley Park for at least two days, and my debriefing would take a minimum of a week and maybe a little more as a lot of important people from various divisions of the services wanted to talk to me.

'Please tell me about Francette?' I impatiently asked. 'You said that you would tell me when I arrived and I am still anxiously waiting for news.'

'Do you want to tell him the news Colonel or will I?' The Major said, looking very seriously at the Colonel.

'No you tell him Major. I prefer to give out good news,' the Colonel added, also with an extremely serious face.

My heart was in my boots. I prepared myself mentally to receive the worst possible news.

'Francette Tranquet went as an agent to France and was based in the small fishing village of Carentan. She was able to report back to us that you had safely arrived in Cherbourg as she actually saw you there walking around the town. So we knew that your little sailing exercise had worked out alright.'

'But is she safe?' I reckoned that he was avoiding telling me something awful.

'Yes she is safe and well. She returned a week ago and will be back, to resume her debriefing, on Tuesday, in two days' time. She has gone to see her parents in Tunbridge Wells for a few days as her father is not well.'

I didn't mind the little trick that they played on me, just to wind me up. A broad grin broke out on my face and immense relief enveloped me.

'I see that you are pleased with our news Markus,' a smiling Colonel added.

'I was so worried as I have thought about her non-stop for the past few months or since she left on her mission.'

'With that out of the way we had better commence your de-briefing. We have specialist people who will be coming in from Monday on to talk to you; however, the Major and I want to hear your story first so as we can analyse the benefit the training had on your mission. We need to hear from you if there is anything that we left out that you needed and any other comments you would like to make. The sessions with the Major and the Colonel continued on every available hour over the weekend.

Francette arrived at Witley Park on the Tuesday as promised and we had a very happy re-union over lunch. I then had to go back into my de-briefing session and she hers until we met again in the evening.

Major Richards told us in no uncertain terms that we were to obey the rules of the house, and there was to be no 'hanky panky' at night!

I had been told that I would be allowed to go home to Yorkshire over Christmas, so I asked Francette if she would like to come with me and meet my father. Thankfully she agreed, so we made plans to travel on Monday 22nd as we both had the whole of that week off.

When Charles Johnson had finished his two day session with me, I was called into the Colonel's office. When I entered the Colonel, Major Richards and Charles were sitting at the round table.

'Sit down Markus we have a proposition for you,' the Colonel said. This time I didn't have to interrupt as I knew what a proposition was.

The Colonel continued, 'Charles Johnson would like you to join their team at Power Jets as an engineer at the start of January.'

'I asked the Colonel what you were going to do now, and he said that he hadn't decided, so I jumped in and asked them if you could be allocated to join me as an engineer,' Charles added. 'You have a lot of inside knowledge about the German jet engine and you have actually flown a jet propelled plane, so you have unique experience. We would like to have that expertise available to us.'

'I don't know what to say. This is an unexpected bonus. Of course, I would love to join your team and assist in whatever way that I can.'

'That's settled then. You can go and see your father over Christmas and then commence in Power Jets at the beginning of January.'

I left the office feeling fantastic. No more combat for me. I would be doing something I loved in a safe environment for the remainder of the war, however long that was.

Chapter 49

I sent a telegram to my father letting him know that I was back in England and that I would be going to him for Christmas. I also told him that I was bringing Francette with me.

The people coming to talk to me were like a procession, and I was kept busy hour after hour. There were officers from the RAF who wanted to know about the capability of the Me262 and when I thought that it would be fully operational. They also inquired about the airplane's vulnerable points and its weaknesses. Officers from the army were interested in its ground attack capabilities. People came to ask me about the morale of the populace in Germany and the feelings of the people against Hitler. It was non-stop, and by each evening I was exhausted.

Francette had a much easier time and was finished before me. She decided to make use of the extra days that she had off to go and visit her parents again as she felt guilty about not going to spend time with them at Christmas. I was talking to people right up to the 21st December when she joined me so as we could travel to Harrogate on the Monday.

For the first time since I returned from Gibraltar, we had time to sit together on the train and just talk about ourselves. The environment of Witley Park hadn't been conducive to talking about our future together, or even if we had a future together.

'What are you going to be involved with now Francette?' I asked her as we were settled into our seats on the train to Harrogate.

'They want me to return to Carentan or some other place in Normandy. They need a lot of information sent back about the German coastal defences in that part of France.'

'Do you want to go back?'

'Well, I don't have much option.' She replied, not looking too happy.

'Surely they can't expect you to back into danger again?'

'I am now a trained agent with experience, so I am valuable to them. There is a war on and they need me.'

'I was hoping that we could get married and settle down near Rugby where I will be working.' I put on my best forlorn look.

'I thought that you were going to ask me that question and I have been trying to work out what my answer would be.'

'Well, have you worked out an answer?'

'I have, but it is not a straightforward *Yes or No*. If I decide to go back to France then the answer is *No*, but if I choose not to go back to France, then the answer is *Yes*.

'When will you make your decision?'

'We will enjoy Christmas together, and I will take my decision before the end of the year, but it could be as late as 11:59 pm on the 31st December.' She smiled, leant over and gave me a kiss.

'I hope the answer is *Yes* as I don't fancy living without you by my side.'

'I love you with every part of me Markus, and that is why I won't marry you if I go back into France.'

We arrived at the station in Harrogate and walked to my father's bakery. I decided to go into the bakery and see him there as it was business hours and he would be fussing around the bakery.

He saw me coming and came towards me. He was about to give me a hug when he saw Francette standing beside me.

'Dad this is Francette who I told you about in my letter.'

'Welcome to Yorkshire Francette.' He shook her hand before he gave me a hug.

'I have a big surprise for you Markus, so follow me into the house. I want to show you something.'

I followed him down the passageway into the accommodation part of the house. He stopped at the kitchen door.

'I am going to tie this towel around your eyes Markus, so as you can't see. You mustn't take it off until I tell you to do so. Francette, I want you to please stay here until I come and get you.'

'What are all these games for Dad?'

'Be patient, but please play along with me.'

He tied the towel tightly so as it covered my eyes. It wasn't like him to play games so there must be a massive surprise coming.

He led me into the kitchen until I felt the table beside me. You can take off the towel now.

The room was dark, and my eyes took a second or two to adjust.

There lying on a bed against the wall was my brother Chris, smiling at me.

My heart exploded! '**CHRIS** I shouted.' I ran across to the bed and grabbed him in a bear hug.

'Chris, Chris, Chris - how on earth are you here. I thought that I would never see you again.' I was choking with emotion, and the words dried up.

'I almost was, but they brought me through, and I recovered. I am still paralysed below the waist, but they think that they can get me back on my feet eventually.'

'Let me introduce you to the love of my life, Francette.' I turned around to bring Francette close to Chris so as he could see her.

My father stood there looking at his two sons, a scene that he thought that he would never see again, grinning like a Cheshire cat. What a Christmas this was going to be.

I turned to face my father. 'Dad, when we met in the house near Harrogate at the time when they wanted my decision to become a spy, you told me that Chris was dead. That was four weeks after the accident so you must have known that he was alive.'

'Yes Markus, I did know that he was alive, but they ordered me not to tell you.'

'But I only became a spy because Chris had died.' I couldn't believe what I was hearing.

'Markus they told me that they would inter me if I didn't go along with their plan. I had no choice.'

'Don't be angry with Dad, Markus. I am so proud of what you did, and you will never know the number of pilots lives that you saved by getting the information for the British.' Chris said with great feeling. 'It makes it even better to know that you did it because you loved me more than your country.'

Francette put an arm around me. 'Markus, looking back at the outcome of your mission and the way that Germany is going, do you regret, for one minute, what you did.'

I got my emotions under control and started to think with greater clarity on what had happened. 'I suppose you are right, and, what is even more important Chris is that you are alive when I thought that you were dead. All I did was for you brother.'

My Dad came over and gave me a hug. 'I'm sorry Markus for deceiving you. It has been on my conscience for over a year now, and I am glad I don't have to hide it from you anymore.'

I relaxed and thought: *Somebody up there must be looking after Chris and I as we had both returned from the dead.*

I now had a family in a free country. I decided to tell Chris about what happened to our mother at a later date.

I dug in my bag and pulled out the model of the jet engine that I had been given when I left Power Jets.

'Chris I want to give this to you. If it wasn't for you, I would have had a very different war and probably would be lying in a grave in Russia. Thanks to you I feel that I have done something useful in my life that will save a lot of lives.'

I handed the model to Chris and gave him a brotherly hug. There were tears in both our eyes.

BOOKS BY PATRICK SLANEY

__Historical Romance__
The Smiles and Tears of Love
__Family/War__
War Brothers
__Vince Hamilton Crime Mysteries__
The Diamond Chain
Heist Season

These books are all available from Amazon in book or electronic format.

Keep up to date with books by Patrick Slaney on his website www.patrickslaney.com

I would also appreciate it if you would take some time to complete a review of this novel. Thank you.